Moments III
Bedtime Stories and Truths

KEITH A. ANDERSON

authorHOUSE

AuthorHouse™
1663 Liberty Drive
Bloomington, IN 47403
www.authorhouse.com
Phone: 833-262-8899

© 2009 Keith A. Anderson. All rights reserved.

No part of this book may be reproduced, stored in a retrieval system, or transmitted by any means without the written permission of the author.

Published by AuthorHouse 11/12/2021

ISBN: 978-1-4389-5176-8 (sc)

Print information available on the last page.

Any people depicted in stock imagery provided by Getty Images are models, and such images are being used for illustrative purposes only. Certain stock imagery © Getty Images.

This book is printed on acid-free paper.

Because of the dynamic nature of the Internet, any web addresses or links contained in this book may have changed since publication and may no longer be valid. The views expressed in this work are solely those of the author and do not necessarily reflect the views of the publisher, and the publisher hereby disclaims any responsibility for them.

Also by Keith A. Anderson

Moments I,
Moments II,
As A Good Soldier &
The Gift (Play)

www.keithaanderson.com

FOREWORD

(Bedtime)
There is nothing like the sound of
Your spouse's voice before
You lay your head down to rest for
The evening. Let these stories of forgiveness,
Love, Compromise and Spirit enable
You to convey your feelings to the
One you love

(Truths)
Though these are my truths, I
Hope that they reach someone by having them
Analyze their lives and desperately applying
What they believe to be true. Like mom
Always says, "it aint nothing but life
Son". Live it and be happy! We're
Only here for a short while.

ACKNOWLEDGEMENTS

First of all I would like to thank Christ for blessing me. There is no way I could have completed this work without you. I pray that my version of bible stories pleases you. From poems like "I Am Ashamed" to stories like JOBE, I hope that they touch someone's heart into repentance or build their faith and reliance in you. All of my failures and all of my accomplishments I give to you. Lord strengthen me to be a better man, a better father and a better husband. I know the bible says, "If you love me keep my commandments," and though I fall short at times, I STILL LOVE YOU LORD!!

Keith A. Anderson

About Moments Bedtime Stories and Truths III

Moments III is my personal best, in my series of Moments Bedtime Stories and Truths. In Moments III you will find some old stories intertwined with new stories. The reason for this is I turned these stories into plays or in the process of transforming them into plays. You will also find that I concluded some of my previous stories. The stories are thought provoking, inspiring and mentoring. I pray that Moments III is as therapeutic for you as it has been for me. Enjoy.

Keith A. Anderson

Contents

THE "BEDTIME ZONE"

(The same thing at home)

Raconteur: *Welcome to the "Bedtime Zone"—where we view the lives of others as they go through various situations. We get to carefully evaluate the decisions that others make and pass judgment because it's not us or at least, not at the "MOMENT."*

What if we had the ability to eliminate the phrase "hindsight is 20/20"? What if we could honestly evaluate the pros and cons of every situation, ask for what we really want, feel how we really want to feel, and stand up for what we really believe in? Would we still make the same decisions? The funny thing is, we probably would. There are five zones that we make decions in. They are the "What ifZone" then there is the choicezone, the decizone, the actzone, and the.... Bedtime Zone. The Bedtime Zone is the time when everything is quiet and you realize what you've done. Most people don't get much sleep during this zone. So I welcome you to the first edition of

The Bedtime Zone

Today, with the assistance of our raconteur, we're going to be passing judgment on the Jordan's—specifically, Malik and Shanice Jordan.

Malik is a successful instructor at the university, and Shanice is a prominent corporate travel consultant. For some, the glitz and glamour of the wedding can disappear just a couple months after the nuptials, but the Jordan's marital bliss lasted for quite a while. They were a match made in heaven…for the first five years at least. Then, they both became complacent within their relationship.

Malik's kisses before heading off to work became sporadic. Compliments on her physique were also few and far between. Shanice, as a result of the absence of compliments, began to feel as though sexy wasn't a necessity. She felt that their relationship had moved past physical appearances. She felt their public accomplishments and status supplemented superficial personal needs. She didn't think anything was wrong. She just felt that their marriage was maturing. So, the showcase of new lingerie rarely made an appearance on the bedroom runway.

Let's check in on the couple as temptation rears its head in order to destroy God's most sacred union.

"Good morning, baby," Shanice said, sticking her head into Malik's study on her way to the kitchen.

"Good morning," Malik said. His words were muffled by the pencil stuck in between his teeth as he typed away on his desktop computer. "Can you bring me a cup of coffee on your way back, baby?" Malik asked, removing the pencil from his lips but not his eyes from the monitor.

"Have you already started the coffee maker?"

"Yes," he replied, continuing to look directly into the monitor.

"I'll bring it right back."

"Okay."

A moment later, Shanice returned to the study with the coffee. "How long have you been up?" she asked.

After setting the coffee down, she began to massage Malik's shoulders while he highlighted and red-inked student papers. This was unwanted attention, so Malik didn't respond by stopping what he was doing and giving his wife his direct attention.

"Oh, I've been up for quite a while. I have to get these midterms graded and input them into the system."

Shanice walked around the desk and forced her way onto his lap. "Would you like to take a midterm this morning?" she asked, in a sexy voice.

Malik stopped what he was doing and looked at Shanice, smiling. "Baby, I would love to take off all these clothes you have on, but I need to get these papers corrected. Can I take a rain check?"

Disappointed, Shanice still managed to smile as she stood up. "Okay, I need to get to the office anyway. I'm going to get dressed."

As she began to walk away, Malik reached for her hand.

"Baby, I promise I will make it up to you."

"I know," Shanice said, nodding her head.

Later that day, in Shanice's office....

There was a knock at the door.

"Who is it?" Shanice called out, hanging up her phone. She had just tried calling Malik with the intention of asking him how his day was going.

"It's Dean."

"Come on in, Dean."

"How are those travel arrangements coming along? I'm sorry about those last minute changes."

"Everything's completed," Shanice said, searching through her files for Dean's itinerary.

"Is everything all right?"

"Yes, everything's okay," Shanice said, but her voice was monotone.

Her tone of voice was the open door for which Dean had been waiting. He immediately shut the door behind him.

"Is there anything that I can help you with?" Dean asked, giving her his undivided attention.

As Shanice began to talk, she noticed that at least Dean was looking into her eyes as she spoke.

Raconteur: *Isn't this the way it happens? It's not the things that you've been doing wrong forever, but the things that you've recently done wrong, that your spouse or loved one notices. Then, when someone different comes along, your spouse will more readily accept the illusion that this person is attentive.*

"I don't know," Shanice said, shaking her head. "I guess I'm just having a bad day."

"Well, let me take you to lunch. Maybe I can brighten the rest of your day," Dean said, clasping his hands in front of him.

"No, I don't think that's a good idea," Shanice said, feeling that Dean was trying to come on to her.

"Come on, Shanice. You're too beautiful a woman to be feeling blue."

Shanice shifted in her seat as if she were slightly uncomfortable.

"Now, I hope that I'm not making you uncomfortable," Dean said, holding his palms up. But, if you ever feel like talking, I am free any time."

Raconteur: *Dean knew that the seed had been planted, and he didn't need to seem anxious. He also knew the power of a seed. The Bible says that faith the size of a mustard seed could move mountains, so planting a seed of genuine concern in the heart of Shanice could eventually pay off. All he had to do was water it every now and then with small, attentive gestures.*

"Thank you for the offer, but I'll pass."

"That's what I expected. Well, I hope that your day gets better."

"Here are your tickets, Dean, and thanks for your thoughtfulness."

Dean looked down at the tickets, shaking his head. "Three days in Connecticut."

"Connecticut is beautiful," Shanice responded.

"Yeah, maybe in the summertime but we're in the dead of winter. Well, I'll see you when I get back."

"You have a safe trip."

Malik stood at the front of the classroom. It was his last class of the day, and during these last few minutes, he struggled to keep his concentration from moving on to his next task for the afternoon.

"All of you did really well on your midterms," Malik said, standing up from behind his desk. "Let's not become complacent and lose focus for the remainder of the year."

Malik looked down at his watch.

"Well, that's all I have for today. Do any of you have any questions for me? Okay, read chapters 9 and 10 and I'll see you guys and gals on Tuesday. Have a good weekend."

As the students left the classroom, Malik took a seat at his desk. Exhaling, he began the final task of organizing his desk before he could head home for the weekend. Just as Malik was fastening his briefcase, Imani walked in. He'd picked up on the vibe that Imani was very attracted to him and before today he had done a good job of fending

her off. She walked in, and today—just today—her smell was making him feel weak, her voice was comforting, and her smile made him want to smile.

"How has your day been?" Imani asked as she walked up to his desk and placed both hands on it.

"It was alright," Malik said, grabbing the handle of his briefcase and bringing it down to his side. "Yours?"

She inhaled and exhaled deliberately. "Exhausting," Imani said. She closed her eyes and ran her fingers through her hair, finally lowering her hand to massage the back of her neck.

Realizing that he was in trouble, Malik began walking to the door.

"Wait," Imani said. She stopped him by grabbing the hand carrying the briefcase. "I know that this is out of line, but Malik, I think you know that I am drawn to you. I'm sorry, Malik, but I've felt this way for quite some time now. I know that we're both married. Well, I'm separated…but I can't help it. Never mind that you have the perfect physique; your demeanor is the most attractive thing about you. You're brilliant, yet humble."

Raconteur: *Is she laying it on thick or what?*

"As I said, forgive me, but I've wanted to say these things for a while now. Look at me. I'm acting like a little schoolgirl."

Raconteur: *Malik doesn't realize it, but he has just been injected with the man-mind-numbing serum called GAS. "GASING someone up" is what we called it in the 80s and 90s. This substance renders most men helpless. This, along with a beautiful woman, is a recipe for trouble.*

"Imani, believe it or not I've known for a while now. But before I got married I did the more-than-one-woman thing, and it took too much out of me to be out there. So I kind of recognized the attraction but I didn't want to act on it."

"That's what I'm talking about. Most men wouldn't be as forthright as you are with me. That's attractive in itself. Well, if there is anything that I can do for you, you just let me know and I'll make myself available. You have a great weekend," Imani said, biting her lower lip and walking away.

Raconteur: *Here's another farmer. Planting seeds of adultery and fornication.*

As Imani walked away, Malik observed the brown pantsuit that extenuated her every curve. And her walk said, *this is the best thing you've never had.*

Back on the home front

"Hello, baby. How was your day?" Malik asked, placing his briefcase on the table and loosening his tie.

"It was okay. I didn't get much done. Do you have a lot of work to do tonight?"

"No not much. I just have to get these lesson plans together, and I should turn in kind of early tonight."

"Okay then, I'll get the kids ready for bed a little earlier so I can spend some time with you."

"Sounds great, baby," Malik said as he stood over the stove to fix himself a plate of food. He peeked around the corner to watch his wife walk down the hall. He noticed that Shanice's walk was totally different than Imani's.

Raconteur: *This guy can't be serious. His wife probably does walk like that, it's just that he's so used to seeing it that he hasn't been paying any attention. If he did notice her sexy walk he would start questioning it. Be careful what you ask for or want—you just might get it. I'm pretty sure he didn't lick his lips the way Dean did today either.*

Malik finished up his work, took a shower, and headed to their bedroom. Shanice was already in bed with the covers pulled up to her neck. Malik climbed in bed and snuggled up next to her.

"Can you give me a massage?" Shanice said, rolling onto her stomach.

Immediately the words *just let me know what I can do for you* came to his mind. To top it off, Shanice wasn't even dressed seductively. Malik tried to shake it off and get into the mood.

"That feels *sooo good, baby,"* Shanice moaned as Malik applied just the right amount *of pressure moving down to her lower back.*

Shanice then reached back with her left hand to massage Malik's manhood. She noticed that it wasn't erect. Opening her eyes, she looked back at Malik.

"What's wrong, baby?" she asked.

"Nothing, baby. I guess I'm just stressed out."

Raconteur: *You'd better think of Imani or something fast, or she's going to think that you're either seeing someone or not interested in her. Neither of the two is going to be good.*

"Let me see if I can help," Shanice offered. She turned over to kiss Malik's chest while continuing to massage him."

Still nothing happened.

"What's going on with you, Malik?" Shanice asked, sitting up in the bed. She was starting to become upset. "You're not the only one that has to work to get turned on here. I think you need to sleep downstairs tonight."

"Baby, I'm sorry. I don't know what's going on with me. It has has to be stress related. This has never happened to me before."

"Whatever! Just please go downstairs. Please."

This was the first time they had ever spent the night in separate rooms. They spent the entire weekend that way, waiting until the kids were asleep before moving into their separate quarters.

The next day at work.

"Dean," Shanice called from her desk as she saw Dean walking by.

"What's up, Shanice?" Dean said with a *yeah, I might be in there* smile.

"How was your trip?" Shanice asked. She seemed to feel a new sense of confidence.

"To be honest, it was better than I thought it would be," Dean said, as he took a seat in one of the chairs in front of Shanice's desk. "I got a chance to check out some Connecticut history."

"Like what," Shanice asked, arranging some papers on her desk.

"I'm a bit of a history guy, so I went to the Connecticut State Library to get an idea of some historical sites to check out. As I was checking out the library, I came across a section that dealt with the Connecticut Freedom Trail."

"What was that about?"

"It was a northern underground railroad, believe it or not."

Raconteur: *Now don't get me wrong—this is a good topic, but not for what the brother is using it for. I'm a firm believer that all it takes is a gimmick, not game, to get a woman's attention. Case in point: in David E. Talbert's Love on Layaway stage play, when the new guy moves into the building with his African Art/beholder of beautiful things gimmick, everyone woman in the building becomes self-aware. I say again, all it takes is a gimmick, not game! And Dean has proven that he has a little of both.*

"Hey check this out, it's already close to lunch time. Why don't we finish this discussion over a bite to eat?"

Shanice paused for a second, but agreed. They were halfway through their meal when the thought of having sex with Dean crossed Shanice's mind. Dean caught the very minute that it did, too.

"So you're saying that the Underground Railroad wasn't just secret passageways to the north, and in fact there were a large number of slaves in the north?"

"Yeah. Crazy, right?" Dean said, licking his lips and shaking his head. "Any place considered a safe haven for fugitive slaves was considered part of the Underground Railroad. They even created the Fugitive Slave Act to force free states to release runaway slaves back to their owners."

"Maybe I just don't remember, but I don't think we covered that in history class," Shanice said. Looking down, she traced around the rim of her glass with her index finger.

Raconteur: *Here it comes.*

"Can I be your safe haven?" As he said this, Dean canted his head slightly, hoping that Shanice would lift her head with a smile and a *yes*.

Raconteur: *What did I tell you?! I am good.*

"I don't have to go back to work today. What about you?" Shanice replied, lifting her eyes with a smile.

"They know that I'm just getting back, so I'm sure that it won't be a problem. Where do you want to go?"

"I don't know. This isn't something that I do."

Raconteur: *Why do women always say that?*

"Okay. Well, I'm sure we can find a nice place to go without the worry of being seen. Hold on, let me ask the waiter for a phone book so I can get an address of a place where we can go."

Raconteur: *Dean wouldn't say hotel because he knew it would cheapen the moment. This guy is good.*

Dean and Shanice found a hotel on the outskirts of the city. Upon entering the hotel room, they began kissing passionately. He then slow unbuttoned her blouse while kissing her on the neck. She then unbuckled his belt to lower his pants. She immediately reached down to touch his manhood to see if he responded. When she noticed that he was all there, this gave her reassurance that she was not the one that was broken at home. All of a sudden, Shanice stopped Dean just before they lay on the bed.

"Will you judge me for the things I'm about to do to you and for the things I want you to do to me?"

Raconteur: *I wonder if she ever asked Malik that question. Even if she did, it's not like Dean is going to be like, "Yeah I'm going to judge you, so please don't be too freaky with me." Come on, that's a really stupid question. Let's be honest. He doesn't care what Shanice does. Malik, on the other hand, has the respect factor against him, because no man wants to treat his wife like a prostitute, but home boy Dean has no problem treating her like that. She's not kissing him when she goes back home. Ladies, you can't compare your man to the man that you're seeing. It's just not fair. Same goes for the men.*

"Shanice, I said that I would be your safe haven, and I meant it in every aspect."

"Thank you," Shanice said, pushing Dean onto the bed.

An hour and a half later they both came up for air.

"You were incredible," Dean said. He smiled and sat up with his back against the headboard.

"You were pretty incredible yourself," Shanice said as she leaned over and laid her head on Dean's chest.

Shanice's phone began to ring. They both looked at one another.

"I think you should answer it," Dean said as he stood up. "I'll give you some privacy. I'll go into the bathroom."

"Hello, baby," Shanice said, answering the phone.

"Are you at work?" Malik asked"

"No. I'm out doing some shopping. Do you want me to pick you up something?"

"Yeah, I need some T-shirts."

"Okay."

"Well I was just calling to let you know that I will be a little late getting home. I have to get some things done, so I'll just grab a bite to eat on my way home."

Raconteur: *Women, if your man doesn't tell you what he's trying to get done, then he's doing something he shouldn't be doing. It doesn't necessarily have to be adultery, but it's*

not good. And Men, if your woman doesn't ask you what you're trying to get done she's doing something she's not supposed to be doing. It doesn't have to be adultery but it's not good.

"Okay, that's fine," Shanice said quickly as Dean walked back into the room. "Love you."

"It seems as though we've been granted more time together. Let's go at it again, and then we'll go out and grab a bite to eat."

"Sounds good to me," Dean said, snatching all the covers off of the bed.

Malik on the phone with Shanice

"Well, I just was calling to let you know that I will be a little late getting home. I have to get some things done, so I'll just grab a bite to eat on my way home. Love you too," Malik said, turning his head a little.

"What did she say?" Imani asked. She was sitting at one of the students desks.

"We're fine," Malik answered. He seemed to be in a kind of daydream.

"Is there something wrong?" Imani got up and walked over towards Malik's desk.

"No…at least I don't think so."

Raconteur: *The sensation that Malik is feeling is the robbery in both what he was about to do and that something had just been taken from him.*

"Come here, professor," Imani said, grabbing Malik by his belt buckle.

Imani began to unbutton her blouse. She then removed her skirt to reveal the most beautiful pair of laced black girl boxers he had ever seen on a woman. Malik began to think, *man, I wish Shanice looked like this.*

Raconteur: *Like I said before. This is unfair judgment. We as men want our women to look like models all the time, while we ourselves could use some work. I'm pretty sure Shanice wouldn't mind running her finger over some hard abs or muscles.*

Malik cleared his desk, lifted Imani, and sat her up on the desk. They had sex for about 15 minutes, then sat and talked for hours about their relationships, both past and present. Because he had already told Shanice that he was going to be late, Malik knew he had some time to take Imani out for a bite to eat.

"Are you up for going to get a bite to eat?" Malik asked as he checked the time on the wall clock.

"Sure. Where do you want to go?"

"Well, we both know that it can't be here in the heart of the city. I think I know of a nice little quiet place on the outskirts called A.D.'s Everything (Authentic Dining)."

"That sounds like a good idea. Let's go."

Dean and Shanice were just finishing up round two and getting ready to grab something to eat themselves.

"You are something serious," Dean said, rolling off of Shanice.

"My drive has always been a reflection of the input of the person I'm with, so that says a lot for you."

""I have the perfect place for us to get a bite to eat," Dean said as he got up to go to the bathroom. "It's nearby, so it will give us some time to get cleaned up and over there in what little time we have left. Are you up for it?"

"Definitely. What's the name of the place?"

"I'm not sure, but they have excellent food. You'll love it."

"Okay. Let me jump into the shower first so I can do my hair while you take your shower."

Dean and Shanice had ordered their food and were in the middle of a conversation about his trip to Connecticut.

"So what do you think of the place so far?" Dean asked. He reached across the table, grabbing Shanice's hands.

"It's really nice. They offer everything."

"Yeah, they actually a variety of chefs, from different bacgrounds, cooking their unique dishes."

"I love the way you look at me when I'm talking," Shanice said, displaying her satisfaction in the form of a smile. "You make me feel so alive and wanted."

Raconteur: *Hello, Shanice. That's what he's supposed to do. Evidently, it was good and he wants to keep getting it. Now, Shanice is probably saying these things because she wants to get some more also but she should just say that because there is no need to beat*

around the bush now. This man is no different from any other man. He has issues, too. Everyone does. At least you know the issues of the one you're with.

"You are so fine," Malik said to Imani as he opened the door to let her out of the car.

Raconteur: *I bet he can't remember the last time he opened the door for his wife. Again men too often get wrapped around how a woman looks. There will always be beautiful women. I don't care if you go out today and find the most gorgeous one you can find—she will only be the most gorgeous one of that day, because tomorrow there will be another one more gorgeous than her. The best thing any man can do is find a booty, legs, a face and a heart that will make him say, this is good enough, and love her for the rest of his life.*

Malik opened the door of the restaurant for Imani. "You are so attentive," she said.

As the waiter walked them over to their table, Malik noticed the back of a woman that looked familiar. Getting closer he recognized who it was and became furious. He then released Imaini's hand and veered towards the table.

"What in the hell is going on here?!"

Raconteur: *Dean must not have been an ugly cat, because he would have used a different word if he was. If he was beneath Malik he would have said, "what's going on here?" If he was on about the same level he would have said, what in the hell is going on here?" He said "hell," so Dean must have presented a challenge.*

Shanice immediately stood up and placed both of her hands on Malik's chest.

"Hold on Malik. I can explain," Shanice said in a frightful voice.

"Well, you need to start explaining."

"We were just having a bite to eat."

Imani caught up with Malik. "What's going on Malik?" she asked, standing next to him.

Realizing that he was doing something that he wasn't suppose to be doing himself Malik took a deep breath and said "Damn," under his breath.

"Is she with you?" Shanice asked, moving towards Imani.

Malik stepped in front of Shanice to prevent her from touching Imani.

"Hold on, Shanice. We need to get out of here before we both get ourselves in trouble."

"Where in the hell do you think you're going? Imani said with anger in her eyes.

"Here. This should be enough to get you home," Malik said, placing money on the table.

"Oh, girl take him," Imani said angrily with slight head movement. "He ain't worth it no way."

"Believe me. I know what you're talking about," Dean said. "She ain't about nothing either."

"Look, man—whoever you are—I'm going to let that one slide, because I'm the reason that the four of us are here. I'm trying to be logical here, because I'm still a man and possessive as hell. I really don't give a damn about me being wrong here so don't push your luck. If I had been doing my job at home, my woman wouldn't be out here with the likes of you."

Raconteur: *That's what I'm talking about. Any man can get a woman. The challenge is can you keep her. What most men don't realize is that every woman that you've slept with, another man has slept with her before, and he probably had less game than you. The job of a man is to be the type of man that a woman would be a fool to mess around on. The job of a woman is to be everything her man needs her to be. That's why the selection process is so crucial. She has to ask herself, can I be the woman he needs? But most importantly, will it change who she is? This is very hard for a woman, because 9 times out of 10 their sexual desire is double that of a man, and it increases with age.*

Malik and Shanice left the restaurant and just sat in the car before taking off.

"I'm sorry, baby," Malik said, reaching over and holding Shanice's hand.

"I'm sorry too, baby," Shanice said as she wiped tears from her face.

"Baby, do you know what I found the most enlightening about this whole thing?"

"Tell me, baby."

"Everything I found myself doing with and to her, I realized that I had stopped doing those very things to and for you."

"I guess this is what irony is about, because I feel the exact same way. Everything that we wanted and needed was right here between us. We just forgot that we used to have the very things that we thought we found in someone else."

"You're right. We just need to continue doing the things that make each other feel special. Most importantly, we have to remember that it is possible that we can fall right back into this trap again. We shouldn't be looking for it to happen, but instead we should let each other know when we start to slip," Malik said. He took hold of both of Shanice's hands. "I love you"

"I love you, too," she replied.

Raconteur: *Well, it looks like Malik and Shanice survived the "Bedtime Zone." Sometimes all it takes is to see someone else with something of yours in order for you to recognize just how important they are to you. This concludes the first of many episodes to come in "The Bedtime Zone". Good Night!!*

THE COMMERCIAL

And cut:

"You don't pay me any attention, do you?" Fancy said, getting out of the car and placing her purse strap over her shoulder. She began to walk away.

"I told you that it slipped my mind," Devon said as he grabbed his laptop carrying case out of the back seat. "Can you wait up?" He closed the door, then pressed the alarm button and walked quickly to catch up with Fancy.

"It didn't slip your mind. You just don't pay me any attention," Fancy said. "I am so tired of repeating myself to you. If you spent half as much time paying me some attention as you do doing other things, you might realize that I'm alive."

"Look," Devon said, gently tugging on Fancy's purse strap to stop her. "I said that it slipped my mind. Let's just go in the restaurant and act cordial in front of my clients. We'll talk about this when we get home."

"Whatever," Fancy said, rolling her eyes and swinging her shoulder, indicating that she wanted Devon to release her purse.

"Look," Devon said, frowning, "I don't need this crap right now. These are some very important clients. If you think this is going to be a problem, you need to take your

15

behind back home. You don't seem to have a problem spending the money that I get doing the things that I do."

"I'm here, right?" Fancy said, turning and looking Devon directly in the eye. "I could be somewhere else."

With a sigh and a giggle Devon shook his head. "You know when you have me, don't you?!"

"What are you talking about? Are you going inside or what?" Fancy said. She folded her arms and examined her finger nails."

"Unfold your arms and come on," Devon said as he walked away from her.

Fancy caught up with Devon at the hostess desk.

"Hello, sir. How may I help you?" the hostess greeted.

"Yes, we're here to meet with another couple."

"Their names, sir, and I will check to verify if they've arrived," the hostess asked.

"The reservation would be under *Moore*," Devon answered.

The receptionist glanced over her list of guests.

"Yes, sir, they arrived a little over 10 minutes ago. Jason will take you to your seats."

And, action:

Devon grabbed Fancy's hand as they began to walk behind Jason. Fancy smiled sarcastically. When they reached the clients' table, Devon and Fancy were surprised to find there were additional people, now seated at two tables that had been pushed together to accommodate the extra attendees. Pete stood up and greeted Devon and Fancy with handshakes. "How's everything?" Devon said as he smiled and returned the handshake. "This is my lovely wife Fancy." Devon indicated Fancy with a gesture.

"Nice to meet you," Pete said. He shook Fancy's hands as he waited for KHajonna to finish a brief conversation with the woman next to her. "This is my crown jewel and future wife KHajonna," Pete said with a brilliant smile.

Smiling and shaking his head, Devon lent his hand to the great KHajonna. "Very nice to meet you," Devon said, continuing to smile.

Then the women greeted one another.

"I've saved two seats right here for the two of you," Pete said. He gestured toward the two seats in front of KHajonna and himself.

Devon then opened his laptop carrying case and removed his laptop and some brochures. He placed his computer on the table and placed the laptop case in between his seat and Fancy's.

"I hope that you don't mind, but I invited the bridesmaids and our parents."

"No, sir. That's perfectly fine," Devon said. He pulled out Fancy's seat for her and then took his own seat. "First of all, I would like to thank you for selecting **Every Occasion Photography** by Lincoln Styles. You won't be disappointed. We have a very large number of satisfied customers. As you can see, we've traveled to a number of locations around the world. Here are some examples of packages that we recently took a little over a month ago." Devon turned the computer screen toward Pete and KHajonna. "I also do wedding videography. Here are some samples our lovely wedding videos."

"These are very nice," KHajonna said looking closer. "You two are a very beautiful couple. May I ask how long you two been married?"

"It's been 10 beautiful years," Fancy said, turning and looking into Devon's eyes.

"Would you do it all again?" Pete asked while turning the computer screen toward his in-laws and other guests.

"There wouldn't be any doubt," Devon said. He put his arms around Fancy and kissed her softly on her lips.

Devon, Fancy, and the Moore's discussed the brochure packages, the timeline, then ate a late dinner to round out the evening.

"We really enjoyed you guys and look forward to doing business with your families," Devon said. As he rose to his feet, he helped ease Fancy's chair from under the table.

"It's been wonderful. I'll be by your office on Monday with the deposit," Pete said. Pete also excused himself from the table to thank Devon and his wife. Devon and Fancy held hands as they left the restaurant.

And cut:

"That was quite a show you put on, Devon," Fancy said. She was smiling as she pulled down the visor to look into the mirror.

"Whatever, Fancy. You put on quite a show yourself," Devon responded. He leaned to his left, putting his right hand on top of the steering wheel and looking forward with a smile.

"Oh, now that it's over you're going to act all bad," Fancy said. She pushed the visor up and looked at the side of Devon's face"

"I bet you would do it all over again. All I ever asked, Devon, is that you pay me some attention and you can't even seem to do that for me."

"I don't know what else to say, Fancy," Devon said. He turned to look at her. "I told you that it slipped my mind. I don't know what else I can do or say. The real question is, when can we get past petty things and deal with bigger issues? I could see if I did

something major, but like I said, it slipped my mind. I didn't forget a birthday or something."

"Whatever I consider important should also be important to you. Wouldn't you want me to consider the things that you feel are important, important to me also?"

"Of course I would, Fancy, but I wouldn't make it into a major argument. God, would you please just let it go?"

"Okay, I'll let it go. I'll let it all go."

"Now it has to be 'let it all go.' Damn, is it really that serious?"

"Stop the car, Devon!" Fancy yelled.

"What? Fancy I really don't have time to play these games with you."

"If you don't, I promise you everything on my momma that I will put this car in reverse."

Devon knew that she could be just that crazy. So he pulled over, knowing that it was about to get real dramatic.

"I'm going to show you how serious I am, Devon. I'm getting the hell out of this car and I'll walk home," Fancy got out. She slammed the door and stepped up onto the curb.

"This is the craziest thing in the world." Devon put the car in park. "Fancy, can you please get back in the car? We're almost home. People are turning on their lights," Devon said, getting out of the car. "Someone's going to end up calling the cops."

"That is the only thing that gets your attention," Fancy said. She turning around and continued to walk down the dimly-lit street.

"Baby, I am really sorry, okay?" Devon said as he caught up with Fancy. He grabbed her hand. "I promise to pay more attention. I'll write it down, or something."

"That's all I've ever asked of you, Devon. Just to acknowledge my feelings."

"Okay, baby. Let's just go home and get some rest."

And action:

"Vereka," Fancy called as she entered the house through the garage.

"Yes, momma," Vereka responded, walking into the kitchen from the living room.

"What's wrong, momma?" Vereka said. She noticed the mascara traces on Fancy's face"

"Nothing, baby. Just a little tired. Are your brother and sister asleep? What time did they go to bed?"

"Just a few minutes ago."

"Okay, you go to bed and get some sleep. You have your meet tomorrow."

"Okay, mom. I'll see you in the morning."

Devon and Fancy went into their bedroom to get ready for bed. Fancy was in the mirror taking off her necklace.

"Let me get that baby." Devon moved Fancy's hand away from the fastener so he could undo her necklace. "You know that I love you more than anything, right?" he said, turning her around.

"You know that I love you, too." Fancy got up on her tiptoes to kiss Devon.

"I love you so much, baby," Devon said, unzipping her dress. He brushed the straps aside from her shoulders while kissing her neck.

Moaning, Fancy said, "I love you too baby. You're my everything."

Devon and Fancy made love for about 15 minutes before falling asleep on opposite sides of the bed. Though they were in an action scene, no I love you's were offered. No passionate kisses and no real touching. It was sort of a band-aid for the evening.

"Good morning," Devon said as he threw the covers back and shifted his feet onto the floor.

"Good morning," Fancy answered. She was straining to open her eyes in order to look at the time.

"Do you want me to fix some breakfast?"

"What are you going to fix?"

"I'm going to fix some blueberry waffles. You want any?"

"Yes, please."

"Did you get my sport jacket out of the cleaners yesterday," Devon said, placing the breakfast tray in Fancy's lap. She scooted forward to eat.

"Oh, I forgot." Fancy cut into her waffle, preparing for a bite.

And, cut

"You forgot," he said, coming out of the walk-in closet.

Fancy wiped her mouth, nodding her head *yes.*"

Devon went back into the closet shaking his head.

"Oh, you have an attitude," Fancy said, becoming angry.

Devon continued looking at her through his side of the walk-in, but Fancy couldn't see him. Fancy slammed her tray of food onto the side of the dresser and it fell to the floor.

"What's wrong with you?" Devon asked as he walked out of the closet.

"I am so sick of this mess!" Fancy began walking out of the room.

On her way out of the room she intentionally—or unintentionally— brushed up against Devon. Devon ignited, pushed her, and held her down on the bed.

"This is some bull----. I am so tired of you being the only one that can forget to do something and it be okay."

"Get your hands off of me! Fancy yelled.

Devon remained holding her down as he stared angrily into her eyes. Fancy bit his hand, and Devon let her up.

The commercial and the show collide:

"Momma, what's wrong?" Vereka asked, coming into the room. Vereka started to cry after seeing a little trickle of blood on her fathers arm.

The other children came in right behind her, rubbing their eyes.

"Vereka, take the kids downstairs, and we'll be down there in a minute," Fancy said.

"Okay, mommy," Vereka said. She gave her mother a hug."

"Its okay, baby," Fancy said, hugging Vereka and patting her on the back. "Your father and I need to talk."

Wiping tears from her face, Vereka rounded up her brother and sister.

"Fancy, this has gone on long enough. Either we acknowledge that we have a problem, or I'm going to have to move out."

"I agree, Devon. There are some underlying issues that we have been ignoring for too long. The strain of putting on a show in front of others has done nothing but push us further apart. I know that you don't like the idea of going to talk over our issues with a therapist, but that is the only way we're going to get an unbiased evaluation of what we're doing wrong in this marriage."

"Is this what it's come to?" Devon said, taking a seat on the bed next to Fancy. "Baby, I'll do whatever it takes to find out how we can get back what we had. I'm sorry for putting my hands on you," Devon took hold of Fancy's hand.

"I'm sorry also, baby."

"We have to make one more promise to each other before we go downstairs to talk with the kids."

"What's that?" Fancy asked. She stood up, still attached to Devon's hand.

"We have to promise that we will never act that way again, especially in front of the children ever again."

"I promise."

"I promise also," Devon said. He stood up to hug Fancy.

Devon and Fancy stood there in each other's arms swaying back and forth for about 2 minutes.

And Cut:

A Way Out II

*P*reviously from Moments II

"How does this clown even know I'm married?" he said out loud. Candice had to have told him. "This crazy-ass girl is putting all of my business in the street and I don't know anything about this cat. What in the hell am I doing? I'm about to mess around and be forced to lose everything I have over some craziness. What is she going to do for me if this crap really hits the fan? Lord I know I JUST got through swearing, and you have given me so many opportunities to do the right thing by this mess, but I keep pursuing it. Lord, if nothing else comes of this, I promise you that I will keep my behind at home. I don't need any more hints."

It had been over a year since Marcus's encounter with Candice until………

Ring, ring, ring, the office phone sounded.

"Sergeant Phelps, can you get that phone for me?" Marcus said, as he was trying to work on some equipment.

"I got you, Sergeant Nelson," Sergeant Phelps said, walking over to the phone.

"Ninety-Eighth Maintenance Motor Pool, this is Sergeant Phelps speaking. How may I help you sir or ma'am?"

"Is Sergeant First Class Marcus Nelson in?" the lady on the other end asked softly.

"Yes he is," SGT Phelps replied. He noticed that this was not the voice of Mrs. Nelson."

SGT Phelps was a devout, saved, sanctified and filled with the Holy Ghost Christian and he was trying to get Marcus to remain on the path.

"Sergeant Nelson, the phone is for you," SGT Phelps said, with both of his eyebrows slightly up in the air.

"Who is it?" Marcus asked. He put his tools down and headed over to the phone.

"No clue Sergeant," Phelps said, looking straight into Marcus's eyes.

"What's up, man?" Marcus asked, looking back at Phelps with a puzzled expression. "Hello. This is Sergeant First Class Nelson. How may I help you?"

"Hello, Marcus," Candice said with a peculiar tone.

"Who is this?" Marcus said, loud enough for Phelps to overhear him.

"Meet me at the shop when you get off," Candice said, as though she and Marcus had been talking on a regular basis.

"Girl, what's going on?" Marcus demanded. He turned the phone away so that no one could hear what he was saying.

"See, there you go again with that same BS. Are you going to meet me or not? I have a client in my chair." She didn't really have a client, but Candice wanted to force his answer.

"Yeah, I can swing through," Marcus said. He knew he had to pick up the kids from the youth center, and Leticia up from work today, because Leticia's vehicle was being serviced.

"Okay, I'll see you then," Candice said, continuing to try to rush Marcus.

Marcus didn't say anything to SGT Phelps, because he knew if he went into an explanation he would look guilty. So instead, he went straight back to the job he was doing before the call.

Marcus thought about his meeting with Candice up until closing time. He flashed back to seeing her beautiful face, her lovely bottom when she was taking her pants off, to the night that he felt like she played him with another guy. Somehow, the games she played and the emotional feeling he had when God gave him a way out a year ago, didn't weigh-in as heavy as they did before. Deep in the back of Marcus's mind he wanted the opportunity again but his spirituality had kept him in check until now.

"I've got to leave a little early, Sergeant Phelps," Marcus said, as he looked at the time on the wall. "Can you close up for me?"

"I got you, Sergeant Nelson," Phelps said. He sensed that something was wrong and was trying to warn Marcus through telepathy.

"Alright. I'll see you in the morning for physical training."

Marcus arrived at the shop nervous, because he knew he didn't have much time, and he didn't want to be seen. Candice unlocked the beauty shop door to let Marcus in.

"Hello, my Marcus," Candice said with a seductive *I already know what I want* look in her eyes.

"What's going on with you?" Marcus asked. He took a quick glance at Candice's face as he walked in. She was more beautiful than he had remembered.

"You," Candice said, walking back over to her client.

"I *bet* it's me." Marcus said, taking a seat in the empty salon chair beside Candice and her client.

"I'm serious," Candice said as she leaned her client's head back into the sink to rinse her hair.

As Candice was talking and working at the same time, Marcus examined Candice's body from head to toe remembering what she looked liked undressed. What she looked like when she hopped up on the bed that day he subconsciously forgot the condoms.

"It's been over a year, girl..."

"I know, I know, and I've missed you," Candice said, using the nozzle to rinse the client's hair. "Have you missed me?"

"Marcus didn't want to speak on that out loud, for fear that her client could be listening, so he frowned and gave a head nod towards towards Candice's client as Candice continued.

"She can't hear you," Candice said softly, continuing to spray.

"You can say that I've missed you. But after you tried to play me, I kind of cut my losses and moved on."

"Hold on. Let me get her under the dryer," Candice said as she raised one finger. She turned the water off.

"Okay," Marcus said with a head nod. He tried to get a good look at the woman as Candice brought her up.

"Go back there." Candice used her head to point, while drying the woman's hair with a huge towel.

"Marcus turned around and saw a door with a sign on it that said, "Break Room, Employees Only." Getting up, he checked his watch and headed toward the break room.

"Here we go again," Marcus said aloud to himself. "The Lord is giving me five minutes to think about what I'm doing. That's all this is. It's time for me to get my head straight. Lord, I promised you that I wouldn't do this. Lord, you were supposed to interfere—have her forget my number, or something. This time, Lord, I do have more pros than cons for doing this. It's a year later and the wife hasn't been as attentive as she used to be. She's not into trying to excite me anymore, and to be honest, Lord, I want to feel what another woman feels like. I want to know if I can still make a woman moan and tell me that I'm everything that she needs. Leticia and I just have sex. I've tried to add some variation but she's not interested. She doesn't compliment me anymore on my physique. From what I remember, Candice loves to kiss, and I would never admit this to any of my boys, but I love to kiss also.

Candice walked in.

"Did you miss me?" Candice said, walking directly up to Marcus and throwing her arms around his waist.

"Yeah, I guess you can say that," Marcus said, smiling.

Looking up at Marcus and smiling back, Candice put both of Marcus's hands on her behind and asked him again.

"Yeah, I guess I did," Marcus said. He squeezed her behind and leaned his head in to kiss her.

They kissed passionately for 3 minutes straight. Marcus reached underneath Candice's blouse and released her eager breasts. Three more minutes passed, and Marcus realized that he had to go.

"Candice," Marcus said. He slid his hands from under her blouse and licked his lips. "I have to go, baby."

"Don't start that again," Candice said, moving back in for another kiss. "I love the way you kiss me."

Grabbing her waist, and Marcus noticed that one of his thumbs was right near her navel. He glanced down and saw that Candice had gotten a tattoo right below her navel leading down into her jeans. Marcus closed his eyes and said a prayer to himself.

"I have to go, Candice, but I promise that I will make it up to you," Marcus said. He pulled her bra back down over her breasts.

"Meet me before you go to physical training in the morning," Candice said, allowing him to adjust her bra over her breasts.

"That's five o'clock in the morning," Marcus said, looking at Candice in disbelief.

"Do you want it or not?" Candice asked, as she backed away, posing.

"You know I do," Marcus said, and pulled her back toward him.

"Then you'll be there," Candice said. She kissed him quickly and walked away. "I'll see you at five. Let yourself out."

Marcus picked his children up first and then went by the hospital to pick Leticia up. Leticia was standing outside with an angry look on her face. Marcus immediately thought, **Oh heck.** *He had already thought about his excuse on his way to pick her up.*

"What took you so long Marcus?" Leticia asked, after getting in the truck.

Leaning in for a kiss, "Oh, we had a late meeting," Marcus said, quickly. "First Sergeant likes to drag things on and on, and then he wants us to come in early for a platoon sergeant meeting."

"Oh really," Leticia said, she rolled her eyes, turning away from his kiss. Take me to pick up my car, please.

"What's wrong with you?"

"What's right with you?" Leticia responded. With her elbow propped up on the door, she held her head in her hand and stared out of the truck window.

"Mommy and daddy, don't fight," one of the children said from the back seat.

Leticia didn't say anything, so Marcus responded to the child. "We're not fighting, baby. Mommy just had a bad day."

Leticia turned to Marcus and stared at him without a word.

Marcus was sure he was going through with his plans now, because Leticia was treating him like she had been for the last few months. The kids got out and rode

with Leticia back home. Before Marcus made it back home he made a stop at the 7/11 to pick up a three-pack of condoms. He wanted to make sure nothing went wrong tomorrow or nothing slowed him down. After making it home, he hurriedly went upstairs to set his clock for 4:30. Marcus couldn't sleep all night. He got up at 4 o'clock and began to get ready. Before he left, he kissed Leticia on the check and told her that he loved her.

Marcus backed his truck in, so no one would see the license tag.

Knock, knock. Marcus heard footsteps coming to the door.

Recognizing Marcus through the peephole, Candice cracked the door. "Did you bring some condoms she said, sarcastically."

Marcus pulled them out of his physical training jacket and showed them to her.

"Come on in," Candice said, fully opening the door.

Candice was wearing black-laced boy short panties with a matching bra. She took him by the hand and led him to her room.

"Damn, girl," Marcus said, checking her out from behind. "I don't remember it being that fat."

After making it to Candice's room, she immediately began to take off his shirt. After taking off his shoes, Marcus began running his hands from her waist to her bottom, and going underneath her panty line. He eventually slid her panties over her perfectly shaped behind and down to her knees. She lifted her feet, and he used one of his feet to finally remove her underwear. They kissed and had sex for forty-five minutes before Marcus said he had to go.

"When am I going to see you again? Candice asked, as she pulled the covers over her.

"I don't know," Marcus said. He walked from her bathroom still in shock from what he had just done.

"How about two days from now?" Candice said, as she slid over to the end of the bed where Marcus was getting dressed.

"We'll see, baby," Marcus replied. He pulled his shirt over his head and stood up.

"We'll see?" Candice repeated. She returned to the head of the bead, where she lay on her back.

"Yeah, I don't know what'll be going on two days from now," Marcus said, putting on his jacket. "Listen, Candice, there are a couple of things we need to talk about before I go."

"What are they?"

"I have a few rules that I need to lay out if we want this thing to work."

"Some guidelines," Candice said, looking down and adjusting the covers.

"Yeah, some guidelines. Number one: I'm not leaving my wife and kids. I don't care how good it gets; I'm not leaving my family. Number two: I'm getting something and you're getting something. Let's not make this out to be that I'm the only one getting something. You and I both wanted sex and that's what we just did and probably will continue doing 'til whenever. I'm not going to be there every time you want to see me, and if you make me feel like I'm doing you wrong every time I can't be there, then I'm going to have to call this off immediately. That's basically it."

"Well I have a few guidelines myself." Candice pulled the covers off of her and got into Marcus's face. "I'm going to win you over Marcus." Then she kissed him.

"Okay, baby. I have to get out of here. I'm late."

"See you two days from now," Candice said, heading to the bathroom.

Candice and Marcus met in the morning and at lunch for about three months straight. Candice was very understanding and didn't put any strain on Marcus and Leticia's marriage. Marcus was starting to develop feelings for Candice and began showing those feelings by purchasing gifts for her. Leticia started to become very suspicious of Marcus. He was easier to get along with. Marcus started to open the car door for Leticia. He pulled out her chair at restaurants. He complimented her more often. He started cleaning up his own messes around the house. He was paying more attention to his finances, and other things she found peculiar, but she eventually decided Marcus must have been simply trying to please her.

One afternoon at Leticia's job.

"Mrs. Natasha Bennett," the woman at the desk called.

Mrs. Bennett walked up to the desk and waited for the woman to tell her where to go.

"Mrs. Bennett, you're going to go through this door and make a left. Follow the hall and go into the second door on your right. Mrs. Nelson will assist you with your referral."

"Hello, Mrs. Nelson. How are you?"

"I'm doing fine. And yourself?" Mrs. Nelson responded.

"I'm fine. My doctor put a referral in for a dermatologist."

"May I have your ID card?" Leticia said, with her hand out.

Handing Leticia her ID card, Mrs. Bennett noticed Leticia's family portrait. She also noticed Leticia's husband but could not quite remember where she had seen him before.

"Beautiful family."

"Thank you," Leticia said, inputting Mrs. Bennett's information into the computer."

As Leticia was finishing with the information, Mrs. Bennett blurted, "I remember where I've seen your husband."

"Excuse me?" Leticia said, handing Mrs. Bennett her referral.

"I'm sorry, Mrs. Nelson," Mrs. Bennett said, wishing she could retract her last statement.

"What were you about to say about my husband?" Leticia asked. She turned slightly in her chair towards Mrs. Bennett.

"I'm sorry. It's none of my business."

"No, it's okay," Leticia reassured her.

"I think I met your husband at the beauty salon," Mrs. Bennett said, shaking her head.

"Oh, he probably had our daughter there getting her hair done," Leticia said, turning back to her computer.

"I don't think so, Mrs. Bennett. He was there with one of the stylists."

"When?!"

"It was about three months ago. He and Candice went in the back for a good little minute while I sat under the dryer."

"You said her name was Candice?" Leticia asked, elevating her tone.

"Yes."

"Can you tell me where she stays?" Leticia said, as she pulled out a piece of paper from her desk.

Mrs. Bennett gave Leticia the address and went on her way.

Meanwhile!

"I only have a few minutes," Candice said, as she opened the door to let him in.

Marcus began to undress before he was all the way inside the house. He had already unlaced his boots and top on the ride over. **They made their way to the couch and began. This time they did things that only married people should do to one another.**

"I love you, Marcus," Candice said, snuggling up in Marcus's arms.

All Marcus could think about was how he was going to kiss his wife after that.

"Did you hear me?" Candice asked, as she looked up into his eyes.

"Um, yes. I love you, too, Candice."

"Let's plan to be with each other," Candice said, sounding as though she were ready.

"I told you that I wasn't leaving my family," Marcus said. He sat up.

"Well I know that I told you that I wouldn't try to make you leave your wife, but I can't continue doing this. If we can't make a decision to be with each other, then I can't do this anymore."

"Candice, I do love you, but how can I leave my family when you can leave me tomorrow? How can I trust you? Who's to say you won't do the same thing to me?"

"You know what, Marcus? Get out. You're trifling! You don't know what you want, but I refuse to let you continue to use me up."

"I told you before we even started this that we were using each other," Marcus said, as he began to get dressed.

"Just get your sorry behind out," Candice said, angrily, throwing his t-shirt and army shirt at him.

Marcus felt somewhat relieved that it was over. He had had his fun. He had not been caught, and he was free—even though Candice could probably describe every tattoo and mark on his body.

Candice called Marcus on his way home from work.

"Are you coming over in the morning? Candice asked with a grin.

Marcus should have known right then that he wasn't dealing with someone who had control of her emotions, but he convinced himself that he could do it just one more time for the road. **Marcus didn't realize that this was his final way out.**

"I can be there," Marcus said, as he turned his car into the driveway.

Marcus opens the garage and notices that Leticia's car was already parked. He runs in and goes straight to the bathroom to brush his teeth. This was another clue that Marcus had been cheating on her. Leticia had cooked his favorite meal and had run his bath water. Marcus became worried, because if Leticia wanted some tonight, he wasn't going to give it to her. He had done some stupid things but he was not going to have sex with his wife and mistress in the same day. After taking a bath and eating, Marcus went to their bedroom to find Leticia asleep.

"Good," Marcus said to himself.

Marcus climbed in bed hoping he didn't wake Leticia. After throwing the covers over himself and getting settled, Leticia opened her eyes and smiled and closed them.

The next morning Marcus went to kiss Leticia goodbye, but she had the cover over her head.

"I'm going to the meeting," Marcus said, grabbing his keys off of the TV stand.

When Leticia heard the garage door open, she jumped up and ran over to the window overlooking the garage. As Marcus was backing out, Leticia took a suitcase and began packing most of Marcus's belongings. She quickly grabbed some sweats, her sneakers, a pullover sweater, and vaseline and ran down to the garage to follow Marcus. She waited for several minutes to make sure he got good and settled at Candice's home.

Ding Dong, Candice's doorbell rang. Marcus's heart automatically went into shock. He didn't have a clue as to who it could be. It could just as well be one of her old flames.

"Hold on, baby. I'm gonna see who it is," Candice said, as she got out of the bed. She threw on her robe that was hanging on the back of her door.

She stepped to the side of the door and opened the curtains to see who it was. It was Leticia. Although Candice had never seen her before, she had an idea of whom this was standing at her front door.

"Marcus, it's for you," Candice shouted to the back room.

Marcus's heart fell to the floor. Candice opened the door, and the two women stared at one another. After Marcus got dressed, he slowly walked to the front door.

"So this is the meeting that you've been going to every morning, Marcus," Leticia said calmly.

"Leticia, what are you doing here?" Marcus said, shaking his head in a worried, angry kind of a way.

"Don't you say anything to me," Leticia said, pointing her finger into his face. She stepped back across the threshold to grab the suitcase. Both Marcus and Candice nearly fell back wondering what she was about to bring out.

"Oh don't worry; I'm not going to do anything to get myself into any trouble. I just wanted to bring Marcus his work and activity clothes. You are a silly-ass man. You work for me now. You are so stupid," Leticia said, as she pushed Marcus's forehead with her finger. "Don't be late for work, because you don't want to mess up our retirement. I mean MY retirement. By the time, you give me half of your retirement, which will be about fifteen hundred dollars, and child support for our kids, you won't *have* a retirement. That's about thirty-six thousand free dollars a year, you idiot. You will have worked for twenty years for me. Jumping out of airplanes, hundreds of field rotations, three tours in Iraq, all for me. So sister, you can have the trifling nigga. Both of you deserve each

other. Now they say that a woman should never keep a man from seeing his children but they did say 'man' and that you are not. You're irresponsible and I refuse to let an irresponsible man be around my children unsupervised. So, looking at the time, I think you need to get to your formation. Have a good day, sister."

A couple of weeks went by and Marcus had moved in with Candice. Leticia hadn't reported him to his command. As the weeks went by, Marcus had become relaxed in CANDICE'S home.

"Can you pick up your boots out of the floor?" Candice said, angrily kicking them to the side.

"Why are you kicking my stuff?" Marcus got up to get his boots.

"Just get them out of the middle of the floor," Candice continued.

"You need to find you something to do," Marcus said. He was becoming upset.

"You're right. I do," Candice said, not quite softly enough.

"What did you say?"

"I said, 'I need to find me someone to do,'" Candice said, continuing to clean up the room.

"What do you mean by that?"

"I mean your wife was right! You are trifling."

Marcus felt like crap. Here he was living with a woman that committed adultery with him, but he was being told that *he* was trifling.

"You're just as trifling as I am. What makes you think that you're any better than me?" Marcus asked.

"I may not be any better than you, but I sure am better off than you. You wife was right, you are a stupid man."

Marcus could have gone over and choked Candice to sleep, but he finally began to listen to that voice in his head that he had been ignoring. Marcus slowly turned his head to the right. What he saw was a door—a door that led to a way out of the path that he had been on. Marcus packed his belongings and left.

"Lord, you must be angry with me. I truly apologize for what I've done. Lord, I want you to know something: I am wiser coming out of this thing than I was going into it. I don't know if that amounts to anything, but I appreciate you letting those women tell me how stupid I had become. Right now, Father, I need you to touch my wife's heart. Help me demonstrate to her that I have recovered from my stupidity. I need to teach my son this lesson. I promise to share my story to other men who I feel maybe heading down the same road. Thank you, father, for giving me *"A Way Out*."

MAINTENANCE MAN

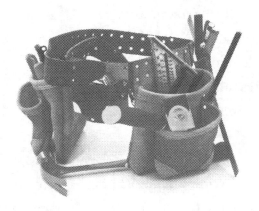

*H*orn blows from outside.

Jamal looks out of the window and sees a service truck in the driveway. He opens the garage door.

"How you are doing young man?" the older gentleman asked, as he walked into the garage.

"I'm doing fine, sir. How about yourself?" Jamal asked. He grabbed his shoes from the rack of shoes left outside.

"Oh, any day that the Lord blesses me with is a good day."

"I hear that," Jamal agreed."

"I appreciate you coming by to help me out with the deck. It's gotten so bad. I need to replace the braces, and put some stain on it."

"Well, let's take a look at it."

"Yeah, if you would follow me around to the back, I can show it to you."

"Your father told me that you needed some help with your deck, and your father's a good man. So I figured he would have raised a fairly decent son."

"I'm alright, I guess. Do you see how the paint is flaking and the wood is starting to split?"

The older gentleman put on the glasses that were hanging around his neck. "Yeah, I see what you're saying. I'm pretty sure we can at least get started on it today. I'm going to get my tools from the truck, and I'll be right back."

"Okay, sir. I'll be right back"

After about an hour of working on the deck, Jamal got up the nerve to ask the older gentlemen a question.

"Excuse me, sir. Can I ask you a question?"

"Yes, son. Go ahead," the gentleman said, wiping sweat from his brow.

"It's kind of personal…if you don't mind."

"I'll let you know if it's too personal," he said, with a smile continuing to work.

"Okay. How long have you been married?"

"This time?" the gentleman replied, with a smile.

"Yeah, I guess," Jamal said, smiling back.

"It'll be 40 years this September. Forty wonderful years with the most beautiful woman on the planet."

"That's what I want to talk with you about. I know that you've seen more beautiful women, but yet you say your wife is the most beautiful woman you've ever seen."

"Are you talking about my wife, young man.?" The gentleman stopped what he was doing and turned to smile at Jamal.

"By no means, sir," Jamal said. He returned the smile. "I'm just saying, sir."

"I know, I know, young man. Just pulling your leg. You're looking at the physical woman. My woman is beautiful inside and out. There is nothing that she wouldn't do for me."

"I feel the same about my wife, also. It's just that…I don't know."

"If you're going to talk to me, son, talk to me. What's really going on with you?"

"I don't know, sir. That's why I wanted to talk with you."

"I think I know what's going on with you," the gentleman said, as he reached into his toolbox for some sandpaper. "Are you insecure in your relationship, young man?"

"What do you mean, sir?" Jamal asked. He was becoming curious.

"I think you're making up excuses because you're afraid of loosing your woman for some reason. I hear self-doubt in your voice. Talking about other beautiful women is a dead giveaway. There will always be a woman more physically beautiful than any woman you find. There will always be a better-looking man than you, too. You don't

know how to go about keeping your woman, do you? This is a classic sign that you would rather jump ship than try to keep your woman interested in you."

Jamal hadn't thought about it that way before, but it made sense.

"Okay. Say that's true. What can I do about it? Hold on, sir. I'm going to grab you a glass of water."

"That would really be nice right about now," the gentleman said, as he wiped the sweat from his forehead with the sleeve of his shirt.

"Okay, sir. What were you saying?"

"Okay. I'm going to make this really simple for you," the gentleman said, looking over the rim of his glasses. You see this deck that we're working on? It requires maintenance every so often, right?

"Yes, sir."

"If you don't make a schedule and check it every so often, you'll forget and you'll end up with what you have here. That's the same approach that we men have to take when maintaining our marriage. We're not going to remember. I mean, think about it. Your house requires weekly services, monthly services, semi-annual services, and annual services. If you don't keep track of those things it can really get away from you. If it goes un-attended for too long, it'll cost you a lot more money to fix it, when it does break, than it would have cost for you to do the required maintenance. If you don't change the batteries in your fire detector when you're supposed to, you create a fire hazard, which could prevent the loss of your home and life."

"I see what you're talking about, Jamal said, smiling. "So I should make a maintenance tracker for my marriage?"

"Most definitely," the gentleman said, looking at Jamal and shaking his head.

"What kinds of things should I include on this 'marriage maintenance tracker?'"

"For instance, opening the door for your lady. This should be a daily routine and shouldn't have to be on the list. But believe me, son, we all get lazy, so write it down. Saying she's beautiful is another daily. A passionate kiss should happen at least weekly. You might want to get a pen, young man. My memory isn't as good as it used to be."

"Hold on, sir," Jamal said, and walked quickly back into the house.

"Okay, that was 'kissing passionately' weekly, 'beautiful' and opening the door daily. Okay, I'm ready."

"A scheduled dinner date at a minimum of once a month. You should try to take her out every two weeks but once a month you should have a scheduled dinner date, just the two of you. Got that one?"

"Yes, sir"

"Make love somewhere different at least once every six months. Go to a hotel or something. Remember that on these scheduled events it's all about her in everything. The first thing you should do with your check is to set aside your money for church then for your woman."

"What?" Jamal glanced up from his list with a confused look on his face.

"That's right. Do me a favor, young man, and think about this: what if your woman knew you were saving money every payday just for her?" If she's a good woman there would be nothing that you couldn't get from that woman. If you follow these maintenance tips that I'm giving you, no muscle-bound man or rich man will stand a chance against you. Don't get me wrong. Women are going to look, just like we do, but a woman knows when she has something special at home. Now you don't let her see the maintenance list. You keep it tucked away and check it everyday. I used to be just like you in my first marriage. I would see guys opening the door for their women and be like, 'It's not that serious.' Then I realized that it wasn't about me. It was about my woman and how special she was to me.

Every three or four years you have to let a professional examine your marriage for you. This is to check for things that can't be seen by you or your wife—things that you can't see that can eat away at a marriage like termites. You can't see it but the foundation could be eaten away and you won't see it 'til it's too late. Learn new protections and deterrents. A marriage should be just like a home. It should "appreciate in value" as the years move along.

You have to do the things you did to get her and new things keep her intrigued. Upgrades so to speak.

Sir, I really appreciate all of this knowledge.

No problem young man. I think that I'm going to stop here for today. I'll come back again next week to do some more. First I need to give you a list of things I need you to purchase. Help me gather up my tools and walk with me back to the truck, if you will.

"Okay," Jamal said folding the paper and placing it into his pocket.

"All right Jamal, here's the list of thing I need you to pick up. Now most of these items can be picked up at Home Depot. Whatever you can't find, just give me a call and I'll pick them up for you. All right."

"Sounds great sir. Sir again, thanks for everything and sir, please don't tell my dad that I asked you those questions," Jamal said, smiling.

Oh I won't. You just follow that maintenance plan and you will be okay. You take care now and I will see you next week.

Thanks and you take care too. I'll see you then.

GOD IS GOD "ALL THE TIME"

*P*reviously from Moments I & II

Theresa told Steven about her sexual abuse and her struggle to shake her promiscuous thoughts. I've made some changes due to reader questions and suggestions. So I decided to start the 3rd chapter of God is God from this scene. In order to get what happened previously, you will need to purchase Moments I & II. Enjoy.

Keith A. Anderson

"Excuse me," Steven said, approaching the nurses' desk.

"Yes, sir, how may I assist you?" the nurse responded.

"I'm trying to get information on Theresa Witherspoon, my wife," Steven said.

"Okay, wait one minute while I get that information for you," the nurse said.

At that moment, another woman approached Steven.

"You're looking for Theresa, right?"

37

Steven turned his head to the left, to address the lady.

"Yes, I am," he said, with a confused look on his face. "Who are you?"

"I'm Naomi, a close friend of Theresa's," she said, looking Steven square in the eyes. "She's in labor and delivery."

"Wait a minute," Steven said, closing his eyes and shaking his head rapidly. "For what," he asked, elevating his voice angrily and then lowering it.

Naomi continued to stare at Steven.

"She's right," the nurse said, lifting her head from her computer screen.

"Just then, the sliding doors to the emergency room opened and Theresa's parents arrived. Thereasa saw her grandmother and ran to her. Mrs. Holmes was not alone. Her best friend Mrs. Ramona was with her. That meant that James was with them also. Ramona was James' wife. In walked Mr. Holmes and James. As they were walking in, James caught up with Ramona and was about to put his arm around Thereasa when Steven yelled out, "Don't you even think about putting your hands on my daughter."

Steven went over to Thereasa and pulled her away.

"What's wrong, Steven?" Mr. Holmes said, in a state of shock.

"He knows, ask him," Steven said, keeping his eyes on James. "I want him out of here now."

"Steven, there's no need to make a scene," Mr. Holmes said.

"And there won't be one, as long as he's out of here. He can either leave on his own, or I'm going to help him out of here."

Normally James would have retaliated, but deep down inside he had an idea about where Steven's anger stemmed.

"Come on, Ramona, let's go outside," James said.

"Yeah, that's the best thing you can do."

The doctor then came out and asked if there were any family members there. Steven turned around and said that he was Theresa's husband.

"Hello, Mr. Witherspoon," the doctor said. "I'm Dr. Jonah. Can I speak to you in private for a minute?"

Steven nodded, and they walked over to an area of the waiting room where, no one could hear them speak.

Meanwhile, Ramona followed James outside.

"James…James," Ramona called out, trying to catch up with him.

"Come on, Ramona, where leaving," James said angrily.

"James," Ramona demanded.

James paused for about ten seconds. Sorrowfully, he then removed his hat before taking a seat on one of the benches.

"What's wrong, James?" Ramona asked, worried.

James looked skyward for a minute, pondering how he was going to tell his wife his dark secret.

"Talk to me, James," Ramona said, turning his head towards her. "Why did Stephen talk to you that way? What's going on?"

James still sat there, silent!

Becoming emotionally infuriated with the entire situation and the feeling that whatever was going on was about to change everything in her life, she began to beat on James, demanding he tell her what was going on. Tears began streaming down James's face as he turned to Ramona, grabbing her hands and placing them on his chest.

"I molested Theresa as a child," James said, shamefully.

With a look of disbelief, Ramona asked James to repeat himself.

"It wasn't the proudest time in my life, but I'm glad that it's out," James said, calmly. I know that you're in pain, Ramona, but even though this is bad for me, I feel relieved." James wiped the tears from his face.

"Why James, why?"

"What reason can I muster up that's going to take away the pain I've just caused you and soon my entire family?" James said, shaking his head regrettably.

"I hate you for this, James. Damn you," Ramona said, crying and running off.

Mr. And Mrs. Holmes were off to themselves, observing the conversation between Steven and the doctor.

"Do you know what that was all about, Gloria?" Jake said, taking a seat in the waiting room."

"I don't think this is the right time and place to bring this up, Jake," Gloria said carefully.

"You don't?" Jake said, shaking his head.

"Jake please," Gloria pleaded.

"Either you're going to tell me. or I'm going to find out myself because I have an idea," Jake said.

Hesitantly, Gloria began to tell the story.

Before she could finished, Jake became enraged.

"And you didn't think it was necessary for you to bring this to my attention?" James stood up, yelling, "My little girl has been living with indescribable pain and you choose not to tell me. How am I supposed to protect my family if you protect the infiltrator?" Jake paused for a minute. Why wouldn't you tell me Jake said rhetorically? "The only reason why you wouldn't tell me is because……………. Tell me you didn't, Gloria! Please tell me you didn't!"

Sobbing heavily, all Gloria could do was put her head down.

"I'll kill him," James said, running outside of the emergency room.

When Jake made it outside he saw that James and Ramona's car was gone.

"Mr. Witherspoon," Dr. Jonah said, "we had to induce labor because Theresa's blood pressure became severely elevated. Theresa's fine now, but your baby needs blood. Unfortunately, the baby was delivered with a common condition called Jaundice."

Steven stood there, not having any idea what she was talking about.

"The baby needs blood immediately. Your wife's blood is a positive, but the child's blood type is B negative. So we need you to give some blood."

"I'm B positive," Steven said, confused.

"Are you sure?" Dr. Jonah asked, bewildered.

"Yes, I'm sure."

"Is anyone in your family B negative?"

Steven had to think fast. He was angry as hell, but he couldn't walk out because Theresa's family would know that there was trouble. He couldn't ask them for blood either because they would figure out that there was a chance that the baby wasn't his. Steven then called Naomi over.

"Naomi, I don't know you and I don't know why you're here, but evidently you know Theresa and the baby needs blood."

"How can I help?" Naomi asked.

"Just tell me you have B negative blood."

"I do."

"Come with me," Dr. Jonah said immediately.

Steven went over to his daughters and took a seat.

"Is Mommy okay, Daddy?" Thereasa asked, her eyes filling with tears.

"Mommy's okay, baby girl," Steven said. He sighed heavily and hugged his daughters close to him.

After giving blood, Naomi returned to the waiting room. Steven was there with Thereasa in his lap and Stephanie leaning on his shoulder asleep.

"I need you to talk to me," **Steven said gently laying the girls down.**
Naomi sat in the chair furthest away from the girls.

"It's a long story," Naomi said sighing while taking her purse strap off of her shoulder.

"Well give me the condensed version," Steven said sitting two chairs down from her.

"It all started about a year ago. I was on a flight back home from Florida when I met Theresa. I was sitting right in front of Theresa and we for some reason or another kept looking into each other's eyes then turning away. It wasn't intentional but we couldn't stop looking at one another," Naomi said with her head down.

Steven just sat there shaking his head.

"Once we landed and began to de-board the plane, I slipped Theresa my number. A few weeks had passed before she called but she eventually did," Naomi said, lifting her head sighing again.

"Can we move a little faster," Steven said in a low infuriated tone.

"I don't have to tell you any of this," Naomi responded.

"And you can leave also," Steven said, looking directly into Naomi's eyes.

"Before long we had developed a relationship," Naomi said sighing heavily. Theresa expressed that she wasn't a lesbian but admitted that she was curious. Eventually, we ended up becoming intimate and we thought we fell in love with each other. We decided that we were going to be together and that we wanted a child together."

"Well we both know that that wasn't possible," Steven said, standing to his feet and walking away then turning back around.

"You're right, that's when we came up with the idea to have my brother......

"Oh hell no you didn't," Steven said, raising his voice.

The security guard started towards the two. Naomi raised her hand as if she was okay and the guard turned away.

"Are you going let me tell you the story or what," Naomi said, with an exhausted look on her face.

"Go ahead," Steven said, taking a seat.

"My brother Jerry agreed and we all slept together. Before we could find out if Theresa was pregnant, she had a change of heart and didn't want to continue with our relationship."

Steven took his seat again and now has his hands covering his face and sobbing.

"She called it off Steven," Naomi said, sliding one chair over and grabbing Steven's arm."

'Get off of me," Steven said, angrily. Get out?

Stephanie awoke rubbing her eyes.

"Can you please leave," Steven said. I don't want my girls to ever see you again."

Naomi grabbed her purse and stood to her feet.

"I'm sorry about everything Steven. Please forgive me," Naomi said grabbing her purse by the handles and walking towards the exit.

"Who was that daddy, Stephanie, said looking up at Steven?"

"Nobody baby. Nobody. "

2 Weeks Later.........

As Steven walked into sanctuary, he noticed that neither Pastor Jones nor the 1st Lady Jones were in their respective seats in the pulpit. In their seats were the assistant pastor, Elder Francis, and his wife, Evangelist Francis. The choir was in the middle of singing "Celebrate," by Smokie Norful. Steven was running late and was surprised that he'd made it before the Pastor began to preach. Today was the day that Steven was supposed to pick Theresa up from the hospital. Steven spent numerous days and nights wrestling with his situation. His new child, Naomi, Theresa's betrayal and her sexual abuse as a child was a lot for Steven to deal with. If it was not for God and the girls, he felt as though he might have left.

The Usher led Steven to his seat. Steven felt as though he was receiving sympathetic smiles from everyone that made eye contact with him. It was a good thing that he had taken the girls to his sister's yesterday to have their hair done. By the time they made it to their seats, the choir had finished singing and Pastor Francis was walking up to the podium.

Pastor Francis was a short man with a low, army style high and tight hair cut. His face was coarse from shaving his heavy beard for so many years. His suits always fit him perfectly. Tailor fitted. His wife was about 1-2 inches taller than he was when she was wearing heels. Today she was wearing her flat shoes, which she normally wore when

Pastor Francis spoke. She was a fair-skinned lady with plenty of curves. I hated when she wore pantsuits to church because you couldn't help but see all of those curves, today she had on a skirt and blouse and her hair wrapped. That was the one thing that I loved about her. It wasn't always wrapped but whenever she was up there with him, it was.

"Amen church," Pastor said, placing his Bible on the podium.

"Amen, Pastor," people near the front of the congregation, responded.

"Celebrate," he said, pausing and looking up from his Bible, smoothing out the pages with both hands. "For this is the day of the Lord," he said, smiling. "How many of you believe that this is the day of the Lord?"

Heads nodded and amen's were heard throughout the congregation. One lady jumped up and began to run around the church.

"The struggle," he said, elevating his voice, "is now finished..............the battle is fought, and the victory is won." He smiled. "I will rejoice at all times," he elevated his voice once again. "For I know that my God is with me. Celebrate," Pastor said, stepping away from the podium. The musicians and the choir began to play and sing the song again. This went on for about 5 to 10 minutes as others from the congregation joined in with the young woman.

Pastor Francis then motioned for the musicians and the choir to fade. "Oh I feel the presence of the Lord in this building. I would ask that you pray for Pastor Jones and 1st Lady Jones in their absence. Pray that they are enjoying their 25th Wedding anniversary in Hawaii. You know that Pastor Jones is checking the web log daily, so you all say nice things about the service on today."

People in the congregation began to look at one another laughing.

"First, I would like to give honor to God, my Father, for strengthening me and giving me reason to celebrate. There is nothing like a celebration. Even in our worldly times, we loved to celebrate. Kool and the Gang said, 'Celebration time…. come on, let's celebrate.' But I'm here to tell you that there's a party going on right here, and THIS celebration WILL last throughout the year." The pastor smiled again with his smile turning into a laugh.

Reminiscing, I picked up Thereasa and put her in my lap.

"Maybe I ought to slow it down a little because I don't want to take some of you too far back because by the look on some of your faces I might lose a couple of you," Pastor said, with a smirk on his face. "I think we need to get into this scripture. If you will, turn with me in your Bible to Exodus the 14th chapter and the 10th verse. When you're there, say amen."

Amens were heard throughout.

Steven opened his Bible and found the scripture.

"As Pharaoh approached, the Israelites looked up and there were Egyptians marching after them. They were terrified and cried out to the Lord. They said to Moses, was it because there were no graves in Egypt that you brought us here to the desert to die?"

Pausing and shaking his head, Pastor Francis continued. "What have you done to us bringing us out of Egypt? Leave us alone."

"Let us serve the Egyptians; it would have been better for us to serve them than die in the desert." Pastor lifted his head from the Bible. "From this scripture, I have titled this sermon 'After the Celebration, how soon we forget.' How soon we forget," he repeated. "You see, church, we have no problem celebrating. It's after the celebration that we have a problem. You, you see," Pastor said, bouncing up and down on his toes, "we quickly forget where he brought us from once we're in the celebration mode. Even when going through, the Lord takes care of you. If you read with me a little further on in the same chapter, about the 17th verse, it reads: When Pharaoh lets the people go, Moses didn't lead them on the road through the Philistine country though it was shorter, for God said if they face war, they may change their minds and return to Egypt. So God led the people by the desert road toward the Red Sea."

Lifting his head back to the congregation and placing one hand on the Bible, he faced the congregation to his left. "I don't know about any of you, but how many of you have ever felt the Lord's hand guiding you? The Lord knew what the Israelites could bear, and church, the Lord knows what you can bear. Some of you even feel like the Lord took you down the long route."

Steven was in total agreement with the sermon, but had no idea that he was in for his own revelation.

Turning to his right, Elder Francis continued. "I know that someone in that huge movement thought to themselves, we're going the long way and wanted to tell Moses and Aaron to make a right turn at the next grove of cacti."

The congregation laughed.

Pastor glanced down at his watch, then said, "I need to fast-forward a little bit. After Moses led them through the Red Sea and they saw the power of God in verses 29 through 31, they feared the Lord and put their trust in him and Moses, his servant. Three days passed, as they journeyed through the desert, without finding water. The people began to grumble against Moses." Pastor Francis smiled and said, "How soon we forget."

At that moment, those four words hit Steven like a ton of bricks. Steven realized that he was quick to judge his wife, when he himself had in the past dealt with a similar

situation in his first marriage. His mind then left the sanctuary and went to a counseling session he'd had with Bishop Odom from his former church home in DC.

Flash Back

"Sis Passmore, may I speak with Bishop Odom," Steven said frantically over the phone.

"He's in with someone else at the moment, and they're his last appointment for the evening," Sis Paasmore said, in her most soothing and concerned voice.

"But I must speak with him tonight," Steven exclaimed.

"You're going to have to call on him tomorrow, Brother Steven," she replied, not wavering.

"Well I'm coming to the church right now. Don't let the Bishop leave," Steven said, and then hanging up.

Sis Passmore pulled the phone from her ear and just stared at it, confused.

About 20 minutes later, Steven showed up at the church's double glass doors, which led to the church offices. Sis Passmore had just locked the doors and was walking away.

Steven walked up and began banging on the glass doors.

A startled, Sis Passmore immediately turned around and stared at Steven.

"Bishop is finished for tonight, Brother Steven," she said walking, over to the doors.

Steven began to bang on the doors, calling out for Bishop Odom. Sis Passmore placed her right hand over her chest and became angry and frightened all at the same time. Bishop Odom immediately came out of his office.

"Bishop Odom," Steven said desperately, "I need to see you, sir."

"Let him in," the Bishop said. "It's okay."

Sis Passmore and Steven stared at one another as she unlocked the door, and then Steven walked through. Steven followed the Bishop to his office.

"Have a seat," Bishop said, as he motioned for Steven to take one of the chairs. "What's going on, Brother Steven?"

"I can't get these images out of my head, Bishop," Steven said nervously.

"Steven, we've gone over this. You've got to let this go!"

"Bishop, the image of my father entering into my room and the things he asked me and made me do won't leave me, and it's gotten worse."

"Talk to me, son," Bishop said, leaning forward and becoming worried about the safety of Ashley and her son." **(Ashley was Steven's ex-wife)**

"Bishop, I find myself thinking about my stepson in that way. I've had disturbing dreams, Bishop," Steven said, beginning to cry.

"Okay, okay calm down," Bishop said, rolling his chair over to me. "Steven, you're going to need some professional help. Do you think this is the reason that you've become so promiscuous, because you're trying to prove your manhood?"

"Bishop, I've had sex with not just women to find this out. Bishop, I don't know, but I feel so helpless," Steven said, sitting back in the chair.

"Okay Steven," Bishop said, realizing that Steven needed some additional assistance. "Let me make a quick call, okay?"

"Okay, Bishop," Steven said, looking up to the ceiling.

Bishop searched through his rolodex and located a number. He then began dialing. After a few minutes of talking, Bishop hung up the phone.

"Okay, I've worked out an early appointment with a friend of mine. His name is Dr. Bill. I need you to be there at 7:30 in the morning. In the meantime, there is some scripture that I would like to go over with you." Bishop handed Steven a Bible from his bookshelf.

"Turn to Mathew the 5th chapter and we'll begin reading from the 3rd verse." Bishop began to read: "Blessed are the poor in spirit for theirs is the kingdom of heaven, blessed are they that mourn for they shall be comforted. Blessed are the meek, for they shall inherit the earth. Blessed are they that hunger and thirst for righteousness, for they will be filled. Blessed are the merciful, for they will be shown mercy. Blessed are the pure in heart, for they will see God. Blessed are the peacemakers, for they will be called sons of God. Blessed are those who are persecuted because of righteousness, for theirs is the kingdom of heaven. Blessed are you when people insult you, persecute you and falsely say all kinds of evil against you because if me. Rejoice and be glad, because great is your reward in heaven, for the same way they persecuted the profits who were before you.

"I've chosen those scriptures to say you are blessed because of your situation. You are blessed because you mourn. You are blessed because you are meek and that you should rejoice and be exceedingly glad because great is your reward. You are blessed because you were abused as a child and because of it, you will be a great father to your children. I know you don't see it right now, but the sun will rise on your life again. We all go through the shadows of death, but remember fear not because the Lord our God is with you. Seek out the Lord's comfort."

Bishop reached over and placed his hand on Steven's shoulder and said, "It's going to be okay, son. The Lord loves you."

Steven lifted his head and tears streamed down my face. "Thank you, Bishop. I feel so much better."

"Steven," Bishop said, comforting, "you know that I'm going to have to ask you to stay here for tonight. I have some sheets and a pillow in the closet, and you can just pull out the sleeper sofa. I also need to call Sis Ashley to ensure that she is okay. Does she know where you are?"

"No, she doesn't, Bishop."

"Well as soon as you call her, I'm going to need to speak with her also. Is that okay?"

"Yes Bishop," Steven said, wiping tears from my face.

"Daddy, do you need another tissue," Stephanie asked.

Steven shook his head and returned his attention to the sanctuary.

"Why are you crying, Daddy?" Stephanie asked. "Daddy, you're always crying." She had tears in her eyes. "Are you crying because Mommy isn't feeling well?"

"Daddy's okay, baby," Steven said, hugging his girls.

By this time, Pastor Francis was further into his sermon.

"If you'll turn with me now to Deuteronomy, the 6th chapter and the 12th verse. The Lord told the Israelites not to forget the Lord who brought them out of Egypt. See, but we only celebrate when things are going great. As soon as things get a little rough, we are quick to forget what the Lord has done for us. The Lord lays out what we should forget," Pastor Francis said, shaking his head. "Job said I will forget my complaint, and I will change my expression. Oh we can say we're not complaining and but Job took it a little further. Job said he's going to smile through his trials," Pastor said, smiling. "Blessed be the name of Jesus. Oh you can say a lot with a simple expression. Complaint all over your face, saying praise the Lord."

A few ladies in the congregation stood up, smiling and clapping and waving their hands above their heads repeating, "Praise the Lord."

"The one thing that I can count on is God being God "all the time." Closing his Bible, Pastor Francis walked down to the front of the church. "Who wants to celebrate on today? Who wants to celebrate remembering and not forgetting what the Lord has done for you? Most sermons end with a nice, slow inviting song as they open the doors of the church, but today I want to bring new children to the Lord celebrating. I don't

want any sad crying and mourning. Not that there's something wrong with that, but I want to bring new children to the Lord singing and dancing so much that he himself smiles. So as the deacons and deaconesses come forward, I ask that you come forward if you want to celebrate in Christ."

Pastor then started singing "Celebrate." The choir and the musicians joined in, and they were having a Holy Ghost celebration.

As everyone celebrated, Steven noticed that it was close to the time for picking up Theresa. So he gathered up the girls and their things and proceeded to the car.

When Steven arrived at the hospital, Theresa's parents were there. Mr. Holmes and Steven hadn't spoken since their incident.

Mr. and Mrs. Holmes had been dealing with their issues of trust and betrayal. They were close to splitting apart but were trying to work out there past issues of infidelity. Even though Mr. Holmes wanted to kill James, he turned him in to the authorities instead. He gave Mrs. Holmes the ultimatum of receive counseling or he would leave because even though he himself had committed the sin of infidelity, he would never place the safety of children before no one. Ramona left James and was in the process of filing for divorce.

"Hello Steven," Mrs. Holmes said, releasing Mr. Holmes's hand and offering hers.

"Good afternoon, Mrs. Holmes," Steven politely responded. He paused momentarily, then continuing to Theresa's room.

"You know, we need to end all of this craziness before Theresa comes out."

"No, Mr. Holmes, or should I say "Jake"—you don't need to be here."

"Now see, you're going to stop disrespecting me," Mr. Holmes said, moving towards Steven.

"Well what are you going to do?" Steven replied, moving the girls out of the way.

Mrs. Holmes immediately grabbed the girls and got in between the two.

"This is not what we need to be doing right now," Mrs. Holmes said, lowering her voice and hand signaling for them to do the same.

"I'm just trying to let him know that I didn't know," Jake said, getting control of his emotions.

"You didn't know?" Steven said, still angry.

"No son…. I didn't," Jake said shamefully.

Steven moved in close. "That's no excuse, it's because of father's like you………………" Steven broke down.

"Come here, son," Jake said, embracing Steven.

"It hurts so bad," Steven said, falling onto the shoulder of his father in-law.

It's okay, Steven. We're going to make it through this son. We all are," Jake said, grabbing the back of Stevens head.

Mrs. Holmes stood by as tears ran down her face, saying to herself, "Thank you, Jesus."

"Mr. Holmes, can you watch the girls while I go in and see about my wife?" Steven said, humbly.

"No problem, son. Go head and do what you need to do, and remember we all have sinned and fallen short of his grace."

Steven and Mrs. Holmes walked up to the NICU to check on the baby.

Staring at the baby through the glass, Steven asked, "How long have you known and how much do you know?"

"I know about it all, Steven," she replied, staring at the baby.

"I don't know how I'm going to make it through this, Mrs. Holmes. This new child, her adultery, and everything else. I don't even know with whom she's been with.

"I know the story, Steven, and it's about time I get it off of my chest."

Mrs. Holmes and Steven had a seat in the waiting room, and she explained what she knew about the situation. Just as she was finishing up, Naomi walked in.

"Hello Naomi," Mrs. Holmes said, pulling back the curtains on her and Naomi's relationship."

Surprised, Naomi responded, "Mrs. Holmes?"

"It's okay, child, he knows everything."

"I want you to know Steven that it's been over between us since the talk that the two of you had when she first told you about her abuse. She loves you."

"If that was the case, how did you know she was in the hospital on that night?"

"I have a friend here that happened to be working the shift when it happened."

"Listen," Steven said, "I understand everything that you're doing and saying, but I'm not ready to accept you. I'm having enough trouble accepting this situation, but I don't have to accept the people involved in this situation. So I'd appreciate and believe that your motives are genuine, but I'm not ready to have a conversation with you right now. So, if you will allow me some space that would be in your best interest."

"Okay, I understand."

Steven stared through the glass door of the room, afraid to enter. She must have felt his presence because she turned towards him. Two seconds after their eyes met, Steven went in and sat on the edge of the bed.

"Hey Theresa, how are you doing?" Steven asked, holding Theresa's hand.

"I'm doing better. How are the girls?"

"They're fine. They're with your father. I met your friend Naomi."

"So you know everything," Theresa said, closing her eyes.

"Yeah, I do," Steven said, continuing to hold Theresa's hand.

"So where do we go from here?" Theresa said, unsure.

"We get counseling and try to move on. We take our children home and we don't look back.

Steven leaned in and kissed Theresa on the lips as Mr. and Mrs. Holmes walked in with the girls.

"I'm sorry sugar plumb," Mr. Holmes said, walking over and kissing Theresa on the forehead.

"I know daddy."

MARRIAGE LICENSE

*M*arriage License is a combination of two or more stories from previous books. The reason for this, is I plan to create a screen or stage play from this story..

"Hello everyone. I would like to welcome you all to our first annual Father's House Marriage Retreat," Bishop Haden said as he stood before the large crowd. And it's befitting that it's a marriage retreat, being that this is Fatience's maiden voyage on the Finger Lakes. For any of you that wanted to know, *Fatience* is a combination of Faith and Patience, which is essential in all stages of a marriage. What I would like to do is give you all a brief overview of what we'll be covering in your four-day Marriage Licensing Course. Your course leaders-slash-instructors were chosen based on your questionnaires that were submitted online. Some of the couples attending need a lot more work than others, so we recruited some serious experts." The bishop offered a

smile. "While we're on the subject of these experts, I would like to introduce one of our premiere recruits. He's a phenomenal well-known couple's therapist. He has four best selling books on relationships, and he hosts his own relationships show on TV ONE. He's a regular on the Lincoln Styles show. He received his PhD and a PsyD in psychology from Chicago State University. He attends The Midwest Star Father's House Ministries, which is our sister-church in Chicago. His name is Dr. Hezekiah Bill. He and his lovely wife Julia will be the class therapists for one of the classes. Let's give Dr. Bill and his wife a welcome round of applause."

Dr. Bill had the charisma and disposition of Laurence Fishburne. He wore a full gray beard and a suit to match. His wife had a tall stature of Michelle Obama and the stance of Condeleeza Rice. They were a beautiful couple.

"Each class will consist of eight couples. That's **one man** and **one woman,** together," Bishop Haden said, smiling and shaking his head. He looked into every eye in the room, smiling again. "Of course, this is Day One, which will be used mainly for in-processing. We need to make sure everyone here is supposed to be here, and to make sure we have your names spelled correctly for your Marriage License. Lastly, we want to issue your meal cards and team shirts. Right after in processing we'll give you a tour of the ship and get you to your cabins. But first, we're going to identify each group and its leaders. Please stand as a couple as I call your family names. I have Sean and Brittany Washington, Tyson and Alyssa Ferguson, Christopher and Faith O'Donnell, Lawrence and Zora Greer, Bianca and Jaheim Johnson, Sheila and Allen Rogers, Diane Watson and Gregg Pierce, and James and Panerva Bailey. Your instructor will be Dr. Bill and Mrs. Julia. Evidently this is the group with the most issues," Bishop Haden said, smiling again.

After getting all of the couples and therapists paired, Bishop Haden began to talk about each day's events.

"Day One, like I said, is in-processing and couple introduction. Day Two, we split the men and women apart to have gender-based discussions. From nine until lunchtime we will have the ladies, and from one until three we will bring in the men. From three 'til five we'll bring everyone back together for a recap. Each group will then chose a song to sing that describes how they feel about each other. Each of your performances will be given here in the Drama Sanctuary. Day Three will consist of intense sessions on building a marriage team, opening lines of communication, defining the relationship, and recognizing signs. Day Four will start where Day Three leaves off. Couples will be given one hour of couple-to-counselor sessions. This means that on Friday, sessions will begin at eight a.m., instead of the usual nine a.m. start. At the end of day four, each

couple will be evaluated by their instructor / counselor to determine if they've shown the ability to take individual and partner accountability in maintaining a healthy and prosperous role in their relationships. In addition, if they've demonstrated the ability to recognized deficiencies individually and as a couple and able to apply what they have learned to their relationship on a daily basis. If so, they will be awarded their "Marriage License" in our first ever Marriage Licensing graduation ceremony. Okay class instructors, they're all yours."

After the tour, Dr. Bill took his class to his classroom. The room was set with one large table in the middle of the room, for the gender-specific classes, and eight two-person couches for couples in session together.

"I have already been introduced, so now it's your turn," Dr. Bill said, as he and Julia walked in behind the class. "I want each couple to stand up together and introduce themselves. I want your names and how long you've been married. I would ask for your ages but I know that would be inappropriate, being that we have women in the room. But men, when we get together, I'm going to get those ages," he said, smiling.

"Good evening, Dr. Bill. My name is Sean Washington and this is my wife Brittany Washington. We've been married for one year. The Bills nodded.

"My name is Tyson Fergusson, and this is my wife Alyssa Ramos-Fergusson, and we've been married for three years."

"Hello, sir. My name is Christopher O'Donnell, and this is my wife Faith O'Donnell, and we've been married for two and a half years."

"Hello, Dr. Bill. My name is Lawrence Greer, and this is my wife Zora Greer, and this is our second marriage. We've been married for seven wonderful years."

"Good," Dr. Bill said. "It's always good to have a couple that has experienced divorce. Not that divorce is good, but to help those that may be contemplating divorce. Next couple," Dr. Bill said, motioning for the next pair to stand.

"Hello, Dr. Bill. My name is Gregg Pierce, and this is my girlfriend Diane Watson, and we've been dating for a little over six months."

"Also good," Dr. Bill interjected. "Okay."

"Hello, Dr. Bill," Jaheim said, smiling.

"Oh, no," Dr. Bill said, as he shook his head. "Why are you smiling?"

"Oh, it's nothing," Jaheim said. "My name is Jaheim Johnson, and this is my wife Bianca Johnson, and we've been married for a little over a year."

"Hello, Dr. Bill. My name is James Bailey, and this is my lovely wife Panerva Bailey, and we've been married for over twenty-five years."

"Congratulations to the both of you. Welcome everyone," Dr. Bill said leaning up against the front of the desk. "I look forward to getting to know each of you, and I pray that we all get what we came here for. By the way, ladies, since you will be here first thing in the morning, be prepared to tell me what you want to get out of this marriage retreat. Make it simple, but if you need to vent your answer, that's fine too. Okay," Dr. Bill said, leaning forward off of the desk. "I start and end every session with a simple prayer. Okay, bow your heads.

"Father, it took a lot for some of your children to acknowledge or to realize that it's important to have you as head of every relationship. Bless every relationship that is under the sound of my voice. I pray Father that you allow everyone here to speak freely and honestly, so that they will leave here better than when they came. I pray for understanding, wisdom and patience. These things I ask in your name, heavenly Father. Amen. I'll see you guys tomorrow."

The Next morning

"Good Morning, ladies," Dr. Bill said, as he walked into the room. The ladies were all seated around the table.

"Good morning," they responded excitedly.

"You guys seem as though you're ready for today."

"Yes we are," Bianca replied, with a smile."

"First of all, I want to find out what each of you really want to get out of this retreat," Dr. Bill said, taking his seat at the table. "We'll start from this side" he motioned, in the direction of Bianca.

"The thing that I want—"

"Hold on," Dr. Bill interposed. "I apologize for cutting you off, but I want to reiterate a very important point here."

"Its okay," Bianca said, giving way to Dr. Bill.

"We can be real here, and you all to can actually get something out of this to take home with you or alternatively, we can be pretty and leave here exactly as we came. With that said, I hope that I have influenced each of you to really speak what's in your heart, because I know you ladies came here for a reason. Again I'm sorry, Mrs. Johnson. You may continue."

"Dr. Bill, I just want my Husband to want me the way he did in the beginning."

"Can you elaborate a little for me," Dr. Bill said. He frowned a little as he looked directly at her.

"I mean it's like I'm not even there. There is no physical or emotional intimacy in our marriage, and it's as if he can go without it."

"Okay, that's good," Dr. Bill said. He had put on his glasses and began taking notes.

"Faith," he said, looking up and in her direction.

"Dr. Bill, my husband and I are basically here to—"

"I have to stop you right there," Dr. Bill said, taking off his glasses. He let them hang down around his neck. I'm not interested in what you and your husband want right now. I want to know what Faith wants to get out of the marriage retreat."

Faith paused for about a minute to think. "I want to find out how I can keep him home for more than an hour," Faith crossed her legs and sat back in her chair. "Dr. Bill, its work, work, work, work, work! Don't get me wrong, Dr, Bill. I love and support my husband in his career, but it's like he lives at the office."

Smiling, Dr. Bill said, "Okay, Faith. That was good. Alyssa you're next."

"Well, I'm not having that problem. To be honest, it's the opposite," Alyssa said, with her arms folded. "Tyson and I worked at the same modeling agency for years, but he's become ridiculously meticulous about the jobs he takes. He's also become very insecure and won't take jobs unless we're in the same location."

"Okay, that's a pretty common issue with couples that are models," Dr. Bill said, putting on his glasses and writing more notes. "I usually wait until everyone is finished, but I'm going to take this one now. Many times, in relationships that I just mentioned for both men and women, both of them have experienced a number of "relationships". Not structured relationships, but bad relationships. A good looking suave man has probably had affairs with married women or a number of women who were suppose to be in committed relationships. The effects that these "relationships" had on him is that now he can't trust women, and this works both ways. He's had his choice of women regardless of their status and now can't find himself trusting any woman, because he feels like none of them are any good anyway. I'm going to prove my point by asking you a simple question."

All of the women around the table were hanging on to every word of Dr. Bill's.

"Has he ever told you that most women are no good?"

"Yes, but he's said it a little differently," Alyssa said. She smiled, as she looked around the table at the other women.

"You're going to have to go above and beyond to prove to him that you can be trusted, if you want this marriage to work. You can't change his past. But you can reassure his

future. Give him tangible reasons to trust you. Not a woman's reason, because that's not going to work. As you ladies already know, men are different."

"Ain't that the truth," Bianca said.

"Let's continue. Zora, you're next."

"Dr. Bill, I'm here to be made aware of the signs and pitfalls that most second marriages fall into."

Taking more notes, Dr. Bill said, "Okay. You're next, Brittany."

"Why do men cheat, Dr. Bill?"

"Now that's getting straight to the point," Dr. Bill said. He put his pencil down and shook his head with a smile. "I'm going to answer your question now, also. First off, I'm going to give you the signs and symptoms of a cheating man. You ladies ready?"

"Dr. Bill, can I have a piece of paper and a pencil?" Diane said with her hand out. She was looking straight into Dr. Bill's face without a smile.

"Me too, girl," Sheila said, looking at Diane as Dr. Bill tore a few sheets of paper from his notebook.

The black women and the Hispanic woman looked at Sheila in amazement.

"Aren't you married to one of the white men in this class?" Bianca asked Sheila, before looking around at the other women.

"Yes, I am," Sheila said, with sista girl attitude. "Oh, white men don't cheat? A man is a man, is a man."

"I hear you, girl," Bianca said.

"I can see you ladies are going to be something else," Dr. Bill said, shaking his head. Here are some telltale signs that your man is probably messing around or preparing to break the monogamous ties of your relationship. Number one: things that use to bother the heck out of him barely affect him all of a sudden. Now everyone over a period of time learns to deal with certain idiosyncrasies that annoy him or her, but if they stop all of a sudden you may want to pay more attention. Now there are levels to these signs. If a man starts to clean up behind himself when he used to leave his things lying around the house, this is a serious sign. He starts to clean up behind himself in the bathroom; he puts his work clothes in the proper place when he takes them off; his pajamas are no longer on the floor by his side of the bed until he gets back home from work. You had better believe something is going on. He may be preparing to be a better man for someone else."

The ladies started looking at one another laughing.

"That makes too much sense," Zora said, smiling in amazement. "I could have used this class for my first marriage."

"If he starts to balance his checkbook more often, that may be another sign," Dr. Bill continued. "Cashing in stocks. He stops putting money into the joint account, cuts back on his spending. These are all signs that your man may be looking for, or in, an affair. You have to pay attention to your man. Just like anything else, a man will tell you when something is wrong. It's very simple, ladies. If you've driven your car for a while but one day it's not picking up speed like it used to or the air-conditioning isn't as cool as it use to be, these are signs that something's changed. Everything sends signals when there has been a change. Does that help you guys understand?"

"Well heck, I should've been in this class months ago," Bianca said. She laughed and shook her head. "My man has cooled down quite considerably."

"Girl, you need to stop," Zora said, tapping Bianca's hand.

"Now, why do men cheat?" Dr. Bill said, with a smile. "This is going to seem real chauvinistic, but men cheat because men are insecure and women are—plainly put—'beautiful.' It doesn't matter what size or shape you are. You are stunningly gorgeous to someone."

"That is so wrong," Shelia said, shaking her head.

"Hold on, hold on. Let me explain. Let me start with insecurity. Every man enjoys the feeling of thinking he's the man. Men are ego trippers. Is that fair to say?" Dr. Bill asked, cautiously.

"Go on," Panerva said, following closely.

"Okay, if you are not stroking your man's ego, sooner or later somebody else will. Pay close attention to what I'm about to say: the key to this whole thing is you know him better than anyone; therefore, you have the advantage. See, any woman can feed his ego with words of flattery, but you know of his imperfections. Those are the areas that you go overboard to encourage him in. Men are afraid of having their inadequacies known. If he is safe and secure with you knowing his blemishes, why risk being judged by someone else? That's what he'll think if he's smart. This goes back to what I was talking about when I mentioned the signs of a man that is cheating. He's working hard to cover up his imperfections before he leaves, but what he doesn't realize is his change ninety percent of the time, is temporary. All of you women sitting here know that you guys get hit on ten times as much as we do. When a man gets hit on, it's like 'this is an opportunity.' She finds me interesting. That's why you have to hit on your man every now and then. You have to think like the clean up woman. It is hard work being a woman, but it is so rewarding. Feed your man and I'm not just talking about food. Find out his weaknesses and erase them. If he does cheat, he will regret the hell out of it. He'll know in the back of his mind, whoever gets her is going to be the luckiest man

in the world. This is also how you keep your man coming home, Faith," Dr. Bill said, looking in her direction. "Have him come home to someone different every other night or something. Wear a wig. Every now and then do something out of your character. Like I said, it's hard work being a woman.

"Okay ladies let's get back to business," Dr. Bill said, as he put his glasses back on. "Diane, you're next."

"I'm here to get information that will better prepare me for marriage. When Bishop Hayden said in one of his sermons that we get licenses to drive and fly planes, but anyone can get married without any training, it really made me think. So I thought it would be something that would help Gregg and I."

"And that statement is so true. Too often I've had to counsel couples that shouldn't have been together from the start. Not only are they not being taught what the Lord says about marriage, but nine times out of ten they came from a broken home with a great deal of arguing, fighting and disrespect. That's all they know, so fighting or disrespect in their home feels like that same love they grew up with. Now, not everyone feels that way. Some of us recognize crazy and do our best to have the dictionary meaning of love. But if you've never seen what right looks like, you will look for TV love. You will be disappointed every time looking for TV love. If you don't know what you're looking for and you don't have the right questions, you will end up with Mr. or Ms. crazy and deranged."

"Well what kind of questions do you ask," Diane asked.

"It's really not about questions. I mean it is, but it isn't. A person will show you who they are. If your man hangs out with men who don't work, if your man spends more time in front of a gaming system than he does spending time with you, if he raises his hand to you one time? Too many women make excuses for men. Yes, and I understand that there aren't many "good" men out there. And yes, there are a great deal of men who haven't had someone teach them how to treat a woman, but your men are here with you. As far as questions go, you can slip in a question like, 'how do you feel about family?' This is a very important question. If you are one that feels as though looking after your sisters and brothers is your responsibility, or you love to go to momma's on Sunday for a home-cooked meal with the family, and he can't stand being around family, you're going to have a problem. Something as simple as that can cause friction in a marriage. He could be a momma's boy and you can't stand his momma. That's going to be a problem for him. Diane, you're the only one that has this advantage. You have to ask your man questions, and when we do our couples session I will remember you and help the both of you out with questions for each other, okay?"

"That would be wonderful, Dr. Bill," Diane said, sounding reassured. "I am so happy that I came here."

"I'm happy for you. The men that you brought here today probably didn't want to come, and some of them did. This is a Christian Marriage Retreat. That says a great deal for the men in your lives. They recognize God in their lives, and God is a way-maker. Let's go ahead and move on. Mrs. Bailey, you're next."

"My husband and I are celebrating an anniversary, and since he took care of me last year, I wanted to do something special for him this year."

"That's very sweet of you. How long have the two of you been married?"

"Twenty-five good and bad years," she said, with a smile. "I must say that most of them were good years or tolerable years."

"That's a beautiful way of putting it. I couldn't have put it better myself. We're going to take a break to get something to drink and stretch our legs. When we return, I'll pick up where we left off by giving feedback to the women I haven't addressed. Then, we'll go to lunch."

"Sound's great," the women agreed.

Meanwhile, the men were in the entertainment room playing a friendly game of cards.

"It's almost our turn to 'go see the doctor,'" Sean said, picking up his cards.

"I'm wondering what the women are saying about us," Jaheim said, smiling as he looked at his hand.

"There's no telling," Gregg said, as he pulled a card from the deck.

"Have you seen the chicks on the boat? Tyson asked, as he looked around.

"Maybe you need to put some cards in your hands and play a hand before you get yourself into some trouble," Allen warned, laying down a spread.

"I have a question for the two older gentlemen in our group," Tyson said, with a peculiar smile on his face.

"Here we go," Gregg said, shaking his head.

"Go ahead, 'young fella,'" James said, while maintaining eye contact with his cards.

"At what age will I stop noticing and wanting beautiful women?"

"I've got this one, James," Lawrence said with a smile. "There are only two ways that you will stop noticing and wanting beautiful women."

"Okay," Tyson said, with an eager smile. "What are they?"

"One is if you're blind," Lawrence said, putting his cards down to look at Tyson. "If you can't see them, you can't want them, right? And lastly, if you're dead and that goes without explanation," Lawrence laughed.

"I can never get a real answer when I ask that question," Tyson said, shaking his head.

James turned to Lawrence. "Do you mind if I help him a little?" he asked.

"Be my guest," Lawrence said. He drew a card and laid another one down.

"That really was a two part question, for one, and no matter what anyone tells you, you're going to do whatever it is you want, because it's about a state of mind. A state of being."

"What are you talking about, James?"

"You're always going to notice a beautiful woman—"

"Then they say that you're lusting," Tyson interjected.

"Can I finish?" James said, turning to Tyson. No, it is not lusting. That was a tool that was used to condemn people and practically pushed people into sin.

"What do you mean?" Gregg said. He was becoming personally interested in James's comment.

"You can't help wanting something. This is bigger than women. You can't stop yourself from wanting a new car, a new pair of shoes, or a beautiful woman. It becomes lust when you do things that go beyond wanting. For instance, I'm going to use a woman as an example, because that's kind of what started this conversation. The woman that you just noticed, for instance. Everyone at this table could want her, but it doesn't become lust until one of us goes out of our way to find out where her room is. When I drive across town to happen to be in the same coffee shop as her. When I find myself going by her job, when I have no reason to be where I am other than to see that particular woman. When you can't control your actions, not just your thinking, that is when you are committing lust.

"But the bible says we are sinning even if we are thinking it," Christopher said, trying to get an understanding.

"And that is true," Lawrence said, to back James up, "But we're talking about lust. We can't control our thoughts—or should I say, as we mature in Christ our thoughts will automatically become more pure—but what we *can* control is our physical selves from being where we're not supposed to be and saying things that we're not suppose to say."

"Hey, Chris, take my hand for me. I need to go and check something out," Tyson said, handing Christopher his cards.

"I don't play cards," Christopher said, pushing the cards away.

"Well, I'm out."

"We have to be in the class in fifteen minutes, Tyson," Gregg called out after him.

"I can see he's going to have some problems on this boat," Lawrence said, as he shook his head.

James lays down the winning hand. "Hey, he's a grown man," he said, as he collected up the cards.

"That's it for me, too," Allen said, as he stood up.

"You're leaving, too, Allen?" Jaheim said, looking over at him.

"Hey, call me Al,'" Allen said, stroking his chin. "I'm going to get freshened up and ready for our session. I'll see you fellas there."

"That's a cool white boy," Gregg said, smiling. "I'm going to do the same. I'll see you guys there."

"I guess we all can do the same," Lawrence said. He stood up to follow the others.

Back to the Ladies

"Okay, ladies. I hope everything has been informal so far."

"This is great," Diane said, sounding pleased with the experience.

The other ladies shook their heads and spoke at once in agreement.

"That's good to hear, Diane, and I hope that it gets better for all of you."

"I think that I need to answer…Zora's question about the pitfalls of a second marriage," Dr. Bill said, as he glanced through his notes. "Is that right, Zora?" Dr. Bill said, looking up from his legal pad.

"Yes," Zora agreed.

"First, I need to get a little history. These are going to be very personal questions and you don't have to answer them right here if you don't want to, but we can get started. Is that fine with you?"

"Yes, that's fine," Zora said. She folded her arms.

"Did you start this relationship before your first one had finished?" Dr. Bill inquired.

"No, it was several years later before Lawrence and I got together."

"That's good! Too many times we start relationships before the relationship that we're in is over, therefore bringing in luggage from the past relationship, which really isn't a past relationship anymore, because what you've done is combined the two relationships together forever. The second rule of starting a successful second marriage

is, respect the previous spouse and the kids of the previous marriage. Disrespecting the partner is not winning points for you, and the only people that get hurt when there is back-and-forth of hurtful words are the children. If there are no kids involved, then there shouldn't be any remaining contact between the divorced couple, if there is hostility. If they continue to have contact, then this is a sign of more trouble on the horizon. The third rule is never believe that he or she is better than your previous partner. This is to say that everyone has faults. Believe it or not, your old partner did some things better than your new partner. It's all about your needs. If your new partner is more emotionally responsive to you, and that's what you need in a partner, then love that about him. But he may not be as good of a cook as your previous partner. Cooking is not what you need, so you may have to cook more. What I'm trying to say is that there are pros and cons to every situation. You just have to ensure that you at least find a partner that gives you core satisfaction. If you're a woman who loves to cuddle, then make sure you find a man who loves to cuddle. So basically when you're trying to avoid pitfalls of a second marriage, do not judge your new relationship based on your previous one and know what it takes to make and keep you happy. Know what gives you comfort. Not what the general censuses of women need to be happy but what Zora needs.   How's that for an answer, Mrs. Greer?"

"That was perfect, Dr. Bill, but I'm going to need for the both of us to hear what you just said."

"That's no problem, Mrs. Greer. That's going to happen tomorrow."

"I think I had one more question to answer and that was…'how can I get my husband to want me the way he did in the beginning?' And that was from Mrs. Johnson, right?"

"Yes, Dr. Bill," Bianca replied.

"Let's see…he's a video game player isn't he," Dr. Bill asked. His arms were partially folded with a hand on his chin.

"Yes, he is," Bianca responded.

"And you're an avid reader, also, right? Dr. Bill added.

"Yes."

"Well, I can tell you part of the problem. Both of you are bored with your current situation. Both of you are escaping this boredom through other means. He lives out his exciting manly fantasies on his Xbox, and you live out your sensual and controversial love situations out of a book."

"Is there something wrong with reading, Dr. Bill?" Bianca was confused.

"If you're using it as a replacement for real life, it is. If you for one minute think your husband is going to be like any of those "characters" you're reading about, you're in for more disappointment. Here I go again, I may sound chauvinistic again, but here goes: Are men visual beings, yes or no?"

Each of the ladies took long deep exhales and some of them shook their heads. "Here we go again," one of them retorted.

"I'm sorry, but it's a fact. Am I right or wrong?"

"You're right," they all agreed.

"And women are emotional beings, right?"

Turning toward Bianca, he said, "You have to show your man what he's been missing."

"Dr. Bill, I've bought lingerie and laid them on the bed so he would know without a doubt what my intentions for the evening were. I've cleaned the house so we would have ample time to enjoy one another."

"I'm sorry Mrs. Johnson but lingerie on the bed isn't doing anything for him. It needs to be on you. Do you guys have kids?"

"Yes, we have a five year old named Jada."

"Well when Jada is in the shower, it would be too easy for you to walk right in front of the game—giving him a chance to pause or you're really going to make things bad—and flashing him. Put them in his face. If he's never seen you in a bra with your nipples exposed, trust me that game is not going to be on his mind any more." Dr. Bill looked around the table. "I know we can be some confusing people. We love the chase. But when the man stops chasing you, I see how you can wonder how to get him back on the hunt for you. You have to surprise your husbands every now and then."

"So what do the men have to do?" Brittany replied.

"WORK! To make sure you don't want for anything. Yes, I did say *want for anything. Now, I didn't say hide out at the office. When I say 'work,' I mean excel at his job to make more money. He's supposed to overlook your craziness.*"

"*What?*" *Sheila responded.*

"Oh, you know you guys can get hormonal craziness."

Zora jumped in saying, "He's right, girl. Well at least for me, because sometimes I lose it and wonder myself, 'what am I talking about?' And he brushes it off and he humors me about it. That's why I love him so much. He knows when I'm going crazy and I know when he's going crazy."

"I don't need to say anything else. That pretty much sums it up. I'm going to let you ladies go for lunch, and I'll see you back here at three o'clock."

"Thanks, Dr. Bill," the women all responded, as they got up to leave the room. "This has been awesome so far," Brittany said as she walked up to shake Dr. Bill's hand.

"Thank you, ladies," Dr. Bill said, collecting up his notes.

As the ladies departed, Dr. Bill's wife, Julia, came into the room.

"How did it go baby."

"It went well. I think we have a lively bunch, but I think there is a lot of desire for love and the willingness to work out issues. Here are the notes that I took down for you and the men this afternoon."

"Oh, good."

"Concentrate on the Johnsons, Fergusons, and the Washingtons."

"Right now I, want to concentrate on some other issues," Julia said, as she seductively removed Hezekiah's glasses and softly kissed him.

"That's why I'm glad you're my wife," Hezekiah said, with a smile. "Lets go."

The Men's Session begins

"Hello, gentlemen," Julia said, walking in with her briefcase.

"Hello, Mrs. Bill," the men responded.

"For the purposes of this session, can you gentlemen please refer to me as Julia?"

Sporadic nods and yeses were offered.

"Are you guys enjoying yourselves so far?"

"This is really nice," Lawrence said, and the others agreed.

After getting situated, Julia took her seat at the table. "So before we get started, I would like to tell you gentlemen a story. Would any of you mind?"

Mumbles of "no" and head-shaking let her know she could proceed.

"Of course not, Julia replied, as little talking as necessary, right?"

Heads nodded, saying *yes*.

"I bet you guys will be talking after this story," Julia said, smiling.

"Okay, you guys know the story of Adam and Eve, right?"

"Here we go," Jaheim said to Chris.

"Of course," Lawrence replied with his hands together.

"All right, we know that the Lord told Adam not to eat from the tree of life. We also know that Adam didn't eat from the tree, to put it plainly, because the Lord told him not to. As a matter a fact, I don't think Adam thought twice about it. He didn't have to. Now enters Eve. Eve was given these same instructions. I'm thinking Eve must have been wandering around one day—I guess window-shopping—when a serpent approached.

Now, we don't know why or if the serpent never approached Adam. We can speculate, but we don't know for sure."

"I know," Sean interjected.

"Hold on, Sean. Let me finish. Anyway, the serpent convinces Eve—"

"I know where this is going," Allen said. He shook his head and smiled.

"Eve is convinced to eat the forbidden fruit. About five to ten minutes later Adam arrives. He's puzzled about Eves actions. 'Why, Eve?' Adam exclaims. Eve immediately says, 'It's not bad, Adam. The Father just doesn't want us to be as intelligent as he.' She then convinces Adam to partake of the fruit."

"They've been deceiveing us ever since," Tyson said, under his breath.

"We must not be that superior, then," James said.

"Now from my understanding, the bible says that after eating the fruit, their eyes were immediately open. If that is the case, then it is safe to say that Eve's eyes were open five to ten minutes before Adam's were. I can imagine that Eve's brain was working at a Pentium One rate while Adam was still on DOS for about ten minutes."

"That's foul, Mrs. Julia," Tyson said, smiling. "Do you all see where she's going with this?" he continued.

"Hold on, Tyson. So with this, we can factually say that when a man is thinking of something, a woman thought about that approximately five to ten minutes earlier."

Everyone began laughing, except Tyson. He just shook his head. "Na, Ms. Julia, that's cold."

"Tyson, you can't argue with the facts."

"Okay, well tell me why have I been able to get over on so many women, huh?"

"How many women have you 'gotten over on,'" Julia responded?"

"Don't you worry about all of that. Just know that my game is tighter than any broad's. Ms. Julia, I'm just telling you what I know. I've had chicks cutting my tires, cursing me out, stalking me and everything."

"You just proved my point even further, but I'm going to spell it out for you, Tyson. And please don't refer to us as 'chicks' and 'broads.'"

"Yes, ma'am" Everyone was now paying close attention. "Do you know why she was tearing your stuff up and cursing you out? Probably not, so I'm going to help you," Julia said. "She was upset because she let you win."

"Let me win?" Tyson exclaimed.

"Yeah, let you win. Women are emotional beings. A woman knows from the start if you're worth keeping around, but on many instances her emotions overshadow her judgment, and she begins to make excuses for a man. She entrusts you with her heart

in hopes that you will take care of it. Deep in her heart she knows if you're capable or not of doing it, but her emotions make it more complicated. Now, when you hurt her she reflects back and remembers that she *knew* you were no good, and that's when she erupts like a volcano. This is shown by example of the things you just described. The cutting of tires, stalking, and cursing you out are all examples of lava. There is much truth in the saying 'Hell has no furry like a woman scorned,' as you can attest to by your slashed tires."

"What about how silly women are about what a man buys them and the type of car he drives? That's pretty pathetic if you ask me."

"Did your father teach you anything?" James said. He shook his head.

"Go ahead, man," Tyson said, looking over at James."

"There are two things that a woman is thinking about when her man buys her a gift. Number one, she can tell how much time and thought he put into purchasing her a gift by what she received. I'm not talking about Jared's. Not that Jared's is bad," Julia said with a laugh. "It's the type of gift. It could be something you both observed together months ago and he decided to surprise you with it. It could have been a pendant that you lost and replaced by putting in a special order. Gifts with meaning. Number two, and the most important, is the fact that she was on your mind. The gift was just a physical representation of his thoughts. The car thing is nothing more than a status symbol. To some women it's a symbol of potential. Men are more prideful rather than emotional. I truly believe that nothing would have fired Adam up more than another Adam in his garden. That's why a woman knows that the best way to get back at a man is to date a man that her man knows. Even the threat of that is enough to set a man off. Another way is to get a man who has achieved more than you. No man wants to think that you can do better than him."

"So Mrs. Julia, you're telling me that we're the weaker person?"

"Not at all. All I'm saying is that a woman is smarter than a man if a man is not being a man. A woman wants her man to be stronger than she is. A woman wants a man she can cast all of her cares upon. You cast all of your problems at the feet of the Father, and she cast her problems, fears, stress, etcetera, at yours. To end this conversation and to take a little break before we get into the session, yes, I believe that men are stronger than women are, but it takes a good woman to make a strong man, either a strong mother or a strong wife, or a combination of both. Okay. Are you guys ready for a break?

Head nods in agreement.

Let's take a break."

Meanwhile, the women are in the gym getting ready to exercise.

"What's up, girl?"

"Sorry I'm late, ladies," Panerva said, walking briskly into the locker room. "But I have a good excuse." She took her water bottle from her pink and gray Nike athletic bag before placing the bag into a locker.

"What was it, Panerva," Sheila asked, as she attached her IPOD to her waist and grabbed her towel.

"Oh, James wanted a taste of his chocolate kiss before I left, and you know I can't leave my man wanting."

"I bet he did," Zora said sarcastically. "You know you wanted it just as bad."

"And you know it, girl." Panerva smiled. "You know that I can't resist him. Anyway, I wanted to give him something to think about before he went back into his session.

"Girl, you are too stupid. I bet you don't have anything left in you for a good workout."

"Girl please, you know I faked my orgasm. I had to do it quick though. It was starting to feel good, and he does this thing . . . " Panerva shook her head, laughing.

"I have to say that I'm impressed that you more mature ladies are still that active," Diane said, smiling.

"We're not that old or dead yet. These are the best years," Zora said. She threw her towel over her shoulder.

"You are better than I am, because once I'm on my way, I'm not turning around," Faith said. "I've already faked enough in my life, so I'm not going to waste a good one."

"Where's Alyssa?" Bianca asked, turning her head and looking around the locker room.

"You should have passed her in the hallway when you came in," Brittany said.

"I don't think I did," Bianca said, frowning.

"I left her at the front desk talking to some guy," Brittany continued.

Sheila shrugged. "She better not let the wrong people see her, because this boat ain't that big."

"Brittany, can I ask you a question," Bianca asked.

"'Why did I marry a black man,' right? "Can I hip you sisters to a little history lesson," Brittany said, as she removed her towel from her bag. "Did you know that one

of the first interracial marriages was between a sista girl and a white dude? The name of the court battle was *Loving vs. Virginia.* Look it up. So it's safe to say that you sista girls started all of this, and we sister girls are just going to the NBA games."

Everyone began to laugh.

"Is that true, Brittany?" Bianca said, surprised.

"Yes, it is."

"Sheila, I'm not trying to be funny here, but I think you two need to exchange spouses because Allen is the coolest white boy I know, and Brittany is the sista girl I never had."

"Are y'all coming out of here or what?" Alyssa said, walking into the locker room. She stuffed a piece of paper into her lemon yellow and black workout support top.

"We were waiting on you," Sheila said. "And what is that you're stuffing down your top?"

"Just a little insurance—nothing big." Alyssa smiled. "Well, I haven't found that out yet."

"Girl, you're going to mess around and get yourself in trouble."

"Whatever, Bianca. It's not like neither of you have never messed around on your men."

It got really quiet.

"So none of you have ever stepped out on your man?"

"If I did, do you think I would actually tell another woman, especially not the clean up woman? I don't think so. Please, let's go work out," Sheila said and walked out of the locker room.

"I thought we decided just to ride the bikes for an hour today?" Bianca said, heading towards the cardio room.

"Sounds good to me," Alyssa said, following Sheila.

They had been riding the bikes for a good thirty minutes when Diane said, "So, what's this insurance thing you were talking about, Alyssa?"

"Diane, why are you still on that?" Alyssa said, sounding like she was gasping for breath.

"Are you okay, Alyssa? Sheila said sarcastically, pedaling faster.

"Stop being a show off. It's not like you developed that body of yours—you were just lucky."

"It isn't lucky staying this fine," she said, maintaining the rate then speeding up. "Alyssa, are you going to answer my question?" Diane continued.

"What is it, Diane? Stop acting like you don't know what I mean when I say 'insurance.' It's for the same reason you get any other insurance, but in this case, it's for just in case my man wants to act up—then I have a back up."

"Well, if your man loves you, and you love him, why would you need prospects for 'just in case?'"

"Because of what you just said, Diane," Sheila interjected. "*If*," she said, stressing the word if. "*If* your man loves you."

"Well, I *know* my man loves me," Diane said, shrugging her shoulders.

"And how do you know this?" Alyssa asked, grinning.

"Because I wouldn't have gotten engaged to him if I didn't feel that he loved me. Plus, he does things for me that no other man has done."

"Girl, feelings are overrated," Brittany said, catching her second wind and stepping up her pace.

"Brittany, you sound as if you agree with what Alyssa is doing," Diane said, frowning.

"It's isn't that, it's just that a woman knows when her man is in love with her. Now I said *in* love with you not just 'loves you,' because any man can love you."

"So, Diane, how do you know your man loves you?" Bianca said, getting down off of the bike and wiping sweat from her forehead and chest.

"Go ahead and school, church girl," Alyssa said, getting off of her bike.

As they walked into the locker room, Bianca began to tell Kim how to tell if a man is in love with you.

"First, you have to evaluate your man's psyche because every man is different. You can't just generalize every man. You determine if he is a giver or a taker, and you give each of them levels. Are you following me?"

Diane nodded. "This is crazy but I'm following."

"Does he take a lot and give a little, or does he give a lot and take little? I'm not going to tell you about my man, so I'll give you an example of one of my men from the past."

"He wasn't that bad of a guy. Whatever happened between the two of you?" Alyssa said, putting the number that she'd gotten into her cell phone.

"Well, he was fifty-fifty. Those are the hardest guys to test."

"This sounds like playing games to me, and Gregg and I are past those days," Daine said, as she put on her sweats.

"Well, if you want to know if your man is in love with you, you'll play this last so-called game." Bianca sat down on the bench in front of them and crossed her legs. "Let me tell you how to do this," she said.

"Tracy and I had been dating for about six months, and I knew that he cared about me, but I was still feeling a little insecure about his ability to make a commitment. I mean, he would buy me gifts, surprise me at work with roses and wonderful dinner dates—"

"Isn't that enough to build on?" Diane said, exasperated.

"Yeah, if you want to be wined and dined for two or three years with no commitment, no ring, and the clock still ticking," Alyssa said, giggling.

"Let me finish, you two," Bianca said, motioning for them to be quiet. "So, I had to find something that was important to him and ask him not to give it up totally but to give me a share in it. See, Tracy wanted to buy a motorcycle before I'd even met him, and I knew that he had been saving up for it. At the time, I was attending RIT and needed some money for my books and tuition. I had most of the money, but I wanted to find out if he was interested in helping me with my future, which I wanted him to be a part of."

Diane shook her head sadly "Don't you know that nigga told me that I might have to wait until next semester? He didn't say he would try and help out or anything, and turns out the very next week he had his bike riding all over town. Then I find out he just wanted to get it for bike week to have a bunch of hoes riding on it. So, you can decide not to test your man if you want to, but I strongly suggest doing so."

"See what I'm saying? Some brothers ain't crap. It's all about new coochie for all of 'em. Let's get out of here," Alyssa said, grabbing her gym bag and heading out of the locker room.

"Well, I'm not playing games with Gregg," Diane said, disgusted. "We have a good thing, and I'm happy with what we have."

Bianca shrugged. "Good for you, Diane. What are we working on tomorrow?"

"Abs," Diane said, patting herself on the stomach.

"All right, I'll see you later."

"You think I should try it, Bianca?" Diane said, hesitantly.

Bianca turned around, one hand on the locker room door. "It's up to you, girl. I'll see you at three."

Back after the break with the men

"You guys ready to get back into this?" Julia asked. She walked back into the class with a drink in her hand.

"I think we've learned quite enough in that last session," Jaheim said, smiling and looking around at the other men. "Let's just come back at three."

"No, we can't do that," Julia said. She walked over to the table and took out the legal pad that Hezekiah gave her. I know you guys are fatigued, and if you give me everything you have with a lot of energy, we can hit this real hard and heavy and we probably can leave a little earlier. How do you feel about that, Mr. Johnson?" Julia asked, looking in Jaheim's direction.

"Let's get hot, fellas," Jaheim said as he smiled and rubbed his hands together, trying to pump everyone up.

"Okay, what do you guys want to get out of this retreat?"

"I want my wife to understand that it's not all about sex when it comes to me," Jaheim said, shaking his head. All of the other men looked at him strangely. "Naaaa, don't get me wrong. I like it as much as the next man, but it's not what it used to be. I know what I'm going to get. How I'm going to get it and how long I'm going to get it. I need some variety and I'm not talking about from other women."

"Believe me, bruh, you don't want to open that box," James said, looking over at Jaheim with a smile. I'm actually scared to have sex with Panerva, because I don't know what she's going to come up with."

"That's what I'm looking for," Jaheim said confidently.

"You say that now," Lawrence said. "Wait until she asks you for more when you don't have any more to give."

"You must be speaking from experience," Sean said, as though he'd never had that problem.

"See, that's what's wrong with you young cats, you set yourselves up for failure. It's not about if you can give her everything sexually. It's about not knowing her limitations. Before long you'll be calling to find out where she is. She'll have you so turned out you'll be paranoid of everything. 'Who did you learn that move from? You weren't doing that last week. What's really going on?' I'm telling you to let *her* open the box. You just take it how you've been getting it. Trust me," Lawrence said. He leaned back in his chair.

"It may not be all about sex for her either, Jaheim," Julia said, turning to him. "Most of the time a woman just wants to feel loved. That's why most of us have sex. The feeling of someone enjoying us brings us all the pleasure in the world. Holding us

while watching a move, whispering in our ear about how beautiful we are, and kissing us passionately is immeasurable."

"That sounds like a fulltime job," Christopher said, while shaking his head. "And I have to go to work."

All of the men began to laugh. Even Julia let out a chuckle.

"Yes, it may be difficult, but the reward for it is like putting in overtime. You get back time and a half. The problem with most relationships is that neither one of the partners understands their strengths."

"Can you elaborate?" Allen said, leaning up and placing both of his hands on the table.

"Please do," Gregg followed.

"It's simple, guys. Give each other what you want and need. We'll take your problem, Jaheim, for example. It's evident that your wife wants more intimacy."

"I can't be intimate with her if all she does is clean the house and take care of the kids. There is nothing attractive or intimate about that."

"Okay, let's take it from there. Let's say she's washing dishes and you're doing whatever it is that you do. I'm going to let you guys in on a little secret of ours. There is a method to the madness."

"I have to hear this," Tyson said, scooting up his chair.

"First, you have to accomplish something."

"What?" Gregg said, with his faced in a frown.

Lawrence and James were shaking their heads, because they knew where she was about to go.

"Hold on, let me finish," Julia said, putting up her hand. "If she's washing dishes and the baby isn't ready for bed yet, it does you no good to go in the kitchen kissing all over her, because the only thing on her mind is that you are slowing her down; she still has a lot to do."

The men smiled and shook their heads.

"Now what you should do is get the baby ready for bed, vacuum the living room floor, iron her blouse for work or something. Then you go into the kitchen and say, 'Baby, I got so and so ready for bed, and I cleaned up the living room,' all the while touching and caressing her. She is definitely going to be more receptive. Does that make sense?"

"Yes it does, but I hope Dr. Bill squared us away like you're squaring the women away," Allen responded.

"I really see what you're saying, Mrs. Julia," Jaheim said, reassuring her that he understood what she was trying to convey to the group. "You are so right about the doing something first. I just never thought about it. So many times I've walked up to her right when she was in the middle of something and tried to be romantic and she was like, 'please, get off of me.' After a few times of that, I kind of figured she didn't want to be bothered, so I kind of don't approach her like that. I wait to be approached…unless it's been a while," Jaheim said, laughing.

"Yes, I've experienced that before, also," Sean said, chiming in. "I felt as though my wife wasn't interested, so I began to look for attention elsewhere. I mean I didn't read the manual before I got married."

"And that's why we're here, Sean," Julia said, confirming his thoughts. "You haven't said much, Tyson," Julia said, looking in his direction."

"I'm good," Tyson responded. "This topic is not one of my issues."

"Well, what issues would you like to talk about, Tyson," Julia said, as she looked at her notes.

"I don't trust women. Point blank."

"I see," Julia said.

"Here we go," Gregg said to Allen, leaning back in his seat.

"Is it more so that you don't trust yourself?" Julia continued.

"That could be true, also. All I'm saying is that women are good liars."

"Can you explain your theory?" Julia asked with a smile.

"Okay, I have slept with numerous women. Sometimes if I feel like it's not going to be a one-night thing or the relationship could evolve into something other than a fling, I ask them about their sexual habits. Most women will say that they've had maybe two or three partners, and I know that they are lying. I know that I've had maybe a dozen one night flings, and if they happen to be in a serious relationship and their man asks them that very same question, I know that they don't count me in that two-or-three partner count that they put out there."

"Did you tell those women that you had a dozen quickies?" Julia asked, looking Tyson in his eyes.

All of the other gentlemen turned their heads towards Tyson, also.

"No, but that's expected of a man. Furthermore, it's easier for a woman to have sex than it is for a man to have sex."

"Has your wife given you any reason to doubt her?"

"No, not really. But I'm not going to wait for her to hurt me either."

"Do you have trust issues with your male friends also?"

"No, not really," Tyson said in a uncertain tone.

"Not really," Julia repeated.

"I'm going to need to talk with you one-on-one, okay, Mr. Ferguson?"

"That's fine," Tyson said, sitting back.

"What do you want to get out of this marriage retreat, Mr. Rogers?"

"I want my wife to accept me for who I am."

"And who are you?" Julia asked.

"I'm a cool white boy that has a lot of female friends."

"Would it be cool if your wife were cool with a lot of male friends?"

"You can't put men and women in the same boat," Allen said.

"Why can't you?" Julia asked. She leaned forward, awaiting his answer.

"If I go out into the middle of the highway and just whipped it out and started taking a leak, someone would probably just laugh at me, but if a woman does the very same thing she would be considered trifling." He looked around the room. "Am I right?"

"Yes, you're right in your analysis, but that has nothing to do with what we're talking about. You should take your wife's feelings into consideration."

"That's how I was when my wife met me, though."

"So you're saying that you shouldn't grow and mature if you want to make your relationship work? You should continue doing the same things that you did when you were younger? Wisdom is one of the most powerful things anyone can attain. The bible says in Job chapter twelve, verse twelve, 'Is not wisdom found among the aged, Does not long life bring understanding?' So as you grow in a relationship, you become wiser. The things you used to do as a twenty-year-old go away. The things you used to do as a thirty-year-old go away. If you want happiness, do things that make her happy and reassured, and she will do the same for you."

"I can attest to that, young brother," James said. "I don't want my wife playing the silly games that we played earlier in our courtship and marriage, and I finally figured out that I don't need to play those silly games that I used to play. There is no greater feeling than knowing that you are with a real person; not a person putting on a front. You can look to being happy because you know the person you are with is one that you enjoy being with.

"When I accepted that Zora was everything I wanted and needed in a woman, there was a sense of peace that came over me," Lawrence said openly.

The other men were looking at him in disapproval. "Don't get all emotional on us," Sean said.

"I'm for real. Tell them, James."

"Certain things they're just going to have to experience themselves."

"Let's move on," Julia urged."

"Christopher, what do you want to get out of the marriage retreat?"

"I want my wife to stop nagging me."

"Man, you hit it on the head for all of us," Tyson said.

"What do you mean?"

"I mean you can't please a woman," Christopher said in frustration.

"Tell me about it."

"You work to give them everything they could possible want, and then they hit you with, 'you're working too much.'"

"And if you're not working, they still complain," Tyson said, jumping in.

"It's like you're wrong if you do and wrong if you don't," Christopher continued.

"Let me help you out," Tyson said. "Damned if you do and damned if you don't!"

"Women tell you wonderful stories about 'it's not about money,' until there is none or there becomes a shortage."

"Mr. O'Donnell, I think you're blowing this way out of proportion. I guarantee that if you were to take one day out of the week to treat your wife special, she wouldn't have any problems. Just one day out of seven. If you tell me that you can't afford to take one day out of the week for your wife you have a problem with priorities because that job can fire you on any given day of the week. Do you know that one person that you can cry on and won't judge your manhood? Your home is your sanctuary. Do you agree?"

"You're right, Mrs. Julia," Christopher said humbly.

"Take care of the one place that you are king, and your queen will take care of you. Mr. Greer and Mr. Bailey, what do you gentlemen want to get out of this retreat being that you two are the more mature of the group?"

"I'm just here to strengthen my relationship," James said.

"My reason is pretty much the same. I've already learned or been made aware of somethings that I've experienced myself but never really thought about in this session. Me being in my second marriage, I don't want to make the same mistakes I did in my first marriage. I also want to be made aware of common mistakes that are made in second marriages."

"That's very good, Mr. Greer. What about you, Mr. Pierce?"

"I just want to make sure I'm making the right decision about getting married. I know this course is supposed to give you training on understanding your mate, tools to aid you overcoming communication barriers, coping skills, and to eliminate stinking

thinking, but I think I need a test run. I mean, you at least get a driving permit before you get your drivers license."

"Well, the bible doesn't say that you can't live together but it does say that you shouldn't have sex before marriage."

"Are you saying that I should have confidence in all aspects of marriage except sex with my partner?"

"I'm going to solve this one before we go any further," Julia said, *with a peculiar smile. The main problem that we have in this area is that we don't restrain from sex before marriage. So, many of us experience different body types* before marriage. If these couples then become saved, they will want to do the right thing by abstaining from sex until they're married. But when they finally consummate their marriage, there are instances of dissatisfaction, because they have subconsciously compared their current mate with the mates that they've had previous relations with. Therefore, to answer your question, Mr. Pierce, many of us would have to go back to the time before they were sexually active and remain celibate until God's choice found them. So if you've had sex before marriage, you kind of set yourself up. I can't advise you to have sex or not. I can say that the bible is against sex before marriage. With that, if no one has any other questions, I'm going to release you guys until three o'clock.

"That was very good, Mrs. Julia," everyone echoed as they got up out of their seats.

"Thank you very much," she replied. "I look forward to seeing you guys at three."

"Hello, everyone," Dr. Bill said as he walked into the classroom. "I've spoken with my wife, and so far we are on track. I'm going to let you guys go for the evening. But first, before the day's session is complete, there is one more thing you guys must do as male and female groups."

Everyone began looking at one another, wondering what Dr. Bill was going to have them do.

"Tonight, you guys will select and perform songs as groups. You could choose a song that tells how you feel after a disagreement, or a song that tells the other person what you want."

"I thought this was a Christian retreat," Sean responded, with a few others nodding in agreement.

"I'm pretty sure none of you are intimate with your significant other to the tune of 'the Mighty clouds of Joy.' There is a time and a place for everything. The Bible itself is

very explicit in describing love in the Psalms. But remember, you should still choose something that's tasteful." "How much time do we have," Sheila inquired eagerly.

"Each of the groups has to be ready to perform by eight o'clock tonight. I hope that you guys really express yourselves tonight. Also, here are the topics that we will be covering tomorrow. Tomorrow's your last day, so I'm going to need for you guys to really talk tonight to bring up things that are important to you as a couple that we haven't covered yet." Changing his mind, Dr. Bill said, "Better yet, I'll wait until tomorrow to give you the topics for tomorrow's session...but don't forget to wear the matching T-shirts with your team's last name on the back of the shirts." "What are the matching shirts all about, Dr. Bill?" Jaheim asked, with a smile. He moved his leg aside as Bianca attempted to smack him on it.

"Good question, Jaheim. The shirts are about team building. When you're on a team, you take care of one another. When you're on a team, you plan for the opponents—in this case, the opponents of marriage. You plan for obtaining spiritual and financial growth, child rearing, strategies against adultery, dealing with sickness and misfortune. In fact, a good indicator that you're *not* a team is when you feel like you're just roommates. Each of you comes and goes as you please. You have separate bank accounts, and there is no support of individual aspirations. We'll talk more on that tomorrow. I'll see you guys tonight at the Drama Sanctuary."

The women performed a song by Keisha Cole entitled " I Remember "
The men performed a song by Troop entitled "Audacity."

The next morning.

Good morning, everyone. We're one day closer to graduation, and I think that everyone is making good progress."

"You guys were awesome at last night's performances." Julia said, with a smile. Who came up with the song selections for each group?" "Well, for our group it was kind of a joint selection," Sean said, as he glanced around at the rest of the guys.

"Well, I don't know about collaboration, because I didn't have a clue on any of the song choices," Christopher said. With a smile, he threw his hands up in confusion. "I would've chosen someone like Toby Keith."

The rest of the guys turned to stare at Christopher.

"Leave my man alone," Faith said, grabbing his arm. "We love ourselves some Toby Keith."

"She has her man's back," Jaheim said, turning away from Bianca.

"Oh, I don't have your back?" Bianca said with attitude.

"Just playing baby, just playing."

"For us it was Sheila. She gave us choices and then made the choice for us," Alyssa said sarcastically.

"Like Julia said, I think you guys did a great job last night," Dr. Bill said. He took a seat behind the desk while Julia sat with her legs crossed on the end of the desk. Okay, underneath all of your chairs are his and her answer boards you that filled out as part of your online applications. We're about to play 'Do I know my Mate?' It is our rendition of the Newly Wed Game. I need all of the women who are sitting to the right of your mate, to move to his left."

All of the women made necessary moves.

"Okay, are you guys ready?" Julia enthusiastically asked them.

Low, unenthusiastic, and hesitant head nods and grumbled yeses were sporadically issued.

"Come on, guys. Where's that excitement and energy that you all displayed last night?" Julia said. Dr. Bill handed her the cards containing the questions as she got down off of the desk.

"I don't know," Brittany said, smiling and shaking her head."

"Well, give me some fake motivation," Julia said, as she prepared to ask the first question.

"Let's get pumped up," Allen said, pumping his fists.

"That's what I'm talking about."

Dr. Bill stood up and grabbed a dry erase marker, preparing to keep score.

"Okay, this question is for the Men." The men turned and looked at one another with smiles.

"Okay, what is your mate's worst fear? We'll start with Tyson and Alyssa."

Sean sat with a smile on his face. He continued to look forward as he shook his head.

"Come on, Tyson. You only have fifteen seconds to answer each question."

"Okay, its gaining weight," Tyson said, covering his head.

Alyssa held up the card.

"That is correct."

Alyssa reached over and gave Tyson a kiss.

"Okay, Sean, same question."

"Success," Sean said without hesitation.

Brittany hit Sean in the side of the head.

"No, that's not right," Julia said. Its...Hold the card up, Mrs. Brittany. It's 'public speaking.'"

"Why would I be afraid of success?"

"Baby, you are. I guess you feel like you'll be obligated to maintain a certain level of success, and you have a fear of failure in public."

"Whatever."

"James, you're up."

"Panerva's worst fear," he repeated. "It can't be a phobia or something like that?"

"It's not supposed to be, but some of the answers that we received online were borderline. It was supposed to be something personal."

"She has no fears that I can think of," James said, as he shook his head.

Panerva quickly held the card up enthusiastically.

"You are correct."

James and Panerva kissed.

"Christopher and Faith."

Christopher smiled, covered up his head, and said, "That I'm going to move my mother in with us."

Faith held up the card.

"You are also right, Christopher. Looks like we're on a roll."

"Lawrence, can you keep it going?"

"That's too easy," Lawrence said with confidence. "It's failure of our second marriage."

"You are correct."

"Alright, Allen. You're up next."

"My wife fears that she's not black enough for me."

Everyone turned and looked at the couple, even Dr. Bill and Julia.

Sheila held up her card, and sure enough it said, "fear of not being black enough."

"You two must bring that up in our one-on-one," Dr. Bill said, smiling at the couple. "Let's move on. Please!"

"Okay, Gregg."

"It's has to be having children."

"You're correct."

"What is this about?" Dr. Bill asked.

"She feels like they would be too much to handle, Dr. Bill."

"What do you mean?"

"Have you seen kids in grocery stores?" Diane said as she placed the card back under the chair.

"Let me write that one down, too," Dr. Bill said, taking notes.

"Jaheim and Bianca," Julia continued.

"Fear of marriage failure."

"Why did you say that?" Bianca said. She held the card up in front of them so no one could see her talking to Jaheim.

"I heard you," Dr. Bill said as Bianca put the card down. "What did you put on your card?"

"I put 'fear of gaining weight.'"

"So which one is it?"

"Fear of marriage failure," Bianca said reluctantly.

"We'll talk about that also in the one-on-one."

"Okay, women. It's your turn. What is your mate's biggest challenge?"

"We're going to start with Panerva and James."

"That's too easy." Panerva was smiling. "It's me!" She said confidently.

"Yes," James said, turning to kiss his wife.

"Hold the card up, James," Julia said.

"Yes, you are right."

"Diane, you're next."

"Ummmm," Diane hummed, looking Gregg in the face. "His biggest challenge is staying organized," Diane said. She was still looking into Gregg's face.

Gregg stared back at her for three seconds and held up the card excitedly.

"We're on a roll," Julia said.

"Okay. Alyssa, what is your mate's biggest challenge?"

"Keeping a job," she said in Spanish.

"What was that?" Julia said with a confused look on her face.

Tyson held up the card, shaking his head. "It's 'gaining weight.' Me keeping a job is one of *your* hang-ups."

"It's keeping a job," Alyssa disagreed, shaking her head.

"Whatever."

"Okay, our next victims—I mean *contestants*—are the O'Donnells. What is Chris' biggest challenge, Julia asked?"

"Christopher's biggest challenge is making time for me and the kids," Faith said. She was making an effort to keep her voice from wavering."

Christopher held up the card. The card read "Quality time."

"That's close enough," Julia said. "You guys are doing great."

"Sheila, what is Allen's biggest challenge?"

"Staying in shape, Sheila said hesitantly."

"Allen held up his card and it read 'working out.'"

"Looks like we're on a role," Julia said. "Alright. Zora and Lawrence."

"It has to be dealing with my sons," Zora said with a smile.

Lawrence held the card over his face.

"'Your children' is right," Julia said.

"Okay, Brittany. You're up next."

"I would have to say, dealing with my father," she said as it popped into her head."

"Dealing with her father," Julia said as Sean held up the card.

"I know, baby," Brittany said, rubbing Sean's face.

"Okay, Jaheim. You're the last contestant. Bring it home for the men."

"Fear of being alone with my wife," Jaheim said sadly.

Bianca held the card up as everyone went silent.

The card read "being alone with me." Bianca slowly slid the card underneath the chair as a tear ran down her face.

"May I be excused?" Bianca said. She was trying to smile through her tears while gently dabbing her eyes with a tissue. As she got up from her seat and began to walk away, Jaheim got up and followed her.

"We're going to take a ten minute break here. Grab a few refreshments, and I'll see the rest of you in a few minutes."

"Okay, this will be the last thing that we do before we get into our one-on-one session this afternoon. Everyone take a look at the dry erase board," Dr. Bill said, getting up from the desk and walking over to the board. "I have three topics that I want to discuss before we go to lunch. This will help us on our one-on-one session later on this afternoon. They are Sex, The Sanford & Son Syndrome and Anticipation. Okay let's begin with Sex. What does the Bible say about sex?" Dr. Bill asked.

Everyone fell silent.

"Don't everyone speak at once," Julia said.

"I think it said something to the fact that neither one of us are supposed to withhold sex from each other, which I have a problem with, because If I'm not into it, then I feel like I'm being used," Sheila said, with her arms folded.

"I hate to say it, but sometimes in marriage you're going to feel that way. The bible says in Corinthians seven and five, 'Do not deprive each other except by mutual consent and that that mutual consent be for a short period of time, so that you may devote yourselves to prayer. Then come together again so that Satan will not tempt you because of your lack of self-control.' It's all about compromise. It also says in the passage before that one that in marriage the wife's body doesn't belong to her, and the husband's body doesn't belong to him. That's one of the most important points that couples miss before they get married—which lets us know that when individuals commit adultery, they're really giving up a body that doesn't belong to them."

"Dr. Bill, why are men so afraid of our sexuality?" Alyssa said, smiling"

"I'm going to let Julia answer that one, being that it will sound chauvinistic coming from me," Dr. Bill said, giving the floor to Julia."

"It took me a long time to accept this; but if you think about it, it makes sense."

"I can't wait to hear this," one of the men said, as they all became very attentive."

"I bet you can't," Julia responded. "Men are insecure beings."

"What?" Allen said. He shook his head and smiled. "That's crazy."

The other men were also shaking their heads, but the women applauded and gave each other high fives.

"Let her finish," Dr. Bill said, putting up one of his hands.

"Can we all agree that men are possessive and women are emotional?" Julia said, trying to look into each of their faces.

"Most of us have premarital sex, right? I'm basing this assumption on averages. During this period of premarital sex, most women don't let out their inner most sexual desires because of fear rejection or judgment. Can we agree on that point, women?"

The women nodded their heads in display of their agreement.

"That's where we go wrong, ladies, besides having premarital sex in the first place. If you feel your man will have a problem with your sexuality before marriage, why wait until after the nuptials to bring out your freaky side? Sex should be thoroughly discussed before marriage. I'm talking about everything imaginable. If you bring Ms. Freaky out after the nuptials he might develop an insecurity to which he may question how freaky you can become. How far will you go? Will you eventually want another man, either with the two of you or secretly? He will never accept this after marriage, and if he does you have another problem."

The men weren't saying anything. Some were smiling, but others were acting as though they were in church, being enlightened by something new that they couldn't yet put into words.

"Most men feel like if you're freaky, be freaky before marriage, or tell him about your freakiness so he can make some decisions. He may feel, 'if we're going to invite some people in, let's invite them in before marriage so I can rule you out now.' Most men will have no problem being freaky with you before marriage. Women, would you want the men to hide the fact that they're alcoholics till after the marriage? I'm pretty sure that you wouldn't."

"That's not the same," Faith said, shaking her head in disagreement.

"Not to you, because men and women think differently. You think emotionally and he thinks logically. You wouldn't want to marry an alcoholic, and he wouldn't want to marry the equivalent of a porn star. He has no problem *dating* a porn star, but he doesn't want to take her to meet mommy. Now don't get me wrong; every man wants a freak. He just has to know how far she will go or has gone in the past. It is imperative that the both of you define your sexual limitations. That's not saying that you won't try new things, but you have to say what things you will absolutely not consider. I hate to say it ladies, but it's about catering to his insecurities—but that's like everything else. You have to find a man who's confident that he is enough for his woman. You have to find that man, or you will never know true complete happiness. Don't settle for a man who's afraid of your sexuality. But remember, we have insecurities, as well. Be careful what you ask for. Intimacy comes in many forms. Did that explain your question, Shelia?"

"Better than I expected."

"I am so glad that someone said it for me," James said. "I just went through that. I was so afraid of Panerva's sex drive but she took care of me. And because I knew she was taking care of me, I did everything I could possible do to please her."

"I have to admit it, too," Jaheim said, looking at Bianca. "That's one of the reasons that I shy away sometimes. Sometimes I feel her desire for me to try different things and I get afraid that I won't be able to handle a freaky Bianca. Here's another thing based on averages, Mrs. Julia. We all have looked at sex tapes at one time or another, and it's hard for me—I don't know about the other gentlemen here—to treat my wife like that. It's hard for me to accept that she may want to be treated like that."

"And that's totally understandable, and that's why these things need to be discussed. If you guys don't take anything else away from this retreat, remember that love and happiness in marriage is just a conversation away."

"That was beautiful, baby," Dr. Bill said. He smiled and stood up to kiss his wife. "I think we've covered that well. Let us move on to the next topic. The SS Syndrome. The SS Syndrome is short for 'the Sanford and Son Syndrome.'"

Everyone laughed.

"It sounds funny, but many marriages suffer daily because of this problem. I know none of you know where I'm going with this, so I'll explain: this is one of the most common and dangerous pitfalls of marriage. It too involves a relationship with insecurity. Many times in a relationship, one person gets motivated and the other may become stagnant. Jealousy can set in and cause animosity in the marriage. If you've every watched *Sanford and Son*, you probably remember that there were so many times that Lamont wanted to leave to better himself, and Fred would find some way to louse it up. This very thing happens in marriages every day. It becomes a *misery loves company* thing. If your spouse is taking college courses during a time when the marriage isn't going well, the stagnant spouse might complain about the time it's taking away from the family, or find some way to make it difficult for you to succeed instead of helping out. There was an episode when Lamont was running for councilman, and Fred was in full support until he realized that Lamont would move away. Sometimes in marriage we won't support each other because of that same fear."

Dr. Bill looked out at his audience. "Does anyone here have indicators of the Sanford and Son Syndrome?"

"I think that I have some symptoms," Tyson said hesitantly. "As a matter fact, I think I have symptoms of everything we've talked about today. Alyssa, there is something that I want to tell you. I've been unfaithful to you. I wanted to apologize to you in front of everyone. Please forgive me, baby."

"I can, baby, if you can forgive me," Alyssa said cautiously.

Tyson got up out of his seat and left the room. Alyssa stayed seated.

"On that note, we're going to take our lunch break here," Dr. Bill said. "I'll see you guys after lunch. This is the order that I want you guys to come in: Jaheim and Bianca at one o'clock, James and Panerva at one-thirty, Faith and Christopher at two, Gregg and Diane at three and so on.

Knock, Knock.

"Come on in, Jaheim and Bianca," Dr. Bill said. Gathered in front of him were all the notes that he'd taken on the couple since the retreat began. Julia was sitting in a chair beside the desk.

"How has the retreat been so far for you guys?" Dr. Bill asked.

"For me it's been a great eye-opener," Jaheim said with a nod. "I mean, with the things that Bianca brought back from her session with you, to the team building, to the open session today, it's been enlightening. We had a talk last night and at lunch, and we both agree that it's been well worth it."

"What about you, Bianca?"

"Like Jaheim said, I wouldn't trade this time for anything. He's been more open and we've been enjoying each other more. I think now we can both be more open with what we want and need to be happy inside of our relationship."

"That's great, guys. But I don't want you two to walk away from this retreat under the impression that there won't be a day that will challenge you and probably make you feel like saying, 'what happened?' Remember, Jaheim, that Bianca loves you more than anything. I can see it in her eyes."

Bianca squeezed Jaheim's hand as she turned and looked into his eyes.

"From our notes it seems like you two just need to take care of the intimacy in your marriage, and everything else will fall into place. Bianca, you noted that you wanted Jaheim to pay more attention to you sexually. And Jaheim, you felt that you guys had exhausted all the excitement in your intimacy. Now it's true that a woman holds the key to broadening the barriers of sexual intimacy, but it's up to the man to give her the reason to unlock those barriers. If your woman doesn't feel beautiful to you, then she's not going to risk embarrassing herself if she feels like the response won't be what she expects. Tell her she's beautiful every day, and I'm sure she will give you everything you need. Okay, Jaheim?"

"Yes, sir."

"I'm going to give you guys an autographed copy of my book. It has more details of other problems that may occur throughout a marriage. Just remember to keep God first. The old saying is as strong as it's ever been: 'a family that prays together stays together.' And we all want to stay together; we want to be happy together. I'll see you guys tomorrow at graduation."

"Thank you, Dr. Bill and Mrs. Julia. You truly have been a blessing," Bianca said, as she and Jaheim stood up.

"You guys be blessed. If James and Panerva are outside of the room, please ask them to come in."

"No problem, Dr. Bill."

"How are you doing, Mr. and Mrs. Bill?" James said, as he and Panerva took their seats.

"We're doing just great. I wanted to thank you guys for being an inspiration to the rest of the group," Dr. Bill said with his hands interlaced on the desk.

"We owe all the thanks to you guys. Like I said during one of the sessions, you guys said so many things that I just didn't realize I was doing."

"I know you just got through thanking us for being a good influence on the group, but the other couples reminded me of the things that I used to think and do. This retreat has been a blessing from every direction."

"Well, I hope that this has been a wonderful twenty-fifth anniversary so far for you, Mr. Bailey," Dr. Bill said with a smile.

"It has been," James said, returning the smile. "She still scares me, though."

"You get him, girl," Julia said, and gave Panerva a high five.

"Hello, Faith and Christopher," Dr. Bill said. He took a drink from his cup. "How do you guys feel so far about the retreat?"

"I'll tell you like this, Dr. Bill and Mrs. Julia: I'm going to go back to tell all of my friends in Buffalo about this retreat. I've learned to relax. I understand that my family is more important than my job—that when it all comes down to it, they will support me no matter what happens," Christopher said, slowly nodding his head up and down. "At least one day out of the week should be dedicated to the one that takes care of my castle...my sanctuary."

"And I understand that I should give him a reason to come home other than I'm there, or to eat and sleep–that every now and then I need to surprise him."

"I'm going to give you guys an autographed copy of my book. It has more details of other problems that may occur throughout a marriage. Just remember to keep God first.

"Thank you, Dr. Bill. We've appreciated everything"

"Thank you, guys."

"My only single couple," Dr. Bill said in appreciation as Gregg and Diane walked in.

"Gregg and Diane, you guys were my most important couple. You two have the opportunity to get it right the first and only time. What are you two going to take away from this experience?"

"For me it's going to be your teamwork concept. It is so true about what you said about a team needing to have a plan. And even though teammates don't always get along, you still have one goal. I think I've chosen the best teammate in the world. She's beautiful, thoughtful, and caring. This retreat has really shown me what I have in my woman."

"Earlier in the session, Dr. Bill, you said, that you would help us ask the right questions of one another," Diane stated.

"Yes I did, and I have them right here," Dr. Bill said, pulling them out of his notebook. Here's one for you and one for you. Let's talk about a couple of them. Here's one: religion.

You don't want to mix religions, because when children become involved, there can be conflict in what religion you will follow. You should follow the man of the house, but it can still cause a conflict.

"Here's another question: is she afraid of sickness? If your woman is afraid of looking at sickness, what happens? God forbid, you become sick. Who's going to take care of you? Bottom line is your man needs to be what a good father is supposed to be to his children. And your woman needs to be what a good mother is supposed to be to her children. What I mean by that is a father provides, regardless of his situation. Children don't want to hear excuses; all they know is what they need and want. A good mother is nurturing and there whenever you need her. This is what you should be to one another in a husband and wife relationship."

"Dr. Bill, you and your wife are a blessing. I couldn't have asked for a better experience," Diane said.

"Hold on. Before you guys leave, I want to give you an autographed copy of my book. It has more details of other problems that may occur throughout a marriage. Just remember to keep God first. The old saying is as strong as it's ever been: 'a family that prays together stays together.' And we all just want to stay together; we want to be happy together. I'll see you guys tomorrow at graduation. I'm pretty sure we went over our alloted time, so please send in Allen and Sheila."

"No problem, Dr. Bill."

"I think you two have the most energy. Sheila really through me for a loop when she said she felt like she might not be black enough for you, Allen. Can either of you elaborate on that for us?"

"As you...What we were—" they both began at the same time.

"Go ahead, baby," Allen said, smiling.

"What I was going to say is, as you guys can see, Allen is not your typical white male. He has dated strictly only black women. I have always felt that he is attracted to the ghetto or urban essence of the black woman, and as I become older and my style becomes more professional, I'm afraid I might lose that urban attitude, and he may loose interest."

"Do you have anything you would like to add?" Julia said, now turning to Allen.

"What I want my wife to understand is that as she gets older and more mature, I will also. Yes, I was attracted to the spirit of the black female, but I'm really not up to battling those same old battles that I use to enjoy being involved in."

"You know most people wouldn't admit that they enjoyed being with or dealing with the urban attitude of the black woman," Dr. Bill said with a smile. I think what

you're really trying to say is that you are attracted to the strength and up-frontness of the black woman. So, it's safe to say that as long as Sheila stays strong, resists being easily submissive, and offers you a challenge, you will remain interested. So Sheila, it's not about you being 'black enough'. It's about you being strong enough. Do the both of you understand?"

"Surprisingly enough, I do," Allen said. Looking at Allen, Sheila placed her hand on his knee and nodded her head in agreement,.

"I do, too," Sheila said, turning to Dr. Bill.

"I'm so glad for the two of you. You are a beautiful couple. I want to give you guys an autographed copy of my book. It has more details of other problems that may occur throughout a marriage. Just remember to keep God first. The old saying is as strong as it's ever been: 'a family that prays together stays together.' And we all want to stay together; we want to be happy together. Baby, I forgot to give the other couples my card," Dr. Bill said, turning to Julia.

"And I forgot to remind you. I'll make sure they all get one, baby."

"Isn't she wonderful? I'd crumble without her."

Mrs. Julia smiled and placed her hand on Hezekiah's shoulder.

"Here's my card. If you have any questions, please feel free to give us a call anytime. I'll see you guys tomorrow at graduation."

"Thank the both of you for everything." Together, Allen and Sheila got to their feet and walked out.

"Hello, Lawrence and Zora. My second-time-around couple. I want you guys to know that you did a good job of being an example of what marriage can be with a *made-up mind*. And that's what it's all about: making up your mind to make things work. What I see in the both of you is one-mindedness. In a marriage you have to be one minded. The bible says, 'because you are lukewarm, I will spew you out.' In relationships you have to make a decision. Either you're with me or without me. Once a couple has made up their minds to be hot or cold for one another, you have won half the battle, and God will take care of the rest."

"Dr. Bill and Mrs. Julia, We wanted to give you guys something for everything you've done for us. Just listening to you help others has helped us." Mrs. Greer reached down into her purse and pulled out a DVD of *the Newlywed Game*."

Dr. Bill and Julia busted out in laughter.

"This is great," Dr. Bill said as he showed Julia the cover.

"We understand that we are one team and one minded, and when we leave this retreat we will plan against those things that can hinder our happiness."

"Baby, I don't think we've ever received a gift," Dr. Bill said to Julia. "This is a wonderful gift, you two, but I want you to know that what you've given me and the others is faith. You guys are an illumination of faith and happiness. I also have a gift for you. I want to give you guys an autographed copy of my book. It has more details of other problems that may occur throughout a marriage. Just remember to keep God first. Remember the old saying, 'a family that prays together stays together?' Well, we really want you to stay together. We want you to be happy together. I'll see you guys tomorrow at graduation. Can you please send in the next couple?"

"Sean and Brittany Washington, my point-the-finger couple. Brittany, you point the finger, saying that Sean may or may not be cheating, and Sean says that since his wife won't give him any attention, others will. In both instances, the each of you needs to look inside, instead of outside, of yourselves for the answer. Sean, for you to blame someone else because you've been looking elsewhere for attention is not only childish but also selfish. Did you try to find out why your wife wasn't giving you the attention that you wanted?"

"I guess I didn't, Dr. Bill," Sean said, raising his shoulders.

"Maybe she's noticed how much you enjoy getting the attention elsewhere and doesn't feel like she should have to compete for your attention, when she's already your wife."

"And how dare you, Brittany, allow anyone to pay more attention to your man? Like I said in the group session, no one outside of your relationship should stand a chance. You lay in the bed with him every night. You cook him meals just the way he likes it. You can bring him lunch with flowers. You can have his son or his daughter. Do you guys already have kids?"

"Yes," Brittany said.

"See! Sean, take that extra time to find out what's going on. No other woman in your case, Brittany, and no other man in Sean's case, should stand a chance if you're doing what you're supposed to be doing! Sean, she's beautiful and she's yours. Make her happy."

"You're right, Dr. Bill," Sean said. He reached over to hug Brittany. "She is beautiful, isn't she?" Sean said and kissed her on the lips. "I really want to thank you." Sean stood up to shake Dr. Bill's hand.

"It's been my pleasure, Sean. I'm going to give you guys an autographed copy of my book. It has more details of other problems that may occur throughout a marriage. We want you to be happy together. I'll see you guys tomorrow at graduation."

"The Fergusons." Dr. Bill stood up and smiled as the Fergusons walked in. "First question," he said, taking his seat. "Have you guys talked?"

"Yes we have," Tyson said humbly. "My wife and I have decided that we shouldn't graduate tomorrow. We have a lot of work to do if we want to repair our marriage. The only problem is, Dr. Bill and Mrs. Julia, we know that it's going to be hard. For me, everything sounds good while we're here. You know we're going to do everything to be considerate of each other's needs, but the fact of the matter is we've both been disloyal to one another. The hardest thing in the world is rebuilding trust."

Alyssa reached over and grabbed Tyson's hand with tears in her eyes. Silence filled the room for several seconds.

"Sometime last year I preached a sermon on wisdom, and the Lord just reminded me of this scripture to give to you both. It says, 'blessed is the man who finds wisdom, the man who gains understanding, for she is more profitable than silver and yields better returns than gold.' That scripture comes from the third chapter of Proverbs, around the thirteenth verse. The two of you have become wiser in the last two days, but let's not discount the wisdom that you gained from the world. The both of you feel like those of the opposite sex are untrustworthy. Hopefully you've learned something from those other men and women you were with that you can use to help rebuild your marriage. Remember why they said they were unhappy with their own partners, and use these things to make your own marriage better. Now, I'm pretty sure that some of them said that they were doing it for some really silly reasons, but if you think about it there is usually a more deep-rooted reason. Try to use these reasons to become wiser in your own marriage. Tyson, in that scripture that I just recited to you it says that she is more profitable than silver and gold. It wasn't just talking about wisdom. It was talking about your wife. The bible says that a man who finds a wife finds a good thing and finds favor with God.

"I wasn't going to graduate you guys tomorrow, but it's pretty clear to me that you've learned something here, and that you're willing to do whatever it takes to make your marriage work. There is only one stipulation that you must agree to, in order for me to include you guys in the graduation ceremony."

"Just tell us, and it's done," Tyson said.

"You guys have to promise me that you will make three monthly appointments to see me at my office. I want to see you two succeed. Do we have an agreement?"

"That's too easy," Tyson said, as he nodded his head in agreement.

"Well, that's just great to hear. You guys have a wonderful evening, and I'll see you tomorrow. Before you leave, I want to give you guys a copy of my book. I'll autograph it at your first scheduled appointment. Deal?"

"Deal, " Alyssa said. Tyson responded by shaking Dr. Bill's hand.

The next day, Bishop Hayden passed out many certificates and blessings. The First Annual Father's House Retreat had been a success.

NAOMI

Now it came to pass in the21st Century AD, that terrorism spread fear throughout the land. There were wars and rumors of wars. In the Holy Ancient city of Babylon (now present-day Al Hillah, Babil Province, Iraq) was where this particular war began. A certain family from a United States military post had its faith tried and tested. The Everett family consisted of Eric, Naomi, Mark, and Charles. Eric was a proud service member who had served his country for more than 20 years. His unit had been called to defend against this enemy called "Terrorism". He was due back any day from a yearlong deployment, and Naomi and the children were preparing for his return.

"Momma, why are we doing all of this for Eric's return?" Mark asked, dusting off all of the furniture in the living room? "

"I've told you about referring to your father as Eric. Don't let me have to tell you that again," Naomi said. She was taking the books from the bookshelf in order for Mark to dust the shelf.

"Okay...*dad*," Mark said, with a sarcastic undertone. "I thought you guys were going to get a divorce. That's what you guys had *the talk* with me about before he left." Mark was 15 years of age and resented his father for hurting his mother. He had spent countless hours trying to comfort his mother after his mother found emails to someone his father was secretly dating.

"Would you please keep your voice down, Mark." Naomi looked around to make sure Charles hadn't entered the room. You know we haven't talked with your brother about that, and for your information your father and I have been talking over the last few months about reconciliation."

Mark began spraying furniture polish in the space where his mother had removed the books. "Momma, you know that I love you and I want nothing but the best for you, but you know that he's never going to change. He practically volunteered for this deployment." Mark finished by wiping the shelf down.

"This is me and your father's issue, and I don't need to explain it to you. I know that you have a little hair on your body, but there is only one parent in this house," Naomi walked over to the shelf with books in her hand and began positioning them in between the bookends. "I've prayed many nights that God would see fit to save my marriage to your father," Naomi said. She picked up the bible and wiped it off before placing it in the center of the coffee table.

"Momma, I can't wait to show daddy my baseball trophy," Charles said, as he rushed into the room carrying his MVP championship trophy and a great big smile across his face. At age 12, Charles was the youngest son. Charles loved and idolized his father. There was no wrong Eric could commit that he wouldn't overlook, as he trusted that his dad was always doing what was best for the family.

"He didn't go to any of your games when he was here," Mark said, cynically. "You don't remember how often he used to say he was 'working late'.

Naomi paused from wiping down the dining room table "I'm not going to tell you again, Mark," She warned him, looking back over her shoulder.

There was a knock at the door.

"Charles, go and answer the door," Naomi said, walking into the kitchen with a handful of china.

As Charles opened the door, there were two formally dressed service members, one with an encased flag and the other carrying a brown document envelope.

Mark looked up from wiping down the glass on the television and noticed the two men.

"Is this the home of Naomi Everett?" one of the service members asked.

Mark immediately new that something was wrong and cautiously walked toward the door. "Yes it is," he answered.

"Son, can we speak to your mother?"

"Yes, sir. Come on in."

"Who's that at the door?" Naomi called out from the kitchen.

Mark turned his head toward the kitchen, but kept his eyes fixed on the two men. "Ma, I think you need to come out here."

Naomi wiped her hands in her apron as she came through the kitchen door. "Who is it?" she asked.

Her facial expression changed instantaneously as she laid eyes on the two soldiers. "Not today," Naomi said, walking towards the men in uniform. "Get out of here. Get out of my house," Naomi said, as tears began to stream down her face. "No, Lord, no. Not today, Lord." Naomi fell to her knees.

"Momma, you have to get up," Mark said, rushing over to his mother. Water was gathering in the wells of his eyes.

The servicemen walked over to Naomi. One of them became very sympathetic.

"Here, son. Let's help her over to the couch."

Once Naomi was seated the couch, the service member with the envelope began to recite what seamed to be a rehearsed message. "Ma'am, are you Naomi Paulette Everett?"

Shaking her head in agreement, Naomi continued to call on the Lord.

"Ma'am, we regret to inform you that your husband, Eric Shuron Everett, was killed in Ramadi, Iraq, on or about 10:37 AM on June 27th, 2007. Here are his personal effects and insurance documentation. All contact information for Personnel Services are located within the envelope. Please accept this flag as a symbol of our condolences."

"Take care of your mom, son," one of the servicemen said, as they departed.

"Momma." Tears were now streaming down Mark's face. "What are we going to do now?"

"Momma, did daddy die?" Charles said, in a state of shock. "Momma…momma." Charles walked over to his mother's side, opposite from his brother. "Did daddy die? What's going on?"

Looking up, Naomi's face was covered completely with tears. "Yes, baby," she replied.

"It's all your fault," Charles yelled at her.

"No, baby. It's going to be okay."

"No, it's not. If you wouldn't have been so mean to him, he wouldn't have left. It's your fault that my daddy is dead, all your fault!" Charles ran to his room.

"Go and see how your brother's doing," Naomi said, beginning to pull herself together.

"Are you okay, momma?" Mark asked, as he gently rubbed his mother's shoulder.

"I'm okay, baby. Just go on and check on your brother."

As the door closed behind Mark, Naomi got on her knees beside the coffee table and began to pray. "Shine your face upon us, oh Lord. Anchor us through this storm of grief. Wrap your arms of assurance around us. Jesus, I know I'm supposed to be strong right now but I'm feeling really week, both in my spirit and in my body. Soothe my aching heart, oh Lord. Lord, I beg you to bless me and my sons with the talents we need to get through this ordeal. Bless me with a talent of patience, because my sons are hurting right now. They're going to need me more than ever. Bless me with a talent of fatherhood, because my children are fatherless. Bless my children with a talent of forgiveness and maturity. Lord, I can't hear you right now, but I'm going to trust in your plan. You said you would be our shelter in the midst of a storm. Father, it's pouring. Shelter us, Father. These things I ask in your holy name. Amen."

After the Funeral…

Sitting at the dining room table were Brandon and Samuel's wives, Gwendolyn and Mona Lisa respectively. Eric's younger sister, Rose was also with them. Brandon and Samuel were Eric's brothers. They're outside with the boys. Brandon and Gwen have a son named Robert around the same age as Mark and Charles

"Girl, I don't know how you are holding up, Mona Lisa said before taking a sip of her sweet tea.

"The Lord is going to make a way," Naomi said. Her legs were stretched out under the table, feet crossed. After tapping her thighs twice with both hands, she said, "He always has."

"This is why I do what I do," Mona Lisa said as she walked over to the couch.

"And what's that?" Gwen asked as she got up and followed her over to the couch.

"You know that joke that every comedian says about walking in from working and just spanking your kids because you know that they did something that they shouldn't? Well, I sleep with a married man or two because I know my man has 'done something that he shouldn't have."

"And that's makes you feel like a woman?" Rose joined them, taking a seat on the love seat.

"No, I didn't say all of that, but it sure makes me feel better! I mean, come, on y'all. Just look at Eric, the way he left things. He changed his insurance when he and Naomi were having problems. Now she doesn't get a dime. What is she supposed to do now? Today's brother has become so trifling. Any long hair-having, young piece of booty that acts interested in them, they lose their minds. Now, this girl didn't have any kids with him and didn't have a mortgage with him, but she's getting paid. Rose, I know that's your brother but if it was me, I would have stabbed his behind when I went up to the casket."

"And what would that have solved, Mona Lisa?" Naomi asked, looking on from the dining room table.

"Not a thing. But like I said, I would have felt better. Heck, I would have felt better for you."

"But that's how it goes," Gwen said. She crossed her legs and leaned back on the couch. "We program our brothers to do what they do."

"What?" Mona Lisa said with a confused look on her face.

"Think about it. When we stand by and let brothers do stuff like this to us, we're sending the message that it's okay. It's starts off at a young age, too. If the majority of our young sisters wouldn't go for the brother with the gold teeth in his mouth and twenty-eight-inch wheels on an Impala, then brothers would drift away from doing that. But we as young black women, we are attracted to that thug-acting bother. And as mature black women, we are attracted to that irresponsible brother—even in the professional world. My experience tells me that we as women would do anything to please that man who just isn't going to do right. Take Naomi right now. Faithful woman. Church-going woman. Man was a straight dog. She did everything she could to win back his heart."

"Now she has to raise two boys into men without a father and without any financial support, because her husband wasn't responsible. You can say what you want to say, Gwen. We haven't programmed men. A man is going to be a dog whether he has twenty-eight-inch wheels on an Impala or factory wheels on a BMW. I was in the military, and I know what these soldiers are doing when they go downrange—married or not."

"Well, I know all of you have your opinions and all of you are right. I would be lying if I said I wasn't upset and afraid right now," Naomi said as she looked around the room. "But there is no reason on this planet for me to disrespect myself because of a man. Yes, I loved and still love my husband. I played the part of the fool, but I promise you I will rise from this situation. I will not let any man steal my joy or my self respect…, Mona Lisa. If I did I would be no better than he was. He has to answer to God for disrespecting me, whom the Lord entrusted to his care. I pray for my husband, because he didn't realize what he had in me. I pray for my sons, because they don't have their father. Yes, he wasn't the best father, but he was theirs. And no, Gwen, we don't like thuggish or irresponsible men as you say, we like positive self-aware men. For our young women, men just seem to come only in those forms that you mentioned. Black women are attracted to positive, strong willed men no matter what they are doing. Eric was that man. If black men knew how to harness that strength, that positivity in their *loins*, they would be the ultimate. Please believe, ladies, that God will provide."

Just then, Brandon entered the house. "Oh, no," he said. "What did I walk in on?"

The women just smiled at one another.

"Are the boys okay?" Naomi said with concern.

"They're both going to be fine. Charles is having a hard time dealing with it, but I'm sure he will eventually come around. Naomi, you know that you and the boys can come and live with us for a while until you get on your feet."

"No, we'll be alright. But I appreciate the offer. We're going to stay right here. I have a few dollars saved up, and I'm expecting a promotion within the next year."

"Okay. Well, you know the offer still stands whenever you want or need it."

"Come on, Naomi," Gwendolyn said, trying to convince her that it would be best for her and the boys.

"I really appreciate all of your support, family. But the Lord is going to see us through this. As much as Eric was deployed, I've had to learn both duties as a parent. I'll call if I need you."

Samuel opened the door and stepped into the doorway.

"What took you so long to come inside?" Mona Lisa said, looking over her shoulder at Samuel.

"I was cleaning out the truck for the trip back."

"Okay, cleaning out the truck for the trip back."

Ignoring Mona Lisa's remark, Samuel asked, "Brandon, are you, Gwen, and Rose ready to go?"

"Yeah, we need to go ahead and get on the road before this bad weather comes in. Again, Naomi, if you need anything, please give us a call."

Gwen, Rose and Mona Lisa altogether gave Naomi a group hug.

"Your faith inspires me, Rose said, holding Naomi's hand. "You were right—my brother didn't know what he had in you." Rose gave Naomi another hug. "I love you, Naomi."

Samuel came over to give Naomi a hug. "You are a strong, good woman. God bless you."

"Come on y'all. Let's go." "Bye, Naomi," everyone echoed.

The house was empty. Naomi plopped down onto the sofa and looked skyward. "Bless us, oh Heavenly Father. Amen"

After Eric's death, Naomi and the children remained in Georgia for ten years. Both Mark and Charles grew up into fine young men. Mark was now married to Regina and Charles to Ophelia. Charles and Ophelia had one child named Sophia. Sophia isn't Charles's biological child. It took many years, but Charles and Mark forgave their father and vowed to make their mom's life as pleasant as possible. It's Thanksgiving and everyone came to visit Ma Nat for the holiday.

"Regina, can you hand me that Turkey baister out of the drawer," Naomi said, putting on oven mitts.

Ophelia chimed in, "Ma, you know that girl doesn't know what a turkey baister is." She laughed, as she continued preparing the macaroni and cheese.

"Leave her alone, Ophelia," Naomi said as she opened the oven door. "Regina, clear me a spot on the counter top so I can set the turkey down." After she set the turkey down, Naomi said, "I'm going to get her squared away," in reference to Ophelia's remark.

"She needs to put some clothes on if you ask me," Ophelia said, looking at Regina in disgust.

"You need to mind your own business," Regina responded. She handed the baister to Naomi. "I can't help it if I look good."

"I can't mind my business if your business is hanging all out for everyone to see."

"She's right, Regina," Naomi said, after sliding the turkey back into the oven. "You have men in the house other than your husband, and regardless of what you might say, you are purposely attracting the eyes of those men."

"A man is going to look no matter what I have on," Regina responded with one hand on her hip and the other on the counter top.

"You may be right, but there is such a thing of advertising too much. You know most women would agree with you—"

"I know, Ma Nat. That's just—"

"...until they have a little girl of their own," Naomi finished.

"You're right about that, Ma Nat," Ophelia agreed, "because I used to dress the same way. That's how I ended up with Sophia at such an early age. Then, I noticed that Sophia was attracted to those same types of clothing. She would give me that same line, but only females know the minds of other females."

"I know that's right," Gwen said, walking into the kitchen. "We can finesse daddy all day long, but momma ain't having it."

"It's about time you guys made it here," Naomi said. She walked over to hug Gwen. "Where's Mona Lisa?"

"She and Samuel had a huge fight, and she decided to stay in North Carolina."

"Those two," Naomi said. She shook her head before walking over to the refrigerator to take out the piecrusts. "Lord, bless them."

"Why do you talk about God all the time?" Regina said, stirring the Kool-Aid. "Who is he to you?"

Naomi smiled as she washed her hands in the sink. "Well, he's a lot of things to a lot of people. To me, he's been a father to my children. My husband, in his absence and a counselor when I'm confused. But you have to know him for yourself before you can truly know him."

Regina continued to stare down into the pitcher of Kool-Aid. "I'm remembering momma taking us to church, at an early age, but that all changed after my little brother died from leukemia. Then momma just stopped taking us to church, because she didn't believe that she could serve a God that could take her only son away. Momma went into a deep depression and my father couldn't take it. He tried everything but couldn't reach her. He eventually left us.

Gwen shook her head "So how's your family now?" she asked, over her shoulder, placing the sweet potato pies into the oven.

"I never heard from my father again and my mother sent me off to stay with her sister in Detroit. My aunty wasn't into church and I eventually lost faith in God, and I'm pretty sure he wouldn't have anything to do with me now, anyway. After I stopped believing, I began to do a lot of terrible things. I just stop caring. My mom is doing better now, though."

Naomi came to Regina's side, lifting her chin up. "Baby, there are a lot of things that we don't understand about God, but we have to trust in his plan. That's why we have to have faith that he knows what's best for us. Otherwise, he would have given up on me a long time ago. The Bible says in First Timothy, one-sixteen, 'But for that very reason I was shown mercy so that in me, the worst of sinners, Christ Jesus might display his unlimited patience as an example for those who would believe in him and receive eternal life.' So, baby, we serve a God who is patient and shows mercy to the worst of sinners. Even you!"

You could tell that Naomi's words touched Regina.

Naomi turned her attention. "Gwen, where's Brandon?" she asked.

"He's in the living room with the guys watching the game."

The men.....

"Smith's open! Throw it. Oh, he's gone," Charles said excitedly. "Go baby, Go.

He's at the fifty, the forty, the thirty, the twenty. He could...go...all...the...way!" the TV sports analyst said elatedly.

"Touchdown, baby," Charles said, mocking Mark. Mark was the only one rooting for the Falcons.

"Hold on. They're throwing the yellow flag," Mark said, still sitting and hoping for a holding penalty.

"Come on, guys. Let's go out back and get this barbeque started before the rest of the food is finished."

"Okay, Uncle Brandon," Charles said, as he sat waiting for the final word on the play.

"Touchdown, baby, touchdown," Charles celebrated, smiling. "I'm going to run into the bedroom and grab the portable TV to bring outside with us."

"Okay, Charles. We'll be outside," Mark said as he followed his uncle out the back door.

"I'm proud of you two boys," Brandon said, putting the coals in the grill. "I mean all the things that you boys been through."

"I know, Uncle Brandon. It took me a long time to forgive my father, but you know what did it for me."

"What's that, Mark?"

"Made me realize that I'm not perfect myself. I've never cheated on Regina, but the temptation has been there."

"Hey, Unc, let's get this grill hot," Charles said, as he walked outside to join them. "How's my boy Rob doing, and why didn't he come down?"

"Oh, he couldn't. He's having Thanksgiving with his girlfriend's people."

"Oh, Rob's still holding out on that marriage thing?" Mark asked, with a smile.

"Uncle Brandon, I have a question for you."

"Shoot," Brandon replied. He stepped back from the grill as the flames grew, the matchbox and lighter fluid still in his hands.

"Why is it that we always tend to gravitate towards the person that we don't want to be like? I mean, I hated the way my father treated my mother, so I did my best not to be like him. But then I married him, so to speak. Charles became like him and he married a woman like momma. It's like this world finds some way to make you face the situations that you try to get away from." Mark said, wearing a look of frustration.

"I know what you're talking about," Brandon said. He's spraying the grill down with Pam. "Your aunt and I were the same way. I was you and your dad was Charles. It took many years and tears for your aunt to make me face myself. She had to show me, me."

"I don't understand what you're trying to say, Uncle Brandon," Charles said as he turned down the volume on the television with the remote control.

"She started treating me the way I was treating her. When I would get mad, she would calmly, this is key now. She would calmly say, 'Baby, isn't this the way you do me?' I mean she would say it in the sweetest voice. She would say, 'If you love me, describe to me what you're feeling right now.'"

"Dag, Uncle Brandon," Mark said, shaking his head. "She came at you like that?"

"Yes!" Brandon said. "Now, it still took me a while to figure it all out. But when it hit me, I was like, 'Man, this woman is *incredible*.' Most women don't realize the power they have over their man. See, Gwen understood that it was all about the approach. A woman can get anything she wants from a man, if she knows how to approach him and has patience. Now, I said 'patience.' No woman should be a fool for a man." Brandon took the cover off of the pan of meat and selected several pieces to place on the grill. "Excuse me, but I love the hell out of that woman because she took the time to learn me.

'I can see what you're saying, Uncle Brandon, but women aren't like that anymore. This patience thing you're talking about doesn't exist. Women want it and they want it now," Charles said.

"That's because you guys don't know how to be men anymore. Just like Gwen had to figure out the power that women have over men, men have to find out the power they have over women. If you know what you're doing, a woman will support you in anything you do. You just have to be sure of yourself."

"Yeah, I'm feeling you on that, Uncle," Charles said, nodding his head. "I don't know about you guys, but I'm about to get back into this game, " he concluded, before turning the volume up again.

After the Thanksgiving meal

"Ma," Mark said, shaking his head in confirmation, "the food was the bomb."

"I second that," Charles said. With his hand under his shirt, he rubbed his stomach. "Uncle Brandon, we really did it on those ribs, right?" he asked, now picking his teeth.

"*We*?" Brandon said turning his head toward Charles. He then got up from the table and head for the living room.

Gwen and Ophelia began clearing off the table.

"Can I help?" Sophia asked, as she stood up from the table.

"Yeah, put that cover over that cake plate and bring it into the kitchen," her mother said.

"Ma, do we have any more ice cream in there for the apple pie?" Charles asked, getting up from the table.

"I gave the last of the vanilla to Sophia. All we have left is Butter Pecan in the freezer," Naomi replied, walking into the kitchen.

Following Naomi into the kitchen. "Ma, me and Mark are going to run to the store real quick." He gave Naomi a kiss. "When we get back, maybe we all can play *Scene It*, or something," he suggested. Walking over to Ophelia to give her a kiss, he said "Love you, baby,".

After coming out of the kitchen, Charles let Mark know about going to the store. Mark then headed into the kitchen to let Regina know that he was going with Charles.

"Baby, I'm going to go with Charles to the store. We'll be right back," Mark said. He walked over to where Regina stood washing dishes. "I love you," he said, and he kissed her on the neck. On his way out of the kitchen he kissed his mother and said that he loved her, also.

"Uncle B, we'll be right back. Be ready," Charles said as he walked out the door.

"I will," Brandon said, looking over his shoulder.

One hour later

"What's taking Mark and Charles so long?" Ophelia wondered, becoming worried.

"Ain't no telling," Naomi said as she sat down on one of the love seats. She was ready for a rest after cleaning up after the big meal.

"Something isn't right," Ophelia said. She began looking for her purse to call Charles's cell phone. Once she found it she immediately dialed his number.

Charles's voice mail immediately came up.

"Regina," Ophelia said anxiously, "call Mark!"

"Ophelia, I'm sure everything is okay," Naomi said.

Gwen and Sophia walked into the living room. "What's going on?" Gwen asked, noticing the serious looks on their faces.

"We're trying to get in touch with Mark and Charles," Brandon said as he began looking for his keys.

Regina began to dial Mark's phone. They heard a cell phone ring from inside the room. Sophia pointed out Mark's phone on one of the end tables.

"I'm going to go and try to find them," Brandon said, putting on his coat.

Suddenly there was a knock at the door. Everyone froze in place for about three seconds. Naomi slowly took her seat, as though she knew that bad news was on the way.

"Who is it," Brandon called as he walked toward the door, continuing to put on his coat.

"Officer O'Malley and Officer Conyers," one of the officers responded.

"Oh, Lord," Ophelia said.

 Brandon opened the door, and there were two police officers standing there without smiles, or even a Thanksgiving greeting.

"Gwen, take Sophia into the bedroom for me, please," Brandon said. He turned around, moving his head and eyes around to find Gwen.

"Not again, Lord," Naomi said, rocking back and forth with her face in her hands. For her, it was a sense of Déjàvu.

"Is this the home of Naomi Everett?" Officer Conyers said as he stepped forward.

"Yes it is," Brandon replied, maintaining his posture.

"Sir, there has been an accident—"

"Lord, no," Ophelia said, becoming emotionally overwhelmed. "Are they okay?" she asked, rushing over to the officers. Regina followed behind her.

"Ma'am, I'm afraid that one of the passengers died instantly, and the other died on his way to Memorial Hospital."

"You must be mistaken," Regina said. She turned and began walking away from the door. "There's no way you could have known that they lived here. There must be a mistake."

"Ma'am, the medics obtained the address from the man who died on his way to the hospital. He directed them to his wallet where his license had this address."

"Oh God, no," Ophelia shouted as she fell to her knees. "Why, God?" she begged.

Fighting back his own emotions, Brandon rushed to Ophelia's side to try to console her. Naomi was still sitting with her face in her hands, silently weeping and praying. When Gwen retuned, Brandon motioned for her to go to Regina, where she was crying and saying, "Why, why, why."

Gwen tried to console her, but after about fifteen seconds Regina shouted, "Don't touch me!" and ran to the kitchen.

"Are you okay, Naomi?" Gwen asked, kneeling down beside her and rubbing her back.

Pointing to the Kleenex, Naomi shook her head yes as she realized that she needed to be strong for her family.

Brandon finally got Ophelia calmed down enough to get her over to the couch.

"Let's pray," Naomi said, grasping Gwen's hand. Gwen then took Ophelia's hand, and so on in a circle. Just as they were getting into the prayer there was a sudden sound of glass breaking, and everyone rushed to the kitchen. Sophia stuck her head out of her room. Seeing that everyone was on there way to the kitchen, she immediately followed.

Walking into the house after placing the "For Sale" in the front yard. Naomi has buried her two sons and has decided to go back with Gwen and Brandon.

"Ma Naomi," Regina said as she and Ophelia took seats on the sofa.

"We've decided that we want to go with you back to North Carolina with Gwen and Brandon," Ophelia said, looking determined to convince her.

"No, now," Naomi said. "I don't know what's going to happen when I get back there. I'm going to stay in momma's old house. As for you Ophelia, it would be best that you keep Sophia in the same school, which is a good school. Sophia has friends here, and that's what she needs now more than ever, considering what she's going through. Don't you agree?"

"Yes, ma'am. It's just that we've become so close to you—Sophia and I both have."

"It's not like we'll never see each other again," Naomi said, taking her sons' picture off of the end table and staring at it. "Plus, I need you to watch the house for me 'til we get everything out of here."

Reluctantly, Ophelia agreed and headed to the bedroom to pack her remaining items.

"You need to do the same thing," Naomi said to Regina. She placed the boys' picture in her purse and sat down on the love seat.

"Ma Naomi, that was a good thing that you just did for Ophelia, but I'm not leaving you." Regina walked over to the love seat. Taking Naomi's hand, she kneeled down beside her. "I don't have a family to go to. You're the only family that I have. Where you go, I will go. Your home will be my home; your family will be my family; your God is now my God. Ma, Mark told me many stories about you. I am a witness to this life-changing tragedy. Things that would normally cause someone to go insane, you still stand strong. Through you, I have learned what it means to have faith. Anyone who can love God after all you've been through is someone that I want to lead me to Him."

"Somehow I knew you would be the one to give me the hardest time," Naomi said. She released Regina's hand before stroking her hair then kissing her forehead.

"Are we ready to go?" Brandon asked, walking in from the kitchen.

"Where's Gwen and Sophia?" Naomi asked as she stood up. "

They're in the kitchen," Brandon said taking a bite from his bagel then a sip from his coffee mug. Naomi walked toward the kitchen.

"So are you going to go back with us?" Brandon asked. He took a seat in the love seat after Naomi had walked away.

"Yeah, I finally convinced her to let me go," Regina said taking a seat on the sofa.

"Regina, I want you to know that I've seen a change in you, just in these past couple of weeks. I know that you still have to be hurting inside, but you're handling it pretty well."

"Well, I've been praying. I hadn't prayed since I was a little girl. Sometimes I get lost for words, but Ma Naomi said that that was okay and I shouldn't get discouraged, because God understands."

"You have a great teacher in my sister. I don't know what I would do if I were to lose Gwen and then lose Robert. She encourages me," Brandon said. He shook his head with a smile, before taking another sip from his mug. "Have you thought about what you want to do?"

"Not really," Regina answered. She stood up and walked around to the back of the sofa.

"What are you *interested* in doing?" Brandon persisted.

"Well, don't laugh, but Mark and I always talked about going into real estate," Regina said, nervously massaging the back of the couch.

"There's nothing funny about that," Brandon said. He put his coffee mug down to go into it a little more. "As a matter a fact, I'm trying to get Robert into the same thing, but he wants to manage and expand the little motel that we own. Gwen has some acquaintances that run the Century 21 Real Estate Licensing School. I'm pretty sure she could get you enrolled right away."

"I don't have any money to pay for school and I'm already staying with Ma Naomi, and I wouldn't know how to repay you guys," Regina said, humbly.

"Well, you're family, and you don't have to pay us anything. But if you feel like you need to do something, you can work at the hotel cleaning rooms or running the office 'til you can get something else. That'll pay for your books. What do you say?"

Smiling, Regina said, "you guys overwhelm me." Gwen, Naomi, Ophelia and Sophia came into the living room to join Regina and Brandon. Brandon then began to load the vehicle.

"I'm going to miss this house," Naomi said, as she took her coat from the closet. "I wish I didn't have to sell it. The Lord has a plan, though. I know He does."

"I'll make sure that I come by every week to check on it," Ophelia said, putting on her hat and gloves. She picked up her bags. "Well, you guys have a safe trip and call me as soon as you all get there."

Everyone came over to give Ophelia and Sophia a hug and a kiss as they got ready to leave.

"The truck is ready," Brandon said, standing in the doorway. "Y'all ready?"

"Yeah, we'll be right out," Gwen answered. She went to the kitchen to turn the lights off and made sure she didn't leave any appliances on.

"Well, Lord, as you close one door you always open up another. Let's go, family."

Regina worked as many hours at the hotel as they would let her. She even took a part time job at the local video store to help with fixing up Mark's Grandmother's house, where she now lived with Naomi. Naomi was unable to work, because she began to have severe back pain from all of those many years she had served as a child care provider at the military post's child development center. Regina vowed to Naomi that she would take care of everything. Gwen came through with getting Regina enrolled into real estate classes. Brandon also convinced Robert to attend the real estate school. It wasn't that difficult, once Robert met Regina. Somewhere between attending classes

together and working together at the hotel, they had become fond of each other, and before long, they began dating.

"What are you all dressed up for?" Naomi asked from the couch. She was watching a DVD of a sermon by Bishop T.D. Olsten.

"Robert and I are going out for dinner and a movie."

"I'm glad to see you two together. You've done so much since you've been here. You are a new person. You dress differently. You speak positively and you carry yourself, as a woman should. I want you to know that I appreciate everything that you've done for us. Through you, the Lord showed me something that I never thought I would see, and that is a renewed mind. Many people change their hearts but never change their minds."

What do you mean by that?" Regina said, confused.

Wrinkling her face and adjusting herself in her seat, Naomi began to explain. "A lot of us change our hearts and turn away from the sins of this world, but our minds aren't transformed. That flirtatious worldly man that changes his heart will be a flirtatious preacher if he doesn't renew his mind. That provocative woman that has spent her life advertising her breasts and curves still believes that it is okay to flaunt her body. You've changed your heart and mind, and we have God to thank for that."

"That's nothing, compared to what you've given me. Through you, I have found life. You taught me that anything is possible through Christ Jesus. Here's something that I didn't tell you."

"What's that, Regina?" Naomi asked, pausing her video.

"I found my mother, and we had a long heart to heart. I told her that I had accepted Jesus as head of my life and that I was happier than I had ever been and that I wanted nothing more than for her to experience the happiness that I was feeling again. No offense to when I was married to Mark, Ma Naomi," Regina said with one of her hands gesturing as she struggled to explain.

"No offense taken, baby. I know that things were different then."

"Thanks, Ma. I knew you would understand. We also talked about my dad, and we even talked about my brother. We cried and talked for hours. She was so happy for me."

"That's what it's all about, Regina. It's about being a witness to someone, because it doesn't do us any good to be Christians if we don't show the world that trials and tribulations come our way just like anyone else. We just have to demonstrate in our daily lives that we can continue to lean on Jesus and pray for understanding and acceptance through those trials and tribulations."

"There was something else that I wanted to ask you, Ma."

"What's that, Regina?"

"Do you mind the fact that I'm dating Mark's cousin?"

"No, I don't mind it because I know that it wasn't something that was in the works before my son passed. I believe what you guys share is genuine and you have all of my blessings."

"I think he's going to ask me to marry him. I don't know what I would've done without Gwen and Robert's help. They gave me a job, got me into school. Rob and I are talking about starting our own real estate business. The Lord has truly blessed me."

The door bell ringing interrupted Regina.

"That must be Robert." Regina said walking over to the door.

"What's up, girl," Ophelia said with outstretched arms. It was Ophelia and Sophia.

Regina and Ophelia embraced with both of them coming to tears.

"Come on in here you two. How's my niece doing," Regina said giving Sophia a hug and kiss also." "Ma Nat, look who's here."

"Hey, Ma Naomi."

Surprised, Ma Naomi stood to her feet coming to tears herself.

Ophelia and Sophia hugged Ma Naomi at once.

"It is so good to see you Ophelia. How's my grandbaby doing? Both of you come over to the couch and take a seat."

"Grand Ma Naomi, I'm on the honor roll and I'm on the gymnastics team, Sophia said excitedly.

"You doing okay, Ophelia?"

"Yes, ma'am. I'm doing okay. Ma, I don't think I every thanked you for being there for me. You taught me what a woman should and shouldn't be. I thank God for you. The world says that there aren't any more Big Mommas out there, but I beg to differ. There probably aren't as many as there used to be, but that's why I feel so blessed to have had you in my life."

"Ophelia, I really thank you for those kind words, but that's just how my mother raised me. I don't know of any other way to be. The only thanks that I need from you is for you to raise Sophie up to be a strong black woman. The Bible says that we should raise our children in the way that we would have them to go. That's why I am the way that I am. You have a tough job, being that Sophie's real father and her stepfather are not here. However, God can teach you how to be a father to Sophie. Don't forget that

your father is still alive. It is his responsibility to give his granddaughter everything that her father would have given her. Now when a good man finds *you* and not the other way around—takes you as his wife–then, he can assume that responsibility. You understand?"

"Yes, ma'am. And I promise to do just that.

Just then, Robert burst through the door calling out for Regina.

"What is it, baby?" Regina said, not knowing what to expect.

"They bought it, baby!" Robert continued excitedly.

"Calm down, Robert," Regina said, grabbing Robert's hand.

"They bought it, baby. The bought the office property off of University and Trianna," Robert said, taking a breath and gathering himself.

"They did?" Regina exclaimed. She was quickly becoming just as frantic as Robert was. They embraced into a tight hug. Then, Robert leaned Regina over, taking her off balance as he planted a long, passionate kiss. "Baby, I have one more thing."

"What is it Robert?" Regina asked, Her eyes were still out of focus from the kiss.

A smile slowly appeared across Naomi's face.

Robert dropped down to one knee. "Baby, I know we just landed the biggest deal in the city, but you can top that if you accept my proposal to love you forever. To love you like you could never be loved by any other man."

"Watching these two makes me want to go and get another man," Naomi said turning to Ophelia.

"You're not the only one," Ophelia said with a slight giggle.

"Baby, I wouldn't want to be with another man. Yes. Definitely yes, baby," Regina said, pulling Robert up to kiss him.

Opening her eyes from the kiss and hug, Regina noticed that Ma Naomi and Ophelia had rushed over to hug and kiss her.

"I love you two," Regina said with tears streaming from her face.

"You deserve it, baby. You deserve it!"

JOBE

JOBE is a combination of two or more stories from previous books. The reason for this is I turned this story into a play.

A Righteous Man

This is one of the greatest stories of faith and obedience ever told. There are a number of Bible stories on faith and obedience. There was the story of Noah, who believed that God would send a rain that would flood the earth. So he collected all the animals on the earth, which made him look kind of crazy. However, he pressed on anyway. Abraham believed that it was the Lord's will for him to kill his own son. That took all the faith in the world. Because of his faith, he was going to do it until God stopped him. None of these acts of faith involved suffering personally, emotionally, and physically until JOB. JOB was an upstanding man that feared God and shunned evil. He was the definitive illustration of what the power of faith could achieve under any circumstance. This was a story in which God showed us his own faith. God believed in JOB. Your ultimate goal here on Earth is for God to be able to look down on you and know without a doubt that you will do the right thing—that you will show JOB-like faith.

JOBE lies in bed asleep. There is a sense of calm about him.
"Look at my son," Jesus said, watching over JOBE. "I am so proud of him. I love him so much and in him I am so very pleased."

"Yes, he does look very content," Satan said, walking up behind Jesus.

"Where have you been?" Jesus said, after Satan made his presence known.

"Oh, I've been here and there," Satan said casually. "I've been in and out of the Earth, and I have found no one worthy of a true test."

"Have you considered my faithful servant, JOBE?" Jesus asked, with much confidence. "There is none like him on Earth, a blameless and upright man, who fears God and turns away from evil."

"It's only because you have blessed him and everything that he touches," Satan said sarcastically. "Have you not protected him and his household? Have you not doubled his possessions? Remove your hand from him. Allow his faith to be truly tested and surely he will curse you to your face," Satan said.

Jesus turned to Satan. After pausing for a moment, Jesus responded. "I will remove my hand from JOBE, and everything he has is now in your power, but do not lay a hand on him."

Satan smiled and left the presence of Jesus.

Theme music from the talk show escalates and tapers, as the commercial ends and the host introduces the next guest.

"Hello everyone, and welcome back to the Lincoln Styles' Show. Our next guest has graced the cover of *Black Enterprise*, *Forbes*, *Jet*, *Eclipse*, and countless other high profile magazines. He was one of the first black Fortune 500 business members from South Carolina. He owns and operates the first black-owned online brokerage firm. He owns 25 business properties. He has an MBA from Howard University and the list goes on and on. Ladies and gentlemen, JOBE Mitchell."

JOBE comes out wearing a perfect smile and a black suit with a red shirt and black, square-nosed shoes, waving his hand in the air to the audience. He shakes Scott's hand and turns back to the audience, who's continuing to cheer. He bows before taking a seat. As the audience begins to settle down, Lincoln begins the discourse.

"Welcome JOBE. You're looking mighty sharp there, man."

"Well, I heard that that's the only way anyone can be on your show," JOBE said, looking down and adjusting his jacket.

"Well, I don't know who told you that, but....it's true," Lincoln said, slowly standing up and opening both of his arms, posing. "This is the latest from my clothing line." Lincoln smiled, flashing his pearly white teeth.

"You are too much, Scott," JOBE said, shaking his head.

"So, what's been going on, brother JOBE?" Lincoln said, taking his seat.

"Nothing much, man, just trying to make it, you know. That, along with trying to keep the wife happy."

"Well, that can be a job in itself," Lincoln said, shaking his head. "How's Yolanda doing by the way?"

"Oh, my baby's doing great. She is in the process of opening her third bed and breakfast. This one is going to be right here in Atlanta. She's sitting right there in the front row," JOBE said, pointing her out.

Yolanda modestly stands up and nods. Yolanda is a very beautiful woman. She is about a foot shorter than JOBE, brown-skinned, and has perfect dimples to go with her perfect smile. She is wearing a black pants suit with a red blouse underneath.

"Come on up here and join your husband," Lincoln said, motioning for her to come up on stage.

As Yolanda makes her way to the stage, stage personnel rush over to attach a microphone to her lapel. Before taking her seat, JOBE slides to the right so Lincoln can talk to Yolanda about the Bed & Breakfast business she has begun to launch.

"How's it going, Yolanda?" Lincoln asked.

"Oh, everything is going well, Scott. The Lord has been truly blessing us."

"Ain't that the truth," Lincoln said, smiling and motioning between JOBE and Yolanda while looking out at the audience.

"Tell me a little more about this INNS & Suites chain that you're starting."

"Well, the name of the company is 'Peaches Bed & Breakfast,'" Yolanda said, looking out at the audience before turning back to Scott. "One of the two is located in Columbia, South Carolina and the other is in Charlotte, North Carolina. Each one has no more than 20 rooms. It has the same upscale feel as the larger INNs and Suites, with a more personal approach."

"Sounds like the both of you are really on the move."

"You can say that," Yolanda said, looking over at JOBE and rubbing his knee as JOBE leaned forward.

"That is so touching," Lincoln said, smiling and nodding his head. "And you know I've noticed that the two of you have on matching attire." Lincoln smiled.

The crowd cooed.

"I'm being serious," Lincoln said. "I don't know about any of you all, but I believe that success is nothing if you don't have anyone special and committed to share it with. It's good to see a couple that has lasted as long as these two have lasted and still be in love, because you can be married for a long time and not be in love. How long have you two been married now?"

"It's going on thirty years this summer," JOBE said. He leaned back on the sofa with his arm draped on the back of the seat behind Yolanda.

"Wow! That's awesome," Lincoln replied. "See, that's what I want. Even when I get to heaven."

JOBE, Yolanda, and the studio audience are quiet as they wait for Scott's explanation.

"I see I have some of you wondering what I'm talking about," Lincoln said, shaking his head and smiling. "You see, I've thought this through. Some people want streets of gold, mansions, and stuff like that when they make it to heaven. I want me a woman. I want the greatest creature made by God. That's heaven to me," Lincoln said, pointing at JOBE and Yolanda.

Women all over the audience begin to clap and cheer. Some even stand.

"I'm not going to get into all of that, but I just wanted to put that out there," Lincoln said, as the crowd began to settle down. "I'm just saying that it's good to see a couple, a successful couple, in love. How do you guys find the time to do all of this?"

JOBE and Yolanda switch seats.

"Simply put, since the kids are all adults and on their own now, she and I have a chance to live out our dreams together. Well, mainly Yolanda. She spent most of her time grooming and raising the kids. So now, I feel like I should support her in all of her endeavors."

"I hear that, brother. You know, most brothers would be afraid to do something like that. Insecure brothers, that is. They're afraid of their woman being in the lime light I guess. How are your three children doing?"

"They're also here," JOBE said, looking out at the studio audience, motioning for them to stand. As they stood, JOBE called out their names. "That's Yasmine, her husband Quincy, and their daughter Egypt; JOBE Jr. and his wife Deborah; and Jerrod and his girlfriend, Shannon."

"Thank you all for coming," Lincoln said, after everyone had taken his or her seats again. "I know you guys are so proud of JOBE and Yolanda. For all of the people out there in TV land, tell us a little about yourself, JOBE."

"Well Scott, I grew up in the deep country of South Carolina."

Yolanda sat there shaking her head, smiling in agreement.

"My father and mother were William and Rachel Mitchell. I had four sisters and three brothers. Eight of us," JOBE said, shaking his head.

"That's a lot of children," Lincoln said.

"Yeah, tell me about it! I know all about head to foot. Mom and Dad, did the best they could buy us though. I can honestly say that if it weren't for them I wouldn't be where I am today."

"You have to have that strong Christian family background," Lincoln said. "Tell me something about your book, which I have here."

Lincoln holds up the book and shows it to the audience.

"The title of the book is *Running Faith-based Businesses*. I co-wrote it with three members of my board."

"Who are the other three co authors?"

"They're here also. They are Blair Knight, Ezekiel Burroughs, and James Washington."

"You guys go ahead and stand up for me also," Lincoln said, looking out at the audience again.

The three men stand up in acknowledgment.

"The book is about putting God first literally. The book discusses how we start our board meetings with a moment of prayer. How we do not make serious financial decisions without praying over them. The book also talks about the pitfalls of becoming wealthy. How we sometimes replace the God that got us to this place of prosperity with the place itself."

"Now that's something for everyone to take home," Lincoln said. "Replacing the God that brought you to a blessed state with the blessing. Awesome! God blesses you with a car, and now you are worshiping the car. Happens every day."

"It's like when God led the Israelites into the promise land. Once they received the promise, they forgot what got them there and began to worship the things of that land. The book describes the signs and symptoms of this disease that most of us catch."

"No, you didn't call it a disease, bother."

"I sure did."

"Well, you know I have the book, and I have read it from cover to cover and, brother, you did a marvelous job. Everyone that wants to become successful or is successful must read this book. As a matter of fact, everyone in this audience will have this book today," Lincoln said, raising the book up in the air.

The audience begins to cheer.

"Now, I'm remembering that the two of you used to sing together," Lincoln said, with a mischievous smile on his face. "Can the both of you please give me, the studio audience, and everyone out there in TV land the opportunity to hear a duet? I already have the mics set up for you guys over there." Lincoln pointed to a smaller stage off to JOBE and Yolanda's right. "Can you do that for us, please?" Lincoln said, with his hands clasped together.

"You know, any time that I can spread the word of God through song, I am more than happy to do so," Yolanda said, looking at JOBE.

"Just give us a little taste, and we'll roll right into commercial. Thank you so much," Lincoln said, standing up to gently shake Yolanda and JOBE's hand.

JOBE and Yolanda sing the song "My Everything" by Helen Baylor and Marvin Wayans.

Quinton and Yasmine Felton had been married going on three years and had one daughter, Egypt. Quinton was a well-built man. He worked out in the gym every day after work. Working at the airport loading planes for FedEx also kept him in shape. Quinton was also taking some afternoon and evening classes whenever he could to get that business degree, which had been eluding him for a while now, but he still found time to enjoy socializing, either at his home or visiting with some of his co-workers.

Yasmine had been working at the local Walgreen's for a little over a year. She enjoyed being a Pharmacist, but her feet had started to give her problems after a year of standing all day. Yasmine had short, highlighted hair. She was a thick girl, too, but she was perfect for Quinton. Nothing was too big and nothing was too small. Quinton called her his Goldie Locks because everything was just right.

"I thought you were going to pick up some snacks and drinks from the grocery store on your way home from work, Yasmine?" Quinton said, coming in from outside and

glancing over at the empty kitchen table. He had been in the backyard grilling chicken wings for that night's Conference Finals, Knicks–Indiana Pacer's game #6. The Knicks were up three to two, and they were playing in Indy.

"You did remember that I have the guys coming over to watch the game with me tonight, right?"

"You did remember that we're supposed to go to daddy's for his book signing in a couple of days, Yasmine said from the bathroom?"

"Yes, I remember, but do you remember that I promised the fellas that I would host the championship series if the Knicks made it this far?" Quinton let an additional five to ten seconds pass before responding, because it was Game 6, and the potential for interruption of the evening festivities had just increased. He quickly realized that he had to play this situation skillfully. The Knicks could be going to the Championship.

Quinton walked over to the bathroom door and knocked softly.

"Are you okay, baby?" he asked. "Yasmine? Baby, I'm going to be able to drive to Charlotte tomorrow. It's not going to be a problem. I've already reserved a van, and I've already picked up the gift that we selected."

Still, he got no answer. He knew that if he called her name again, it was just going to aggravate her into exploding with an answer. So, he just continued with a question.

"What's wrong? Do you want to talk about it?"

Quinton knew that any wrong move here would mean making some phone calls to cancel the playoff party.

Yasmine still was not answering.

Quinton immediately stopped to go over every step in his head, ensuring that he had covered every base. Had he been attentive, patient, planned for the trip to Pop Mitchell's book signing, and not noticeably been patronizing to her? He desperately wanted to keep from blowing this situation totally out of proportion because this was the Conference Finals.

"Baby, that's okay; I'll just run to the store and grab some things. Do you want anything?" Still no answer. "Okay," he said softly. "I'll be right back."

As the guys started showing up, Yasmine and Quinton had barely said more than five words to each other.

"Oooo weeee! Did you see that pass from Maurberry?" TJ said, his hands up to his mouth as he leaned back into the couch. "Give me some love on that one, Q."

"You know it," Quinton said. "I knew we made the right choice in picking up this cat."

Quinton and TJ were rooting for the Knicks; Perry and Sylvester (Sly) were pulling for the Pacers. The fellas could feel that there was some tension going on between Quinton and Yasmine, but as normal when you go over to your boy's house, you ignore it.

After Yasmine put Egypt to bed, she began to wash clothes. Quinton knew that once she started washing clothes at 9:30 at night, the game was about to be over.

"It's half-time, baby, and we're up ten points," TJ said, walking over to Sly to get a pound.

"Back up off of me, TJ," Sly said, pushing his hand out of the way. "We still have another half of the game left, and Reggie hasn't even shown up yet. You know once Reggie gets started, you and Spike Lee will have your heads hanging low like you do every year ya'll play the Knicks playoff hope killers."

"TJ, grab me a drink while you're up yapping about those soon to be tied for the series 3 to 3 Knicks," Perry said.

Just before the second half began, Quinton went down into the basement to talk with Yasmine.

"Baby, is everything okay?"

"What do you think, Quinton?" Yasmine replied abruptly.

"I don't know. You won't talk to me."

"Do I have to tell you everything, Quinton?"

Quinton realized that he was at the beginning of the end of his playoff party.

"Apparently so, because I'm not a mind reader."

"You knew that I didn't feel like company tonight," Yasmine said, raising her voice a little.

"Girl, if you don't keep that mess down . . . . I asked you if there was anything wrong," Quinton said, whispering forcefully, "and you didn't say a thing."

"Well, I'm saying something now. And I don't want any company tonight." We need to get ready to take this trip to see Daddy. His book signing party is in two days, and I don't want to wait until the last minute to get everything we're going to need to take with us."

"I have already taken care of all of that, plus I had this party planned weeks ago."

"That sounds like a personal problem," she said, looking him in the eyes and loading the dryer at the same time.

"See, you're trying to start. I'm not about to tell these guys that they have to leave. We're in the middle of the game."

"Well, either you're going to tell them or I'm going to tell them. You decide."

Quinton was as furious as he could be. He didn't want to tell the fellas, and he definitely didn't want Yasmine to tell them. So he had to come up with something quick.

"Are you serious, Yasmine?" he said, hoping that she would finally give in and say something like, *Just don't let this happen again.*

She just stared at him.

Quinton spun around angrily and walked back upstairs.

"Hey Quinton, you're just in time, man. The second half is about to start. We don't want to jinx us, so you have to be sitting down in your same seat at the inbound," TJ said.

"Hey TJ, um, I going to have to call it a night, man—the wife isn't feeling well."

"What?" Perry said, putting his drink on the end table.

"Quit playing, Q. Sit down and watch the game, man," TJ said, shaking his head.

"I'm serious, man. I hate to do this, but the ball game is over."

"I'm not going to give you a hard time right now because I feel your pain, and I've been there. But you can best believe, bro, that I'm going to give it to you on Monday," TJ said, giving Quinton dap.

"Thanks, man."

Once everyone was gone, Quinton didn't say a word as he went into the linen closet and grabbed a blanket. He then walked into the bedroom, took a pillow off of the bed, and went back to the living room.

"Oh, so you're going to sleep out here tonight?" Yasmine said, as she walked by with a stack of folded laundry in her arms.

Quinton politely gave her the same stare that she had been giving him since she'd gotten home from work, and then continued to watch what was left of the game.

"So you can't hear me talking to you?" she said, moving in front of the television.

"Look Yasmine, you got what you wanted, so now I want to be left alone. Can you do that for me?"

"So you wanna be left alone, huh, then be alone. I can't stand you anyway," she said, throwing the laundry on the floor and heading for the bedroom.

Normally Quinton would at least go behind her to console her, but not tonight. He felt as though what she had done on this night was going to take some time to get over.

The Trip to JOBE's

Everyone has arrived at Yasmine and Quincy's home for their trip to JOBE'S book signing party. The only people that are not there are Quincy and Hilton. Calvin and JOBE Jr. are in the bonus room playing pool.

"What's up, JJ?" Calvin asked, as JJ walked over to one of the stools and took a seat.

"Nothing much, Uncle Cal. Just came up to see what you were doing. What's going on with you with your **PHAT FARM** jeans and hoody, trying to look all young and what not?"

Calvin smiled. "Talking about the way I'm dressed—you're looking pretty DMX yourself, with all that Akedemic gear on, as you young cats would say . . . knowing that nothing about any of y'all is Akedemic." Calvin placed chalk on the tip of his cue. "Is this the latest professional wear for up and coming lawyers? Come on over here and rack'em so I can school you."

"You want me to break or you, Uncle Cal?"

"You'd better break because that might be your last shot."

"You're talking mad trash for someone who probably hasn't shot pool in a while."

Calvin laughed. "I probably haven't, but I know that I can take you," Calvin smiled. "So, what's going on with you? You seemed a little upset walking in?"

JOBE Jr. shrugged. "Shannon started trippin' last night," he said, jerking a pool cue from the cue stand.

"About what?"

"About nothing, Uncle Cal."

"You know what, I've been married for a little while now, and I've never known a woman to trip about nothing."

"It's like this. Yesterday, me and a couple of my colleagues went to check out the Tarheel-Terappins game. I planned it two weeks ago, so I figured it wouldn't be a problem. So, you know how I do—I got dressed and went to do my thing. When I got back home, she's sitting on the couch waiting up for me. After she makes eye contact, she doesn't say a word to me and heads upstairs."

"That's a good thing, JJ, being that she waited up for you. It's when she doesn't wait up that you should get worried. So, what time did you come home?"

"No, Unc—it *used* to be a good thing when she used to do it wearing a satin gown, a thong, smelling like my weakness, and all of this while reheating my plate that she'd put aside for me. Know what I mean, Uncle C! Now she waits up in a wool robe, an old scarf, and the leftovers are still in the pots stuck in the frig. She's on some old different sh—" JOBE Jr. caught himself before cursing. "Sorry, Uncle Cal, but she's got me pretty hot right about now."

"So, what time did you come home, JJ?" Calvin asked, realizing that JJ was avoiding his question.

"There used to be a time when it didn't matter what time I came home."

Calvin leaned over the table, preparing for his shot. "Are you going to tell me what time you came in or what?"

"I think it was around three-something," JJ said, shifting the pool cue back and forth between his hands smiling.

"Three in the morning? Come on, JJ. What if she came in at three in the morning? Wouldn't you be tripping?"

"Come on, Uncle Calvin. Don't hit me with the 'JOE.' What would you do if your woman did the things you do song. You and I both know that there is a difference between how a man handles his thing and how a woman handles hers."

"True that, true that," Calvin said, as he walked around the pool table trying to find his next shot. "Combination 5 on the 9, side pocket," he said, using the end of the cue to point out the shot.

"Did you know that there is a difference in how men and women define love?" he said, bending over the table again.

"Of course, Uncle Cal. I know all about that."

"Well, break it down to me, Mr. Professor of Love," Calvin said, as JOBE Jr. took his shot and missed.

"Yeah, let me break it down to you, old school." JOBE Jr. grabbed his cue with both hands and began to explain. "You see, a woman thinks love is what you buy her. You know, like jewelry and clothing. They like things that symbolize how their man feels about them," he added. Walking around the table, he bent, nailed his final high ball, and began chalking his stick. "Are you following me, Unc?"

"Go ahead, I'm listening," Calvin said, folding his arms and smiling.

"And men, all we want is understanding. Take my situation for example. I would know that my woman loved me if she wouldn't question what I do and just understand that a man is going to do things that she's not going to understand. Like hanging out

with my colleagues or just getting lost for a minute or two doing nothing. Know what I mean, Uncle Cal?"

JOBE Jr. leaned over the table again. "8 ball, side pocket," he called. "Come on, baby, get there." JOBE Jr. tilted his head in the direction of the ball as if it was going to help the ball along.

Calvin smiled when the ball missed the pocket. "First of all, I'm not that old for you to be calling me old school. Secondly, you're in the ballpark, but you won't be hitting any homeruns thinking like that. Let me break it down to you." Calvin called out the 14 ball, corner pocket, and then watched as the ball rolled gracefully into the hole before turning back to JOBE Jr. "A woman knows her man loves her by the sacrifices he makes for her. Now, you were close with the jewelry thing, but it's what you have to give up getting the jewelry that counts. Long payments or holding back on those dubs or a big screen TV for a while are some of the things that shows her that her man loves her."

"I think I see what you mean, Uncle Cal."

"But the sacrifices don't necessarily have to be that big either. Like you said, let's take your situation for example. What do you think would have happened if you had surprised her by telling her that you'd decided that you'd rather spend time with her yesterday instead of hanging out with the fellas? I bet you probably would have had to beat her off you because it lets her know that no matter what, no person or thing comes before her. Every woman loves that feeling. I'm not saying do those things all the time, but you have to demonstrate your love to a woman every now and then. Believe me when I tell you, it's not all about sex with women. Oh yeah, they like sex, but it's not a measuring tool for them. If it was, we'd come up short half the time."

"I don't know about you, Uncle, but I'm handling mines."

"So why are we having this conversation? You have to give a woman something that no other man can give her, and this comes through the sacrifices you make for her. The way you take care of her. Oh, she's going to play games just to test your sacrifice level. You have to be prepared for that at all times and go along with it. Some games are healthy."

JOBE Jr. nodded. "I think I'm beginning to understand where you're coming from. So last night was a test?"

"I'm not saying it was or wasn't. But I do know that your lady was and probably still is upset with you, and you haven't done anything to ease her pain."

"So you're saying every time she gets upset with me, I have to fix it?"

Calvin shook his head. "I thought I taught you better than this . . . . Heck yeah, of course. You're the man of the house, right? Should it be her job? All I'm saying is that

you should sit down calmly with your lady and explain to her exactly what you did and why and figure out how the both of you can avoid the same situation."

"I got you, Uncle Cal."

"Hold on, let me finish. Check this out," Calvin said. He knocked his last low ball into the corner pocket and chalked his cue. "Now, the way that a man knows his woman loves him is by the number of times she gives him what I call, 'Undeserving Love.'"

"What do you mean, Uncle Calvin?"

"Let me give you an example. Way back in the day, I used to pull the same bull crap you're pulling. Your Auntie used to do the same things your wife did. I'd hang out with cats all night and show up whenever. Food would be warming on the stove because even though I was out real late, she always knew about the time I would get home. I mean it would be various times of the night, too. I thought she was psychic or something. That's just how in sync she was with her man. She'd still get up the next morning and cook me breakfast. My uniform was already ironed, boots were where I could find them, and my lunch was already prepared. But just like you and many of us, I eventually wore out my undeserving love. A woman is not going to continue to be a doormat for her man. Nobody's going to continue to be a doormat for anyone that doesn't show any sign that they are going to change their behavior. I found that out when those things that used to happen stopped happening."

"So, how do you fix it, Uncle Cal?"

"You end up doing both," Cal said shaking his head.

"What do you mean?" JOBE Jr. asked, confused.

"You end up sacrificing and giving up undeserving love. When you're messing up, sometimes you're going to have to suck it up. That video game you used to play all day will be replaced with washing dishes when it's not your night—or going shopping in the mall for hours at a time looking at 100 pairs of shoes. Oh, you got to pay. Eventually, if she is a good woman, she'll lengthen your rope little by little and you just take it, slowly. It's all good though because you know what you have in your woman."

Calvin leaned over the table again. "8 ball, side pocket."

"Don't scratch," JOBE Jr. said, as the ball rolled into the pocket.

"Game, youngster," he said, smiling. "Have you learned anything, JJ?"

"Yes, sir, I have," JOBE Jr. said humbly.

"Well go ahead and rack'em up one more time before everyone else arrives."

"All right, but I'm going to beat you this time," JOBE Jr. said, reaching down to place the balls back on the table.

Meanwhile, the women are in the kitchen preparing snacks for the trip.

"Shannon, how has my brother been since he got out?" Yasmine asked, looking in the cupboard for snacks for Egypt.

"Two days ago, he was tripping, but he made up for it."

"I bet he did," Deborah said, placing the sodas into the cooler.

"Where is he anyway?" Francis asked, bouncing Egypt on her lap.

"He forgot to pick up Papa JOBE's present, and he's trying to turn in a few applications before we leave," Shannon said.

"How is he though?" Aunt Francis asked.

Shannon was hesitant, but she eventually responded. Taking a deep breath, she said, "You guys know that he's been looking for work since he got out, but it's been hard for him. His record follows him everywhere. For the past three weeks, he's been on an emotional roller coaster."

"God bless him," Aunt Francis said, shaking her head. "There's nothing more difficult for a man than feeling helpless when he's trying."

"Sometimes he would be so happy, as if everything was great, and then there were times when he was angry at the world. His depressive states were the scariest and lasted the longest, Shannon said with a worried tone."

"You know you can call me or any of us when you're afraid," Yasmine said, trying to reassure Shannon.

"No, that would only add to his humiliation. I know that he would never hit me. He walks out and sits on the stairs whenever it gets too much for him."

"Okay," Deborah said. "But remember, we're here. I've been in a couple of relationships, and I believed that very same thing until he went upside my head. I'm just saying, we all love Jerrod, but he's been through a lot."

"I've spent numerous nights consoling him because he would cry uncontrollably. I knew that after the depression came the anger; whenever it gets too bad, I go to my mother's. Since we've been going to Bible study on Wednesday nights, he's been doing much better. Pastor Reed has him in the drama ministry and on the choir."

Listening to Shannon talk about how tough of a time her favorite nephew is having really begins to upset Francis.

"I didn't know he was having this hard of a time," Aunt Francis said, putting Egypt on the floor and standing up. "Let's all join hands and pray for Jerrod.

"Father, we come together as a family, as one voice speaking on behalf of your son, Jerrod. Lord, you promised that you would never put more on us than we could bear. Lord, we all have to reap what we have sown, Lord, and your son Jerrod has done just that. Let us stand in for him, Father, and ask you to pour blessings of confidence, positive thinking, and obedience upon him. Bless your son with the unimaginable. Touch his spirit, Father, because it has grown weary. Touch his mind, Lord, so that he may make wise decisions because the devil is cunning, Father. Touch the company that he keeps until he can see the devil for who he really is. Bless him, Father, so that he may be a blessing to the company he keeps. These things we ask in your name, Father. Amen."

Everyone echoes the Amen.

"I see that nice arrangement of flowers in the living room," Deborah said, trying to get Yasmine to talk about the flowers as she continued making sandwiches.

"Oh, I got those yesterday," Yasmine said, smiling and taking a seat to brush Egypt's hair.

"What did he do?"

"Oh, it wasn't him. It was me."

"What did you do, girl?" Shannon said, going through her purse looking for her file.

"Girl, I came home...with an attitude. Ruined his playoff party and had him send his friends home, and then he slept on the couch."

"So why did he send you flowers?" Deborah asked.

"Because he knew I was wrong," Yasmine said.

"Now that's a man that knows what he's doing," Aunt Francis said, smiling and nodding her head. "You women don't know what to do with a real man."

"Oh I know what to do with him. I gave him an apology that would satisfy the worst mistake."

"That's the answer for all of you young women." She shook her head. "Believe me when I tell you that one day it's going to take a little more than that."

"What do you mean, Aunt Francis?" Yasmine asked, placing the hair pomade, comb, brush, and unused hair accessories into a clear container.

"I'm talking about realizing what you're doing before it gets that far. Unnecessary arguing," Francis said, looking right at Yasmine.

"You know what, Aunt Francis?" Yasmine said, figuring she had a revelation.

"What?" Francis said, knowing that Yasmine was about to say something crazy.

"I think I intentionally do it."

"You intentionally do it?" Francis said, with a confused look on her face.

"Yes ma'am, I really believe that deep in my subconscious, I know what kind of sex we're going to have if I do something crazy, so it drives me subconciously, knowing what I want. One of those subconcious days I started to call Shannon at the hotel because I made 'mister' really mad," Yasmine said, smiling and laughing.

"Girl, I know what you're talking about," Deborah said, smiling herself. "I think we all do that. I started to go by pharmacy to see if Yasmine could fill me a prescription."

"A prescription for what?" Yasmine said.

"Girl, an hour or two more never hurts."

"You are too much," Shannon said, joining in the laughter. "JJ has a problem?"

"Lord no, but like I said, an hour or two longer never hurts when you've been as bad as I've been," she said, getting up from the table and walking over to the kitchen sink. "I think I need a glass of water," she said, shaking her head.

The *doorbell rings.*

"Let me see who's at the door," Yasmine said, heading to the living room. "Who is it?" Yasmine looked through the peephole.

"It's Hilton."

"Hey, Uncle Hilton," Yasmine said, as she opened the door. "Did you decide to go with us to Daddy's party?"

"No, I still can't make it. I just wanted to bring my gift over before you guys got on the road. Is Quinton here?"

"No, he went out to get the van. Uncle Hilton, why aren't you going?"

"I have my reasons," Hilton said, handing Yasmine JOBE's gift. "Who else has made it here?"

"JOBE Jr. and Uncle Calvin are upstairs in the bonus room playing pool."

Jerrod walks in the door.

"Hey Uncle Hilton, you just getting here, too?"

"Yeah, I just wanted to drop off JOBE's gift and to see everyone off."

"I'm going back into the kitchen. Let me know when Quinton gets back, Jerrod," Yasmine said, walking toward the kitchen.

"Hold on, big sis. Here's Daddy's gift. Where do you want me to put it?"

"Just hold on to it. We'll put it with the others when we load the van."

"All right, big sis," Jerrod said, turning back to Hilton.

"Uncle Hilton, I need to talk with you for a minute."

"Yeah, what's up, Jerrod?"

"Let's play a game of chess while we talk."

Quinton always has a chessboard set up on a small chess table in the corner of the living room.

"What's going on?" Hilton said, turning the board so that Jerrod had the white pieces.

"Shannon getting on my nerves. She always has a laundry list of things for me to do. There is no way I can get the things she wants done and find a job at the same time."

"You can work with me," Uncle Hilton said, raising both eyebrows.

"No disrespect, Uncle, but I'm not trying to be cutting no grass in that hot sun," Jerrod said, frowning.

Hilton moved his queen into position.

"It's not just cutting grass. It's called landscaping."

"Well, I'm not trying to be "landscaping" in that sun either."

"Well…the Bible says that a man that doesn't work doesn't eat."

With the pressure of the game and what seemed like someone else preaching to him, Jerrod was becoming agitated.

"Jerrod, I'm not saying make a career of it; I'm just saying stay long enough to get yourself together."

Now focusing directly on the game board, Jerrod placed his left hand on his forehead, barely covering his eyes, and moved a piece.

Uncle Hilton took about one minute to examine the board and then he moved again. "Checkmate."

Jerrod looked the board over, and then closed his eyes, sighing in disgust. He realized that he could have blocked his uncle's move.

Uncle Hilton smiled again. "I understand—"

"No, you don't understand," Jerrod said, suddenly swiping the pieces from the board while standing up and looking at Hilton.

"I'm so sick of everyone telling me that they understand. Please tell me, Uncle Hilton, what you understand. Tell me how everyone can understand that I feel like I let my family down. Tell me how everyone can understand not being able to get a job

because of a record that follows you everywhere. Hell, I'm having problems getting a job at a pizza place. Uncle, I read an issue of *Jet* that said a white man in New York with priors has a better chance of getting hired than a black man without priors. So you tell me where the hell that leaves me?" Tears began to run down Jerrod's face.

The ladies came into the living room from the kitchen and Calvin and JOBE Jr. came in from the bonus room.

"What's going on?" Yasmine said, looking at Jerrod and Hilton.

"What bothers me the most, Uncle . . . " Jerrod paused and turned his head. " . . . is the fact that I know this isn't what my life should be like. I didn't have to sell drugs, and I damn sure didn't want to get caught, but I did. I had so many opportunities to stop but I didn't. Nobody, I mean *nobody*, can understand my pain." Jerrod wiped the tears from his face.

Uncle Hilton now became serious himself. "Sit down," he said forcefully.

"Number one, you didn't let your family down. Everyone here has made mistakes. Hell, I've made plenty of them. You're right, Jerrod. No one can understand your pain, but it's time to move on, son. You are a man, and I know it's a hard job being a man. It's the hardest job on earth. I'm glad that you finally got it off of your chest though. Now let's move on. No, you're not going to like every job you take, but do it until you can do better. You have a son and a woman that loves you. They are your first priority. So pick yourself up, brush yourself off, and keep your head up. You can handle it. You're smart, young, gifted, and have a family that loves and cares about you. Do something with it."

A few seconds of silence passed.

"I understand what you're saying, Uncle, but it gets so hard at times." Jerrod sat back down. Shannon sat down beside Jerrod and began caressing his head.

"I bet it does, Jerrod, but I want to see you accomplish the things that I know you have the ability to accomplish. Show everyone that you're not going to let this thing beat you. Come on, man. I have faith in you. We have faith in you. What you need is faith in the man above and faith in yourself."

"I feel you, Uncle Hilton, and I apologize for knocking the pieces on the ground and raising my voice."

"I got you," Uncle Hilton said, picking up the pieces. "Things like that happen. You're a man. I thought I was going to have to knock you out though."

They began to smile. Aunt Francis came over to Jerrod and placed his head on her chest.

"Everything's going to be okay, son."

Just then, Jerrod's phone began to ring.

There was silence in the room.

"Hello?" Jerrod said, slowly walking away to hear what the person on the phone was saying. "Yes. Yes, I can do that."

Everyone began to get smiles of hope.

"Wednesday at eight thirty will be great," Jerrod said, turning around and smiling at Shannon.

She immediately walked over to his side.

"Thank you, sir, and I'll be there. You have a wonderful weekend also." Jerrod hung up.

"I have a job, baby," he said, grabbing her and lifting her up, swinging her around.

At that moment, Quinton returns.

"What's going on in here?" Quinton said, looking around. "Are we ready to go?"

"Yeah, we're ready," Yasmine said, breaking the silence.

"Well, let's go!"

Hilton helps everyone load the vehicle and sees them off.

It's the next day, and JOBE and Yolanda are getting ready for their day. JOBE is coming in the house from getting the morning paper. Yolanda is already dressed in a business suit coming into the living room from the kitchen.

"Good morning, sweetheart," Yolanda said, handing JOBE a cup of coffee and a bagel before he sat down in his favorite chair.

"Good morning to you, too, baby, and thanks, love." JOBE took a sip of coffee.

"You're welcome, baby."

"You've been up for a while now," JOBE said, opening the paper.

"Yes, I need to go to the bank this morning."

"Why?" JOBE said, turning on the TV.

"I received a call around 4:30 yesterday from Jason, our loan officer, saying that there was an issue with the application."

"I thought that it had already cleared?" JOBE said, flipping through the channels.

"I thought so, too," Yolanda said, handing JOBE a coaster.

A newscaster from the television begins to speak.

"And in local news, all assets associated with JOBE, Inc. have been frozen. We have an unconfirmed report this morning that JOBE, Inc. financial records have been confiscated due to unconfirmed reports of fraud and embezzlement. Let's go to Harold on the scene at the office of JOBE, Inc."

JOBE immediately puts down his cup and gets to his feet.

"Harold, can you shed a little more light on the story?"

"Yes. There is alleged proof that JOBE Mitchell steered a number of unconfirmed clients into purchasing several properties and stocks. Jason, we also have unconfirmed reports, but through reliable sources, that JOBE Mitchell collected funds from these said kick backs from these alleged purchases of stocks and real-estate deals."

"Oh my God," JOBE said, staring at the television. "What is going on?"

"I don't know, but I think you need to call the office to find out," Yolanda said, placing her purse on the coffee table and taking a seat on the sofa.

JOBE gets up and walks over to the phone, still keeping his eyes on the television.

"Let me call Zeke to find out what's going on. He should've gotten to the office early this morning and at least given me a call."

After about four rings, JOBE hangs up.

"I didn't get an answer," JOBE said, looking at Yolanda, bewildered. "Zeke is never late."

"Call his cell phone," Yolanda said.

"It went straight to his voice mail," JOBE said a moment later, becoming concerned.

"Let me call his home. Maybe he's there."

A young lady answered the phone. "Hello, this is the Burroughs residence."

"Christian, is your father there?" JOBE asked, trying to stay calm.

"Yes, sir," she answered. "Who may I ask is calling?"

"Who's that on the phone?" someone shouted from a distance.

"Someone looking for Daddy," Christian said, before her mother took the phone from her.

"Who is this?" Vivica said.

"Vivica, it's JOBE."

"I'm sorry, JOBE, but we were advised that we were not supposed to be in contact with you."

"You were advised?" JOBE repeated. "What's going on, Vivica? Is Zeke there?"

"I'm sorry, JOBE, but I have to hang up now."

Dial tone!

"She just hung up on me," JOBE said in disbelief.

"Well what did she say, JOBE?"

"Much of nothing."

"Was Zeke there?"

"I couldn't tell you," JOBE said, picking up his cellular phone to call Blair or James.

Just as he locates Blair's number in his phone contacts, there is a knock on the door.

"What could it be now?" JOBE said, frustrated.

"Sir, my name is Detective Weeks, and this is officer McIntyre. We have a search warrant to search your premises." The detective held up the search warrant.

"For what?" JOBE said, with an angry look on his face.

"Sir, if you just step aside, myself and my crew will be out of your home in no time."

"What's going on Hilton, Yolanda asked?"

"I don't know but I'm about to find out, JOBE said turning to heading upstairs to get dressed."

JOBE brother Hilton walks in

"Honey guess who decided to show his face today, Yolanda said before Hilton made his way up the stairs? Hilton, we don't want you here and we don't need you here right now."

"Yolanda, I can see that you're upset with everything that's going on but I have something that I have to tell the both of you."

"Just what do you have to tell us Hilton? We barely see or hear from you any other time but on our worst day here you are."

"I'll accept that Yolanda because I'm bigger than that and I know that you're hurting."

"What is it Hilton, JOBE asked coming back down the stairs?"

"I don't know how to say this, Hilton said with his head down trying to hold back the tears."

"What's wrong Hilton, JOBE said walking over to his brother's side."

"The kids were in a terrible accident and everyone…….."

"What about the kids, JOBE said grabbing Hilton in his collar and pushing him against the wall so he could see Hilton's face?"

"Quinton………. And everyone was ….

"Was what Hilton, Yolanda said impatiently?"

"They're all gone JOBE, Hilton said lifting his eyes."

"No God no, Hilton said falling face first into Hilton's chest and pounding on the wall."

"Oh God, Yolanda said falling to her knees."

 "What's going on here, Detective weeks inquired walking over after witnessing Yolanda falling to her knees?"

"Sir we just found out that our entire family died in a car accident."

"I'm sorry to hear that, Detective Weeks responded. We're going to get out of here so that you may grieve in private. Again, I'm sorry sir. Is there anything that I can do sir?"

"Pray for us, Hilton responded."

Hilton made his way over to Yolanda

"Why is this happening to us, Yolanda wept?"

"Why God, Why? I know you have a plan Lord but I'm lost here Father, JOBE said shaking his head. My entire family's gone."

"I'm going to leave you two alone. I'm going to get some more details and I'll be right back, Hilton said wanting to give them some time.

JOBE, Yolanda continues their embrace as tears run from both of their eyes.

It's a week later. JOBE, Yolanda and Hilton are returning from the funeral.

"JOBE I'm gong to go ahead and get out of here. I need to get on the road before it gets too late," Hilton said still feeling some tension between him and Yolanda.

"You sure you don't want to get some sleep before heading out, JOBE asked taking off his tie?"

"Yeah Hilton I know that you want to beat the traffic," Yolanda said sarcastically.

"I'll be fine. Call me baby brother if you need me?"

"I will Hilton."

As Hilton opened the door, JOBE's intern Andre' was standing there about to knock on the door.

"JOBE There's someone at the door," Hilton said opening the door.

"Who is it?"

"It's me Mr. Mitchell," Andre said walking in

Realizing that there may be more trouble, Hilton decides that he's a little hungry. JOBE, I'm going to grab a bite before heading out. I'll be in the kitchen to give you all some privacy.

"Mr. Mitchell, you wont believe what's been going on down at the office," Andre said walking over to JOBE.

"What's going on son," JOBE said leading Andre over to the couch?

"Mr. Mitchell, you won't believe what's going on down at the office," the young man said, shaking his head.

"What's going on, son?" JOBE asked, sitting the young man down and taking a seat right beside him.

Yolanda sat on the sofa adjacent to them but near the edge to hear what was going on.

"It's okay, David," JOBE said, reassuring him that he could say anything in front of Yolanda.

"Well, I'm pretty sure you've heard the accusations of misuse of the company's money, but there is more," David said hesitantly.

"What is it, son?" JOBE asked.

"Well um, there are rumors that one of the clients that you received money from for real-estate purchases was Mrs. Foster."

"Who?" Yolanda said, getting to her feet.

"Baby, it's nothing," JOBE said, looking up at Yolanda.

"What about Mrs. Foster?" Yolanda said, looking directly at David.

"They found email conversations, and they pulled phone records of calls made from your office to her cell phone and home phone. Most of them were dated around the time many of the purchases were made. They even pulled her past year's itinerary and matched them with yours. They found out that quite a few of them matched from departure date to return date."

"So this is what's been going on under my nose?" Yolanda said, angry.

"David, thanks, son. You can leave now," JOBE said, exhaling heavily and standing to his feet.

"Tell me this isn't true, JOBE," Yolanda said, tears forming. "Is this what you do when you're going on your so-called business trips? Is she what you do when I'm out of town handling our businesses?" Yolanda leaned toward him. "Is this your so-called support?" Tears streamed down her face as she sat back down on the couch.

"Why Lord, why?" JOBE exclaimed. "Yolanda, none of this—"

"Don't say anything, JOBE, and get out," Yolanda shouted.

"What's going on, Hilton asked walking in from the kitchen?"

"Ask your adulterous brother."

JOBE makes his way over to Yolanda and attempts to console her.

"Don't touch me, JOBE," Yolanda cried out. "Your sins have caused all of this. Get out," she screamed, placing her head back on the sofa.

"Baby, it's not what you think," JOBE said, trying to explain.

"I said get out," Yolanda said, gnashing her teeth.

JOBE went upstairs to change clothes and to pack an overnight bag in hopes that he would be back home by the next day.

"I am truly sorry about all of this. You know that none of the things that they are accusing JOBE of is true," Hilton said.

"And how would you know Hilton?" You're never around to know anything, Yolanda said angrily,

"Yolanda, you and I both know why."

"That is no reason to stay away. Your brother needs you."

"Do you know how I feel when I look at him knowing what happened between us?"

"That was decades ago Hilton and keep your voice down."

"It doesn't matter how long ago it's been. It still hurts to know that I betrayed my brother with his wife. I still look at you and want you."

"I still want ....

JOBE can be heard walking back down the stairs.

"What's going on here, JOBE said sensing the tension?"

No one spoke for about 3 seconds. Yolanda then grabs her purse and ran out of the house.

"Follow her Hilton and make sure that she's okay."

"Okay JOBE. I'll be back to check on you."

"That's okay Hilton. I need some time to be alone. Just make sure Yolanda is okay.

JOBE and Hilton hugged each other and Hilton went after Yolanda.

Picking up one of the family portraits JOBE fell to one knee beside the sofa and began to pray. Father I know you have a reason for the things that has happened and I know that you are going to reveal it to me in due time. I just ask, Father, that you look upon my wife tonight, Lord. Wrap your loving arms around her. Comfort her for me, Lord. Lord, you know that nothing that happened that was due to any fault of my own, so I can still trust in your word without any guilt in my heart. I can come boldly to you because I have done what you have asked me to do. You told me that you would never leave me or forsake me, and I still believe you, Lord. Speak to the storm that is tearing this family apart. God, sing to my wife tonight because I can't be there, Lord. Ease her soul for me, Father. I know this is all going to work out because you are God."

Immediately, a song that JOBE used to sing all the time began to play over and over in his head. He began to hum the tune to "You are God." He hummed it until he fell asleep clutching one of the sofa pillows. As JOBE slept, Jesus came in to see how his son was doing.

"Oh my son," Jesus said, kissing JOBE on the forehead. "It's not as long as it has been, son. You make me so proud."

"Yes, he is doing better than I thought he would," Satan said, walking up behind Jesus.

"Where have you been?" Jesus said, after Satan made his presence known.

"Oh, I've been here and there," Satan said casually. "I've been in and out of the Earth, and I have tried your son to no avail."

"Yes you have, and yes he still stands."

"It's only because you have not allowed me to touch him. Have you not protected him from true sickness? Allow me to touch him, and surely he will curse you to your face," Satan said.

Jesus turned to Satan. After pausing for a moment, Jesus responded. "I will remove my hand from JOBE, and everything he has is now in your power, even his flesh."

Satan smiled and left the presence of Jesus.

The next morning, JOBE travels to his office to find out more about his financial affairs. He eventually makes it to the boardroom where Blair, James, and Zeke are having a conversation.

"Hello Blair, James, Zeke," JOBE said, walking into the boardroom.

"Good morning, JOBE," Blair said, taking a seat where JOBE usually sat.

"What's going on, Blair? What is this all about?" JOBE asked, placing his briefcase on the table.

"It's about you, JOBE. It's about you paying for your sins, my man."

"WHAT SINS…I mean, what sins are you talking about?" JOBE said, catching himself and trying to maintain his cool.

"Did you really think you could get away with all of this?" Blair said, reaching down to pull paperwork from his briefcase.

"Blair, you and I both know that I haven't done any of the things they are accusing me of."

"Not from where I'm sitting," Blair said, preparing to read from one of the documents that he'd pulled from his briefcase. "We have proof that you were taking kickbacks from deals, having an affair with Mrs. Foster, and I personally have the emails that you yourself sent and received."

"Why am I not surprised that you have them personally? I'm slowly figuring out what this is all about," JOBE said, remaining standing.

"What is it all about, JOBE?" Blair asked, collecting the papers and tapping them against the table to even them out.

"Jealousy! You've always been jealous of me, and it's finally coming out," JOBE said, looking directly at Blair.

"No! This is about you and your conduct, JOBE," Blair said, standing up and becoming angry."

"Why are you the only one that's talking, Blair?" JOBE said, looking at James and Zeke. "Are you the only one that feels this way? Do you feel the same way, James?" JOBE asked, looking at him.

"It's all there, JOBE," James said, supporting Blair.

"You don't sound too sure, James," JOBE said.

"Can you honestly tell me why I would do something like this to my family?"

Bair quickly interjected. You don't have a family anymore, which further proves that your sins are catching up with you. The Bible says that you reap what you sow"

"Now you're going to quote the Bible. Well here is another quote. The Bible also says that the sun shines on the evil as well as the good. He sends the rain on the just as well as the unjust."

"Well, there's a monsoon going on in your life right now. You're losing your business and you've lost your family," Blair said sarcastically. "Just make me the designee of your portion of the book, and we'll take it from there."

"Zeke," JOBE said, pausing for a moment to look Zeke in the face. "I can see it in your face, Zeke," JOBE said. "You know that this is wrong."

"I want to believe you, JOBE, but how can I when there is so much evidence against you? Trust me, brother, when I say that I've prayed over this since the beginning. My heart goes out to you JOBE, and Yolanda, and I'm deeply sorry for your loss. My suggestion to you is to repent now and ask God for his forgiveness," Zeke said, really believing in his heart that all the tragedy that had occurred in JOBE's life was a direct reflection of his sins.

Just as Zeke is finishing his sentence, one of the secretaries walks into the room.

"Excuse me, Mr. Knight, but you have a ten o'clock in your office," Nancy said, walking a few feet into the boardroom.

"How are you, Nancy?" JOBE said, trying to remove the negativity that had filled the room."

"Should I let him know that you're on the way, Mr. Knight?" Nancy said, disregarding JOBE's greeting.

"Yes Nancy," Blair said, smiling and putting the documents back into his briefcase."

As Nancy left the room, Blair continued. "That pretty much sums up how everyone feels about you, JOBE," Blair said, closing his briefcase and removing it from the table. "Let's get out of here, fellas. We have work to do."

"Hold on, Blair," JOBE said, facing the wall and slowly turning around. "You know what's ironic about this whole thing?"

"No, but hurry up, I have a company to run."

"The scripture that I spoke on earlier also says, 'But I say unto you, love your enemies, bless those who curse you, do good to those who hate you, and pray for those who spitefully use and persecute you.' With that I say you gentlemen have a blessed day."

"It's amazing to me that you still quote the Bible after committing the sins that you have committed," Blair said, shaking his head. "You can let yourself out."

JOBE sat there for a moment, slumped over with his elbows on his thighs and his face in his hands. He then inhaled and exhaled deeply before deciding to go through the mail that he had taken from home. One of the envelopes was addressed from Carolina's Medical Center. It included the results of his Periodic Health Assessment. The letter said that JOBE should come in immediately for a second screening. JOBE quickly turned the envelope over and saw that the date of the letter was almost two weeks old. JOBE promptly pulled out his cellular phone and dialed the number on the letter header.

"Hello, you've reached the urology department at Carolina's Medical Center. How may I help you?"

"Yes, my name is JOBE Mitchell. I had a PHA done four weeks ago, and I'm just reading that I was supposed to come back in for a second screening."

"What is your name again, sir?" the woman asked.

"JOBE—JOBE Mitchell," JOBE said, suddenly worried.

"Yes, sir. Dr. Ferdinand wants you to come in immediately. Can you come in right now?"

"Can you tell me what's going on?" JOBE asked.

"No, sir, I can't. Can you come in now, Mr. Mitchell?"

"Yes I can," JOBE said. "I should be there within an hour."

"Okay, sir. We'll see you then."

As JOBE was leaving, the young intern appeared again.

"Mr. Mitchell," he said, getting in front of JOBE.

"Son, whatever it is that you want to tell me, you're going to have to tell me later."

"This is very important, sir," the intern stressed. "I think I can help you find out how this came about. I never believed that any of the lies were true. I think I can get some of my friends down in IT to look into the email, if that's okay with you?"

With his mind somewhere else, JOBE replied, "Son, do whatever you have to do, but I have to leave."

"Okay, Mr. Mitchell. I'll let you know what we find out."

In JOBE's haste to get out of the room, he left his PHA on the boardroom table. The intern picked it up, read it, and inserted it inside of his jacket pocket.

JOBE's house is on the way to the hospital. He makes several attempts to call before his arrival, but Yolanda doesn't answer her cell phone or the house phone. He decides to stop by to make sure she isn't there. JOBE knocks on the door. Looking through the peep hole, Yolanda sees that it's JOBE.

"What do you want?" Yolanda said through the door.

"I need you to—"

"You don't need me to do anything, JOBE, but file the paperwork."

"Can you be quiet for a minute?" JOBE yelled. "let me in. I need to talk with you?"

Yolanda waited for about a minute without answering before opening the door.

"You need to say what you have to say and leave, JOBE," Yolanda said, as JOBE walked in.

"Okay Yolanda, I know that you are hurting, but I'm telling you that I didn't do any of this," JOBE said, turning around at the sofa to look at her. "I need to be with you right now, woman. We need to be with each other right now."

"Maybe you should have thought about that before you and Mrs. Foster were taking trips together," Yolanda said, looking JOBE directly in the face as she passed by him.

"This is the last time that I'm going to tell you this! I didn't have an affair, and I haven't been receiving money under the table."

"Well you're—"

"I said listen."

Yolanda stopped and looked at JOBE.

"Our family has passed in a terrible accident, my business is under investigation, they've frozen all of my assets, and I just spoke with the hospital and they said that I must come in right now. I need you by my side, Yolanda."

"Well, they've put a lien against each one of the Bed and Breakfast houses, and I end up looking like a fool to my family and everyone that I know. For God's sake, JOBE,

you had me on national television. I guess your sins have ruined us all. If I were you, I would curse God and—"

"And what, Yolanda?" JOBE said, shaking his head. "Like I said, I didn't do any of the things that they are accusing me of, and I'm on my way to the hospital. I want you there by my side. I'm not going to be able to make it without you. I still love you, and I still trust God to make this right. I need you, Yolanda."

"I want to believe you so bad, baby. Tell me that you've taken care of my heart. Tell me that you would never deceive me like this, JOBE. Tell me," Yolanda said, now in tears.

"Falling on his knees in front of Yolanda and placing his hands on her waist, he said, "Baby, I promise you with everything in me that I love and have only loved you! You are my reason for waking up; you are my reason for breathing, and you are my reason for living."

Still on his knees, he throws his arms around her waist and places his head in her abdomen, crying. They wept together for close to an hour before heading to the hospital. The tears are long overdue over the loss of their children and their families. After making it to the hospital, they find out that JOBE has developed Cancer, and it has already spread throughout his body. After weeks of staying in the hospital, JOBE decides that he doesn't want to stay at the hospital, so he turns one of his spare rooms at home into a hospice-like room. JOBE still remains faithful, prayerful, and praiseful throughout weeks of treatment and sickness. Yolanda spends all of her time caring for JOBE.

"Yolanda," JOBE called out from his room.

"What is it, JOBE?" Yolanda answered, heading his way.

As she entered the room, JOBE turned the television down and began to speak. "Yolanda, can you bring me something to eat and turn the radio on for me?"

"JOBE, can you turn the TV off before I turn on this radio?"

"Okay baby," JOBE said, smiling. "You still love me?" JOBE asked, continuing to smile.

"You and I both know that you are in no condition for anything like that," Yolanda said, turning the radio on and walking out of the room.

"Well, you know the Lord works in mysterious ways," JOBE said. He coughed roughly.

JOBE then reached over to the nightstand and grabbed a glass of water to help clear his throat.

Radio Personality:

"That was Shirley Caesar and Dottie Peoples singing, **I'm Blessed.** *For continuous Gospel music that keeps your spirits lifted all day, keep it locked on 103.9 FM* **The Light.** *We're going to keep it going with one of my personal favorites by Pastor Smokie Norful,* **Still Say Thank You,** *the live version. Ain't that the truth. No matter what's going on in our lives, we still have to say thank you."*

JOBE began to hum the tune, closing his eyes and shaking his head as he said, "Thank You, Jesus," over and over.

All of a sudden, a familiar voice abruptly entered the room, singing the song. He made his way over to his brother's side, and they both began to sing the song together. Tears began to flow from both of their eyes as they poured their hearts and souls into the song. Yolanda heard them, and she came into the room. They all began to sing the song, giving God the glory for all they had been through.

After the song was finished, Hilton wiped the tears from his face. "How are you doing, brother?" Hilton said, smiling. "It's been a long time since we've sung together."

"Too long, my brother," JOBE said, grabbing his brother's hand and squeezing it.

"I have something to tell you," Hilton said, smiling.

"Oh no," JOBE said, smiling back. "Do you remember the last time you had something to tell me?"

"It's good to see that you still have your spirits up," Hilton said, shaking his head in disbelief.

"The Lord's been too good to me for me not to, brother. I have my beautiful wife and my brother by my side. What more can I ask for?"

"I have something," Hilton said. "Andre, come inside."

JOBE lifted his head to see who it was. It was his intern.

"How are you, Mr. Mitchell?" Andre said, walking over to JOBE's bedside.

"I'm doing well," JOBE said, making a fist and covering his mouth as he coughed. "What brings you here, son?"

"I don't know if you remember, but I told you that I would get my friends down in IT to check out your computer. What they found out was that your computer had been broken into."

JOBE closed his eyes and said, "Thank you, Lord."

"They also found out that Mrs. Foster's email had been broken into also. All of your credit card information and banking information had been stolen. They made flight arrangements for you and paid them themselves in order to keep you from checking into things. Money was deposited in accounts bearing your name to make it look like you were receiving additional monies."

"I knew you would make a way, Jesus," JOBE said, turning and placing his face in the pillow.

"I'm sorry that I didn't believe you from the beginning," Yolanda said sorrowfully, with tears streaming from her eyes.

"It's okay, baby," JOBE said, coughing some more. "Satan is good at dividing the family."

Just then, the doorbell rang.

"I'll get it," Hilton said, collecting himself and heading out of the room.

In walked Blair, James, and Zeke.

"JOBE..I don't even know where to begin," Blair said humbly. "Envy overtook me, and I couldn't control it. James and Zeke had nothing to do with any of it. I'm on my way to turn myself in. I want you to know that there are a couple of reasons why I am here, and one of them is not because I was caught but because I still envy you. How can any man go through what you've been through and still be as devoted to God as you are? Another is I know that you are dying, and I wanted to tell you in person the things that I did. I couldn't live with myself if I didn't get the opportunity to see you face-to-face to ask for your forgiveness."

"Number one, Blair, I'm not dying," JOBE said, coughing roughly. "Number two. If you remember, I told you on the day that I met you in the boardroom that I forgave you. I pray for you, Blair. I pray for your soul. I loved you and still love you like a brother. Don't get me wrong, there is a part of me that wants to tear you apart. I would be lying if I told you that this wasn't the trial of my life, but when I think about all the Lord has done for me, all of that hurt and anger goes away. I love you, Blair."

"I love you, too, JOBE," Blair said, dropping his head and leaving.

After Blair left, JOBE looked to everyone and asked it they could sing, "Still say thank you," once more.

Hilton, Yolanda, James, and Zeke sing the song like it is the last song they'll ever sing. Near the end of the song, Yolanda smiles, then looks to JOBE and notices that his eyes are closed. He's not singing anymore. She smiles, gently leans over, and kisses his face.

"Thank you, Father," Yolanda said, standing up again and asking everyone to join hands in a moment of silence.

JOBE lies in bed asleep. There is a sense of calm about him.

"Look at my son," Jesus said, watching over JOBE. "I am so proud of him. I love him so much and in him I am so very pleased."

"Yes, he does look very content," Satan said, walking up behind Jesus.

"Where have you been?" Jesus said, after Satan made his presence known.

"Oh, I've been here and there," Satan said casually. "I've been in and out of the Earth, and I have found no one worthy of a true test."

"Have you considered my faithful servant, JOBE?" Jesus asked, with much confidence. "There is none like him on Earth, a blameless and upright man, who fears God and turns away from evil."

"It's only because you have blessed him and everything that he touches—"

"No, Satan! That is not the reason that JOBE doesn't turn to evil."

"Then why?" Satan said, awaiting Jesus' answer.

"It's because JOBE expects Life and life more abundantly."

"That's what all who follow God expect," Satan said, trying to discredit Jesus' reason.

"You're right, Satan, but JOBE isn't tying to obtain it on Earth. JOBE understood that none of the things he obtained on Earth meant anything if Jesus wasn't a part of it. JOBE could have nothing, and he would still be happy. You took his fine cars and land. You took his standing in the community. You took his health and his life, and yet he still smiled. He left you with nothing else to take away from him, and he still praised God the Father."

Jesus turned to Satan. "I will give JOBE three times what he had and bless all the days of his life. I will bless his nations not only with money but also with wisdom and happiness forever. Leave me, Satan, for I want to be with my son."

Satan left the presence of Jesus.

JOBE lies there in bed asleep, with calm about him.
JOBE lies in bed asleep. There is a sense of calm about him.

"Wake up, JOBE," Yolanda said, shaking him.

"Give me five more minutes," JOBE said, turning over.

"The kids will be here today, JOBE. We need to get up and get things ready," Yolanda said, sitting up in bed.

JOBE turned over to Yolanda. "You know, I had the strangest dream last night."

"What was it about?"

"I can't remember," JOBE said, looking confused and shaking his head, "but I do feel so blessed. Thank you, Father!"

DAVID

(Also A play)

*P*reviously from Moments II

Theresa told Steven about her sexual abuse and her struggle to shake her promiscuous thoughts. I've made some changes due to reader questions and suggestions. So I decided to start the 3rd chapter of God is God from this scene. In order to get what happened previous to this particular scene you will need to purchase Moments II. Enjoy.

Keith A. Anderson

For months, David preached as if he was a man on a mission. Most of the time, he would cry during the sermon. Eight months after Lt. Stokes' death, David's request

to finish up his command early was granted and he took over a small detachment in another unit. Now he was able to date Brenda openly. Brenda was to have the baby any day. His anxiety over what he had done began to fade over time.

David paid for a cab to pick up Brenda and bring her to an upscale Italian restaurant.

"Sorry I'm late," David said, as he approached the table from behind her, adjusting the buttons on his jacket to take a seat. "How are you feeling today?"

"I've had some Braxton Hicks contractions all day and my feet are hurting me something awful," Brenda said, kicking off her shoes under the table.

"I know, baby, and I'm sorry for bringing you out, but I wanted to treat you tonight."

"You could have treated me at your house just the same," Brenda said, rubbing her belly.

Just then a waiter approached.

"May I take your order?" the waiter said, pulling out a pen and paper from his apron. David gestured, suggesting that he start with Brenda's order.

"I'm really not hungry," Brenda said, continuing to rub her belly. "I'll just have a glass of water for now."

"And you, sir?" the waiter said, turning to David.

"I'll have water also," David said, looking up and smiling.

"Well I'll just leave the menus here until you decide, and I'll grab those waters for you," the waiter said, tapping his pad and then placing the pad and paper back into his apron.

"David, let's just go, okay?" Brenda said, sounding exhausted.

"Okay baby—this is not how I wanted it to go, but...."

David reached into his jacket pocket and began to pull out a ring-sized case.

Brenda opened her eyes in anticipation of what was inside. David walked over to her side of the table, kneeled down, opened the case, and said, "Brenda would you make me the happiest man on the planet tonight?" Inside the case was a stunning engagement ring. All eyes in the restaurant were on Brenda and David by now. Brenda's eyes began to water and a tear fell from her left eye. Looking back into the eyes of David, for a moment both of them began to flash back to the time when they'd first met.

David had time to prepare for the event. He did love, Brenda but he really felt as though this would make it right in the eyes of God. That it somehow washed him clean

of his terrible decision-making. Brenda on the other hand had to do the calculations on the spot. Though this was what she wanted, and had come up with so many reasons why marrying David was the right thing to do, how they had gotten to this point really bothered her.

"Yes, yes, yes," Brenda said, grabbing David by the face and pulling him closer to give him a kiss.

David took the ring out of its case and placed it on Brenda's finger. He kissed her passionately again before returning to his seat. He then reached across the table with both hands to grasp Brenda's. Looking deep into her eyes, David began to say words that he had wanted to say for a while now.

"Baby, I know that how we got to this point was far from perfect, but we do love one another. I'm asking that tonight we pray together and ask God for forgiveness and understanding. I think we need to do this together, being open with God about how this came about and together ask for his forgiveness."

This made Brenda feel much better about their situation. She became overwhelmed with David's commitment.

"Thank you, baby," Brenda said, with a look of love and admiration. "That's why I love you so much. You seem to calm all my worries without me wearing them on my sleeve by complaining or becoming depressed. Sometimes I believe that it was fate that he did come back when he did, because it still looks as though this is his child. Some of the women in his family have given me second looks but for the most part, they've been supportive."

"I know, Brenda," David said, gently massaging her hands, "and it's going to be that way, but the Lord will see us through. Are you ready to get out of here?"

"Yes, David," Brenda said with a smile.

David quickly rushed over to her side of the table, pulled out her chair, and helped her stand.

The next day, David went to work feeling as though he had set things right with God. He felt utter relief. In the back in his mind though, David still knew that he would reap what he'd sown.

There was a knock at the door.

"Come on in," David said, rolling his chair back over to his desk from his bookshelf.

"Sir, there's someone her to see you," one of his soldiers said, sticking his head just inside the door.

"Who is it?" David asked.

"I think it's someone from the Criminal Investigation Division. Wrinkling his face with confusion, David said, "send him in."

The man was dressed in civilian attire and he looked familiar.

"How are you, sir? My name is Nathan," the gentleman said, shaking David's hand.

David gestured for him to take a seat. "I'm fine, sir, and how are you?"

"I'm doing great. I just want to speak to you; it won't take long at all," Nathan said, taking a seat.

"How may I help you?"

"It's about a soldier in your command," Nathan said, with a little bit more aggression in his voice.

"What happened now?" David replied, leaning back in his reclining chair.

"Someone in a leadership position was having a relationship with one of his soldier's wives."

"What?" David said, becoming upset.

"Yes, sir," Nathan said, frowning. He continued to look directly into David's face. "He had been seen with the soldier's spouse on numerous occasions. It is even suspected that the child she carries is not her husband's but the adulterer's."

David became enraged.

"There is zero tolerance for this type of behavior in this command," he said, raising his voice.

"Who is it?" David asked.

Nathan stood up from his seat and walked to the edge of David's desk. "It's you," he said, looking directly into David's eyes.

David almost lost all bodily functions. His heart fell to the pit of his stomach. His life actually passed before his eyes. Well, his future did. Complete humiliation was imminent. He then recognized Nathan. Nathan was a face from the congregation at church but more importantly, he faintly remembered Nathan's face from the CVS where he'd picked up Brenda on a couple of occasions. So not only had he been found out in his Army life but also in his spiritual life.

"I was sent here to tell you that what you did in the dark will come to light."

David began to cry in fear, shaking his head.

"The Lord gave you everything! Soldiers to influence on the Lord's behalf and a great ministry. Now he's going to take it away from you. All of it! You have a good day,

Captain," Nathan said. He examined an award that had been given to David, read the inscription, then shook his head and walked out of the office.

David quickly stood up and hurried over to the door to lock it. Walking slowly back to his seat, he noticed that he had a wet spot in the front of his Army Combat Uniform. Immediately the phone rang. David couldn't answer it. In the middle of ringing, it stopped. One of the soldiers from the adjourning office answered it.

There was another knock at the door.

"Yes?" David responded.

"Captain David, it's for you."

"Take a message for me, please," David said.

"It's the hospital sir," the soldier retorted.

"Transfer it to me," David said, wondering what it could be now.

"Okay, I have it," David called out.

"Hello this is WOMACK Army Medical Center," the person said. "Your wife is in labor, and your name was listed as an emergency contact."

"Is there something wrong?" David exclaimed.

"Sir, can you please come to the emergency room entrance of the hospital? There will be someone there waiting for you."

"Okay, I'm on my way."

David began to pray as he headed toward the hospital. "Lord, please don't take my wife and child. I'm begging you. Take me instead, Father. I don't deserve your grace and mercy."

David ran in from the parking lot directly to the emergency room receptionist. "Ma'am, can you tell me where I—"

"Excuse me, sir," a nurse said, walking up quickly to get David's attention. "Are you Captain David?"

"Yes, what's going on?"

"Come with me, sir," she insisted, as she headed towards the elevator.

As soon as the doors opened, the nurse hit the appropriate floor number and the doors closed.

"How's my wife doing?" he asked.

"She's doing fine," the nurse said, "but your son isn't doing well. That's where we're headed to now."

Once the elevator doors opened, they immediately turned to the right and headed towards the Neonatal Intensive care unit. As they got closer to the unit, an alarm from one of the infant incubators became louder and louder. Four of the nurses began to react

in a controlled but hurried pace. After two to three minutes of unsuccessfully bringing vitals down to normal, they immediately began to move the infant to an operating room. David noticed the last name taped to the incubator and face of the child as the nurses whizzed by.

David instantly reached out to the child, falling to one knee, sobbing. A couple of male nurses aided the young lady in assisting David to a chair.

"What's wrong with him?" David demanded, his eyes red and filled with tears.

"He has what is called RH Disease," the nurse said, trying to console him. She then asked someone to bring him a glass of water.

"What is that?" David asked, rubbing his forehead.

"It's a blood disorder caused by the incompatibility of blood types between an unborn child and the mother."

"I don't understand," David said, sounding confused. "She's already had the baby."

"Mr. Stokes—"

As soon as Stokes left the nurse's tongue, David's demeanor shifted. He didn't feel like crying anymore and for a minute, he wasn't thinking about the baby or Brenda. He was thinking, *What in the heck is gong on? More secrets! Here I am being called by another man's name, and I can't say a thing or I'll bring un-needed and unwanted attention to myself.*

The nurse continued. "—Mr. Stokes, what happened was because of the incompatibility of the child and your wife; your wife's body treated the baby's blood cells as a foreign matter and released antibodies to attack the foreign matter."

"But like I said, ma'am, she's already had the baby!"

"I understand, Mr. Stokes—"

"Apparently, you don't," David interjected.

"If you'll calm down, Mr. Stokes, I'll explain it to you. Will you let me explain?"

"Yes, I apologize."

It's okay, we are all under stress. As I was saying, during delivery the baby's blood combined with Brenda's."

"Could any of this have been prevented?"

"Yes, but from looking at your wife's records, we didn't feel the need to treat your wife as a risk factor for this particular disorder. From your wife's information, she is O negative, but so are you."

All David could do was shake his head.

"Mr. Stokes, I think it would be a good idea for you to visit your wife for now. I will personally come to your room with any updates on your child's status."

David sat there for about 15 seconds, rubbing his forehead and shaking his head in disbelief.

"Mr. Stokes?"

David immediately snapped to attention. He thought that if she called him Mr. Stokes again, he'd probably go off the deep end.

"Yes, take me to her."

As David walked by the empty bed in the two-bed room, he noticed that Brenda was asleep. David quietly took a seat beside the bed and began to pray. Right in the middle of praying, David's phone rang, waking her.

"This is Captain David," he answered.

It was Nathan.

"I know about your situation, David, and I'm not going to turn you in yet. I'm giving you seven days. On the seventh day, you need to tell on yourself or I will." Then Nathan hung up the phone.

David stayed in the hospital for the seven days praying and pleading morning, noon, and night with God to spare his child and to forgive him for his sins, but on the seventh day, David and Brenda's baby died.

After days of praying and begging God for his forgiveness, David finally realized that God had forgiven him the very day that he'd repented. He even thanked God for his mercy. He loved God even more because he realized that he served a merciful God that would forgive and accept him no matter what he'd done. He'd always known that you can't un-plant seeds of deceit, lust, and idol worship. David vowed before God that he would never betray God's mercy again, and he begged the Lord to cleanse him from head to toe. Losing his career and ministry was a part of his own seed sowing, and he accepted it.

WHERE'S DADDY

*M*e'Shone is in the kitchen preparing a special surprise meal for Amen. Me'shone had been planning this evening in her head all afternoon. She made last minute arrangements to have Charlotte, her niece, to pick up Keyshawn to babysit for her. Her mind and body were yearning for Amen's attention. She was daydreaming in and out of how the events of the evening would take place as she glided happily from the kitchen to the stove and in and out of the refrigerator.

Doorbell rings.

"Keyshawn, I'm not going to tell you anymore to get these toys up out of this floor and go and get your overnight bag packed, Me'Shone said walking towards the door."

"I'm packed all ready momma; Keyshawn said, continuing to play with his trucks."

"Well go and grab it, Me'Shone said." Your cousin is here to pick you up.

"Okay", Keyshawn said, picking up his toys and heading upstairs.

"Come on in Charlotte. Keyshawn will be down in a minute, Me'Shone said wiping her hands in her apron. Is that Wanda in the car, Me'Shone said waving?"

"Yeah, momma told me to ask you if you would take Grandma to pay her bills tomorrow." Me'Shone waved to her sister Wanda sitting in the car.

"Tell your mother that she could have called me earlier to ask me about that. Your momma always does that to me. Anyway, Make sure Keyshaun is in the bed by nine and I will be by in the morning to pick him up, Me'Shone said, walking towards the kitchen."

"How much are you paying me this time Aunty Me'Shone, Charlotte said following her Aunty into the kitchen?"

"The same amount I paid you last time you kept your cousin."

"But he's a year older and worse since the last time I babysat for you."

"I'll think about it Charlotte, Me'Shone said, smiling."

"I'm ready, Keyshaun said, coming down the stairs, with his overnight backpack on his back continuing to maintain his game on his Nintendo DS."

"Okay Keyshaun you behave yourself, Me'Shone said, walking Charlotte and Keyshaun over to the front door." After opening the door, Me'Shone began to adjust Keyshaun's clothes on him. "Tell your momma that I'll be there in the morning to pick Keyshaun up okay."

"Okay, Aunty."

As Charlotte and Keyshaun walked towards the car, Wanda rolled down the window and began to speak.

"Did Charlotte tell you about momma, Wanda shouted, as she waved from the car."

"Why didn't she just get out of the car Me'Shone said, returning the wave and nodding her head yes. "

"Bye momma," Keyshaun said getting into the car.

"I love you, Me'Shone said waving."

Just as she closed the door, the phone rang.

Me'Shone checked the caller ID and recognized the telephone number. Deep inside her woman's intuition, she felt that something was wrong but choose to ignore it.

"Hey baby, I have a surprise for you, Me'Shone said, with excitement, making sure she spoke first." She wanted Amen to know that she had something planned before

Amen said anything that would bring an end to her romantic evening that she had all ready began and hopefully that would make him adjust anything that could interfere with her romantic escapade.

"Baby I have the perfect evening planned for us, Me'Shone said, continuing with the excited tone."

Me'Shone I hate to tell you this but.............

"Wanda and Charlotte just picked up Keyshaun so we have the entire house to ourselves, Me'Shone said in a seductive tone."

Baby that sounds great but…

"I am also cooking your favorite dish. I also stopped by Fredrick's of Hollywood and I bought several of your favorite outfits for dessert. I picked out Chocolate, cherry and Banana flavored outfits if you know what I mean."

Baby can you please just listen for a second………

"Do you know that Wanda had the audacity to ask me to take mamma to pay some bills, all last minute, as if I don't have anything else to do? You know that I don't mind but she could have at least told me a day in advance. I have a mind to……..."

"Me'Shone," Amen said stopping Me'Shone before she said another word. I'm trying to tell you that I'm going to be working late tonight. I'm sorry baby."

Silence

"I promise that I will make it up to you tomorrow baby."

"It's okay," Me'Shone said, as her excitement deflated. "Just do what you have to do."

"I'm going to finish up here and I promise that I'll be home as soon as I can, okay."
"Okay."

Amen knew that that okay was not okay. "I'll see you when I get home."

"Yeah," Me'Shone said, sharply.

"I love you," Amen said but before he could get it out Me'Shone had all ready hung up.

One hour and a half later.

"Honey I home," Amen said coming through the door.

As he hung up his blazer and put away his briefcase, he noticed that the table was still set with candles and dinnerware. That's when Me'Shone came through the kitchen door and began clearing off the table.

"Me'Shone, Amen said taking off his tie and heading over to the table." He knew that this was just like being in jail. In jail you get one telephone call and in this situation he has a one question limit. He also knew that that one question could never be, "Are you okay or what can I do to help." So he came up with another approach. He decided to use a statement instead of a question.

"Baby I apologize," Amen said humbly. He also knew not to say that he was sorry because that would leave him open for, "Yeah we know that you are sorry." It was all about what to say, how to say it and what words to use when saying it. None of it was going to work tonight though.

"Why are you apologizing?"

"Because I know you had an evening planned for just the both of us and I couldn't be here."

"People apologize when they do something wrong. Did you do something wrong Amen?"

No I didn't do anything wrong but I wanted ....

So what are you apologizing about?

Me'Shone, can we talk?

"Talk about what Amen," Me'Shone said, walking back through the kitchen door.

"I can tell that you're upset," Amen said, talking to the kitchen door.

"I'm not upset," Me'Shone said, walking back through the door.

"Okay," Amen said. "I can't force you to talk to me," Amen said grabbing the remote and turning on the television.

Five minutes later.

"So what did you have to do tonight that was so important," Me'Shone said, standing by the couch?

Taking a deep breath, Amen explained. "Baby we had a meeting that ran a little bit longer than normal. A number of things that came out of the meeting needed to be resolved and it took longer than expected."

"Is this tie going to put itself away or do I look like the maid," Me'Shone said, not even addressing his explanation?

"Well I guess that since you can't beat me up over what helps pays the bills around here, you're going to nitpick me to death. I thought that you weren't upset?"

"I'm not upset. I'm frustrated."

So now, we're going to play the word game?

That's your problem Amen. You think that everything is a game.

I didn't say this was a game. I said you were making a play on my choice of words.

You need to start putting in a little more overtime at home.

I am so sick of having this argument with you.

Not as sick as I am.

"Me'Shone, I'm asking you to leave this one alone. No I'm begging you to just drop it. I can see if I was out messing around or if I did this on a constant basis but you know that I was doing what I was supposed to be doing."

You were supposes to be home. I am so tired of being put on the back……..

"I am supposed to take care of my family," Amen said, standing to his feet. I am so tiered of feeling like a failure to you, when you know that I am trying to please you on every level. No, I am not going to be perfect at all the things that I do for my family but I need my wife to see my efforts and equate them to love. Yes, every now and then, I am going to need you to reel me back in but I need you to know how to go about doing it."

Why does it always have to be about you?

See that is what I am talking about. Here I am trying to reach out to you and you're still pointing the finger. I have to get up out of here.

Well leave Amen. You're no different than any other black man. It was just a matter of time. Yeah you put on a good good-man front but you're no different than anybody else.

So now you're going to attack my manhood. I want you to listen and listen very close. I have been a good man, husband and father in my house. Not perfect. Not by far but I try. If you were smarter about this situation you would've come at me differently and maybe just maybe I would've been more understanding towards your feelings. I am busting my ass for this family and all I'm getting is a hard way to go. Maybe I'm not what you need in a man but I refuse to let our son grow up believing that a man works his behind off to give his family everything and then his wife questions how he does it, is the way it's supposed to be. So if you need me I'll be in a hotel.

I knew you were just like every other black man, looking for a reason to leave. I've been expecting it anyway. I've been preparing for it. My daddy did it, what makes you any different.

You know what? That's the problem. You can't want to be happy with me, all while planning for the day that you will leave. If you can't see us being together forever then you're wasting your time and mines. While you're at work tomorrow I'll come by to get the rest of my things.

"Oh you can find time to do that," Me'Shone said, becoming resentful.

No I don't have time for that either. It's just that I don't want my son watching me pack my things to leave.

I hate you. I never should have married you. I need a man in my life.

If you think your personal attacks are going to provoke me to put my hands on you you're wrong. I guess you witnessed that too growing up. Well you're not going to get it. As a matter of a fact, I don't need anything. I'm leaving now. On his way out the door, Amen punches a picture of himself and Me'Shone and it falls to the floor.

Me'Shone begins to pray.

I don't need him Lord. I don't need any man but you Father. My mother didn't need a man and I don't need one.

Three days later in Amen's break room.

"What's up Bruce," Amen said, walking into the break room taking a seat at the table with his friend.

"Nothing much man," Bruce replied.

Female co-workers in the break room. They watch Amen walking into the break room.

"Grasping her cappuccino with both hands, have you all heard about Amen," Venus said, leaning in to whisper to her friends?

"Yeah I read the email that you sent out," Treece said shaking her head.

"Email," Paula said, with a confused look on her face.

"Yeah, I forwarded it to yo," Treece said, turning to look at Paula. The title of the email was Amen.

Girl I thought amen and not Amen.

Paula you're out there sometime.

I was thinking it was another chain letter that I would have to pass on to ten more people including myself, to receive a blessing.

"No it wasn't one of those," Treece said, shaking her head smiling.

"So what did the email say," Paula asked, looking at Venus and Treece?

Inconspicuously looking over at Bruce and Amen's table, "Amen left Me'Shone and Keyshaun," Venus replied.

"Are you serious," Paula said, shocked of the news? I just saw them in church last Sunday and they looked like they always do, like the perfect couple.

"Well I saw him on coming out of the hotel on Juniper AVE a couple of days ago," Venus said, taking a sip from her cup.

"How do you know," Paula said, looking at Venus as if she knew a little too much?

It's not what you think Paula............ You know that Starbucks that I go to every morning, well it's off of Juniper also. It's right across from the hotel that I saw Amen coming out of two days ago.

"He could've had his family there with him," Paula responded.

"In town," Treece said ruling that out.

"It sounds like you are hoping he's staying in a hotel," Paula said.

Well like they say, you don't put what you think is trash on the curb unless you're sure you want to get rid of it because somebody will find some use for it.

Don't you mean one person's trash is another person's trash treasure?

You say amen I say Amen!

They all laughed.

"Well I don't need another trifling man in my life," Venus said. Half of the black me I know don't want to be married anyway. To me he's just another black man that walked out on his family.

"That's not fair," Paula said, taking a look at the clock on the wall. Would you like for black men to put us into one category and say that all of us suffer from Angry Black Woman Syndrome?

"Well I know I do," Treece said taking her hand and rubbing her neck and shoulder area.

"Why do you say that," Venus said, with a confused look on her face?

Girl the police stopped me a month ago and I wanted to give him a ticket.

"What were you going to give him a ticket for," Paula said shaking her head.

"For making me late for work," Treece said, as they all began to laugh.

"Treece I don't even know why I asked you," Venus said.

"As I was saying Venus, every marriage or relationship is different. We don't know what happened between Me'Shone and Amen to cause him to leave or for her to put him out."

"All I'm saying is that most black men find a reason to leave," Venus said with a convinced look on her face.

Back to the men's conversation

"You sure everything is all right," Bruce said opening the lid on his left over's.

"Why what's up," Amen said with a confused look on his face?

So you haven't seen the email?

No I haven't seen any email but you know I'm off of the email friendship distribution list.

What are you talking about man?

Well you know how busy I've been right.

Yeah, okay.

For the last month, I haven't had time to forward all of the latest gossip, chain letters, and spiritual poetry or media files with black people doing something crazy; therefore I've been removed from the distro. Eventually emails stopped coming. If you really want to know who your friends are, stop forwarding emails. It's easy to get them back though, Amen said pausing and looking at Bruce.

Okay, I guess you want me to ask you how?

Oh that's easy. Just send about three or four consecutive emails and in about a day or two you will start to receive emails again, Amen said ending his statement with a bite of his deli sandwich.

"You have taken this email thing to a whole different level," Bruce said shaking his head.

"Maybe but it's true." "Try it if you don't believe me," Amen said, taking a drink from his soda.

Anyway, word is out that you're staying in a hotel.

"Pausing and smiling Amen replied. It wasn't anybody but Venus. I knew she saw me the other morning with her gossiping behind. That's why she doesn't have any business. She's too busy in everyone else's."

Well you know if she saw you she was going to put it out there. You know you really can't blame her for being bitter. Rob did do her wrong.

So that gives her the right spread another person's personal business. I am so tired of women using past relationships with men, whether it be their man or their father, as an excuse to give any other man hell. I'm not even in a relationship with this woman but you're saying because Rob messed her over she has the right to put my business in the street.

Amen, chill bro……. I wasn't saying all of that. I was just saying that she's hurt and to validate her theory that all men are dogs, she subconsciously seek out men who may

be doing the wrong thing. "You know what Rob did was ...." Bruce said shaking his head.

"Crazy," Amen said, finishing Bruce's sentence. Messing around with her hairdresser and turning around and getting the woman pregnant. The woman that you make an appointment with is scheduling you around the time she's out with your man and you're paying her.

"So she was using Venus' money to taking her husband out," Bruce said, smiling and shaking his head.

Crazy!

So if you don't mind, what happened between you and Me'Shone?

My Father's business.

What?

That's what I was doing. My Father's business.

What? Who are you trying to be now?

Check this out. Taking care of my family, making sure they have everything they need and most of their wants is what the Lord want me to do. Me taking care of my family is me doing, "My Father's Business".

So you were working late again, Bruce said sarcastically.

Smiling, Amen answered Bruce. Must working late equate to doing something wrong? Bruce, I can look myself in the mirror and pray without any reservations.

What happened?

Well to make long story short, Me'Shone had planned an evening for us but I ended up working late. Words were exchanged and I left.

You left?

Yes I left.

"Can I be straight with you," Bruce said as if he disagreed with how I handled the situation.

Oh, here we go.

See you're thinking negatively all ready. That's not good. Are you going to be open minded?

Yeah, Bruce go ahead.

Okay, can we both agree that women are emotional beings?

Slightly showing his palms and tilting his head to the side he showed that he was in agreement.

Okay let me tell you what you should've done.

"I'm listening," Amen said, putting away the wrappings from his sandwich.

You were supposed to just take it. Being a man, we have to have broad shoulders. We have to take things that we don't necessarily want or deserve. Everything she said was based solely on hurt.

Amen sat there as if he already knew what Bruce was talking about. The first night alone in the hotel had already began to teach him a few things. Hearing it from Bruce was sort of a confirmation.

When you came home you should have brought home something for her to break.

What? I was with you until you said that.

Listen. You bringing her a card, flowers or something would have given her something to direct her anger towards. It didn't have to be in your face it could've been when you went to sleep. She would either through the flower to the floor giving her some satisfaction or she would have talked to the flowers after you went to sleep.

She would have talked to the flowers? Man you are too crazy. What would she say to the flowers?

Something like, "If he think these flowers saved his a** he has another thing coming. Walk up in here with some flowers and everything supposed to be all right. These flowers don't even smell good. He must have picked these himself because aint no flower shop open this time of night. I have a mind to drown him with the water in water in the bottom of this drinking glass." You know something like that.

They both laughed.

Man you are too stupid.

But it's real though. This helps her even the score a little. Now after she rips the card up in your face, you should clench your teeth and apologize again.

What?

Listen Amen. Clinching your teeth is key because if you just apologize without showing some frustration she can take it as weakness and continue but if she sees your manhood she should acknowledge it .

You thought I had the emailing thing down to a science. You have lost your mind.

Hold on this is the coupe de gra. Now I don't know if you know it or not but I think this entire episode was about sex. I'm not trying to get into your personal business but I'm just telling you what I think. All of the planning that she put into that evening was a prelude to you handling your business. Now don't get it twisted. It wasn't solely about sex. She needed your undivided attention. When a woman is planning to give you some and the end result of what she was planning is halted, oh you have a problem. What you were supposed to do was to find a way to ensure that she at least got what she wanted and you let her scorn you for messing up her plans.

So what should I do now, send her some flowers?

No! There's a lesson in this for Me'Shone too.

So how will I know if she's learned her lesson?

Has she called you?

Not yet.

Well she hasn't learned her lesson.

I thought you said that I was wrong.

I never said that you were wrong. I said that you handled the situation wrong. If you apologize now she's going to think that this is how things are supposed to end up. Like they say, "you teach people how you want to be treated." You will be telling her that this is an acceptable way to treat you.

Man where did you learn all of this?

Trial and error. You know what?

What's that?

After ten years of marriage, I started keeping a journal of all fights. I began to analyze each and every one of them. Not saying that the outcome will be the same but someone once told me that, "if you "want "a different outcome you have to approach situations differently.

I got you but this hotel thing is getting expensive.

Don't worry about that. I'll help you out if you need it. Hey, Amen I have to get back to this desk. I'll get back with you later.

Bruce thanks.

No problem man. We're supposed to be there for one another. I'll see you after work.

All right man.

Sunday Morning. Walking into the church, Amen noticed that Me'Shone was in the choir. She also noticed him coming down the aisle. She was wearing his favorite Sunday outfit. Today was exceptionally hard being that it was Father's Day! On holidays, Bishop Kittles usually lets one of his up and coming ministers deliver the message and today was no exception. Minister Harris was going to be delivering the Father's Day Message. Bishop Kittles stood up to introduce Minister Harris.

"Blessed the Lord saints," Bishop Kittles said, walking up to the podium.

The congregation responded, with bless the Lord.

I said bless the Lord Saints.

The congregation responded faster and louder.

I know that it's Father's day and we normally don't get as fired up as we do on Mother's Day but I'm here to tell you Saints that Father's Day is just as important and should be celebrated just as much or more so than Mother's Day. I know I may have ruffled some feathers with that one so let me explain. You see only the women and children here with good husbands and fathers, understand what I'm saying. You see they can look around the congregation and see the families that are here without the man of the house. So any day that you can celebrate having something that most families don't have is a day to go overboard with your celebration. Can I get an amen?

Amen's were heard all over the congregation.

"That's what I'm talking about Bishop, Minister Harris said," standing in front of his seat."

You don't have to worry about a rock crying out in some of these men's places because they understand how hard it is being a real man. A man of God! You see it takes a real man to fight of the temptations of this world. You know I feel like preaching on today but on that note I want to thank Minister Kittles for volunteering to bring us the Father's Day message, Bishop Kittles said turning around and smiling at Minister Harris. I didn't even have to look over his message today because I know Sister Harris has already done that a couple of times.

The congregation laughed.

Well with no further a due, let's give the Lord a hand praise for Minister Harris.

The congregation stood to their feet as Minister Harris made his way to the podium.

I know Bishop was saying that as a joke but Sharlinda was looking over my shoulder every time I started to work on my message, Minister Harris said smiling and opening his bible and placing in on the podium. ....Praise the Lord. First and foremost I want to give honor to the father because it's his day. Because he is the Father. I know we normally don't look at it as such but he is the ultimate father and father figure. When I take inventory with myself, he is the measuring stick and though I fall short at times when I take inventory, I make sure I haven't fallen back to where I started, Amen. Like the old saying goes. I may not be where I want to be but thank God I'm not where I used to be. Amen

The congregation responded with smiling amen's.

If you will, turn with me in your bibles to Proverbs 27th chapter and the 15 verse. And it reads, a continual dropping in a very rain day and contentious women are alike. Now women stay with me. It's not me saying this. This is straight from scripture. Now

it didn't say all women. It says a contentious woman. Now we know every woman here is fire baptized and Holy Ghost filled. Right, Minister Harris said smiling.

Me'Shone and Amen's eyes met as Minister Harris said those words but they quickly turned away.

"With those scriptures I would like to entitle this message, Where's Daddy."

Preach that thing one of the men shouted from the congregation.

Now I want to go into what may cause a woman to be that contentious woman that the scripture is speaking of.

Most of the couples within the congregation began to look at one another.

First of all what is contentious? When I researched the word it uncovered words like arguable, controversial, litigious and most important debatable. Like I said earlier, I know none of the women sitting here fit the description of a contentious woman so I'm going to move on, Minister Harris said smiling.

The men in the congregation tried to maintain a straight face as Minister Harris continued. Ensuring they didn't look at their spouses.

Again I ask the question, why would a woman become contentious. Now if you will turn in your bible to Proverbs the 21st Chapter and the 8th verse it reads, the way of a man is froward and strange. Now I knew the definition of strange but I didn't know the definition of forward. When I looked it up there were a couple key words that appeared that immediately got my attention. The words were headstrong and stubborn. With the word strange, that gives us three things that could cause a woman to become contentious. "Or do we," Minister Harris said, looking up from his bible. If we read on it says "but" as for the pure his work is right. Which is basically saying, but as for the man that's upright in his going and coming, his work is right. Basically the bible says the way of a man is strange. It's a known fact that men are more logical thinkers than women and women tend to be more emotion driven.

The congregation is very quiet. Me'Shone is paying very close attention.

Therefore a man's way of thinking is bound to drive a woman to be contentious if she finds herself trying to argue or debate the thought process of her man. His way of thinking is strange to her. Which leads us into the next verse, Verse 9, and it reads it is better to live on the roof than share the house with a nagging wife. The nineteenth verse reads it is better to live in the desert than with a nagging and complaining with. Now these next statements I'm about to make aren't in the bible but they are safe to say statements. I'm not saying they're right but it's the thought process of some of our men. So is it safe to say, it is better to leave my kids behind than to live in the house of a nagging woman? Where's Daddy?

You preachin now Minister Harris, another man shouted from the congregation.

Is it better to be broke and alone but with a piece of mind than be in the house with a contentious woman? Where's......Where's Daddy?

Men throughout the congregation began to stand up all over the congregation as the words of Minister Harris hit home for a lot of married and single men in the congregation.

Is it safe to say that a man would rather walk out of a marriage than to let a woman push him to hitting her? Where's Daddy?

Minister Harris has to pause for a second or two as men continued to stand and applaud.

You see some women, not the women here, are carrying the hurt and pain of past relationships into their marriages. Relationships with their fathers and boyfriends. They're waiting for or they're anticipating that their man is going to leave or mistreat them like the men in their past.

Me'Shone placed her face into her hands as she began to tear up.

You see my bible says, without vision the people perish. Again is it safe to say, without vision your marriage fails. If you can't see yourself being happy with someone or if you're planning to leave how can you expect a marriage to work. Just because your daddy left doesn't mean the man you chose is going to leave. Just because your last boyfriend or husband cheated doesn't mean your current boyfriend or husband is going to cheat. Without vision your marriage with fail.

"Amen Preacher," Bishop Kettles said, standing to his feet behind Minister Harris.

"The bible says in the second chapter of Genesis and the eighteenth verse, an excellent wife, who can find? Her worth is far above jewels. There's a worldly saying that says a good man is hard to find but the scripture says an excellent wife, who can find, Minister Harris says shaking his head smiling. The bible says her worth is far above jewels. When I first read this scripture, I couldn't help but to think of that old temptations song. Once again I know you all have been holy all your life so please just bear with me because I had to be delivered, Minister Harris said," stepping away from the podium.

Some of the members in the congregation began to feel the Holy Spirit.

You see I wasn't always covered by the blood.

The music ministry had taken over and the congregation was up and praising God. Minister Harris had even begun to dance. As the music died down Minister Harris continued with the message.

164

As I was saying, every time I read that scripture I would think of the Temptations. They use to sing a song entitled, "My Girl." I always thought that was that was the most beautiful poem ever written. There was a verse that said, I don't need no money, fortune or fame, I've got all of the riches in the world that "One Man" can claim. I use to think, what kind of a woman makes a man say he doesn't need any money? Can you imagine that? That's when I met my beautiful wife Sharlinda. With Sharlinda I have so much honey, the bee's envy me, Minister Harris said looking over at Sharlinda smiling. All I really want the women to understand on this Father's Day is that we're strange, headstrong and stubborn. There are some men out there trying though. If you think your man is trying, give him your support. Men take care of your women. Try to understand their feelings. Before I close I would like to leave you all with a poem I read a long time ago. The poem is entitled, "I am a Man". It was written by Keith A. Anderson.

I Am A Man

YOUR WORLD WILL COME TOGETHER,
WHEN YOU REALIZE THAT, YOU ARE A MAN.
KNOWING AND ENSURING THAT,
ON YOUR OWN TWO FEET YOU CAN STAND.

NOW SAYING YOU ARE A MAN,
DOES NOT NECESSARILY MEANS THAT YOU ARE ONE.
HOPEFULLY YOU'LL BE ABLE TO SAY YOU ARE
BY THE TIME THIS LETTER IS DONE.

I AM A MAN
BECAUSE I'VE ACKNOWLEDGED MY WEAKNESSES
AND I'VE ASKED GOD TO HELP ME CORRECT THEM,
IF YOU DON'T KNOW YOU WEAKNESSES
THEN THIS IS WHERE YOU SHOULD BEGIN.

A MAN DOESN'T CHANGE DIRECTION,
WITH THE BLOWING OF THE WIND.
GOD, LESSONS LEARNED AND PERSISTENCE
ARE THE TOOLS THAT HE USES TO GUIDE HIM.

NONE OF HIS DECISIONS
ARE BASED SOLEY AROUND A WOMAN.
IF IT IS, HE'S DESTINED TO FAIL
OF THIS I AM CERTAIN.

A MAN SEARCHES FOR A WOMAN
THAT CAN BEST SUPPORT HIS LIFE'S MISSION.
THIS TAKES TIME AND PATIENCE
AND WITH THE UTMOST PERCISION.

YOU SEE THE WORLD HAS IT ALL TURNED AROUND
WE HAVE WOMEN LOOKING FOR MEN.
YOU WANT TO KNOW WHAT'S WRONG WITH MARRIAGES
WELL THIS IS A GOOD PLACE TO BEGIN.

A MAN SEARCHES FOR THAT WOMAN
THAT MEETS HIS EACH AND EVERY NEED,
FOR THAT PERFECT BODY AND SOUL
IN WHICH HE WANTS TO PLANT HIS SEED.

A REAL MAN IS IN CONTROL OF HIS SEX DRIVE
NOT HITTING ANY AND EVERYTHING THAT MOVES.
HE TAKES PRIDE IN HIS MANHOOD
BECAUSE HE KNOWS THAT HE HAS NOTHING TO PROVE

IT TAKES A REAL MAN,
TO LOOK A WOMAN SQUARE IN THE EYES
AND BE TRUTHFUL WITH HER
NOT TELLING HER UNNEEDED LIES.

I AM A MAN
BECAUASE I CAN STAND ALONE IF I NEED TOO
I DON'T NEED CLICKS AND A WHOLE GOUP OF PEOPLE,
TO DO WHAT I NEED TO DO.

A MAN IS A PROVIDER.
HE NEVER NEGLECTS HIS RESPONSIBILITIES.
ALWAYS MAKING SURE,
HE'S TAKING CARE OF HIS WOMAN'S NEEDS.

A MAN TREATS HIS WOMAN
LIKE THE JEWEL SHE REALLY IS.
HE NEVER PUTS HER SECOND,
SECOND BEHIND THE KIDS.

HE STUDIES HIS WOMAN,
AS IF HE WERE STUDYING FOR A TEST.
HE WANTS TO MAKE SURE,
THAT HE'S GIVING HER HIS BEST.
MAKING A VALIANT EFFORT TO
PLEASE HER SPIRIT AND TEASE HER FLESH

HE TAKES CONTROL OF EVERY ARGUMENT
BECAUSE HE KNOWS IT IS UP TO HIM TO SET THE TONE.
BECAUSE HE KNOWS THAT HE HAS TO ANSWER,
FOR EVERYTHING THAT HAPPENS IN HIS HOME.

HE UNDERSTANDS THE IMPORTANCE,
OF PLAYING A SIGNIFICANT ROLE IN RASING HIS KIDS.
NOT USING THE EXCUSE THAT HE DOESN'T KNOW HOW
BECAUSE HIS FATHER NEVER DID.

NOW EVERDAY SHOULD BE USED AS A LEARNING PROCESS
BECAUSE IT'S HARD BECOMING AND BEING A MAN.
I KNOW THAT WITH GOD AS THE HEAD OF MY LIFE,

WHITH HIS GUIDANCE I KNOW THAT I CAN

SO I HOPE THAT I'VE BEEN SUCCESSFUL
IN HELPING YOU ASSESS IF YOU ARE A MAN.
NO ONE THING OR PERSON CAN TELL YOU IF YOU ARE ONE
ONLY YOU CAN.

God bless you all and men you have a wonderful Father's day.

The congregations stood to cheer for the word and the beautiful poem.

The choir director came out from amongst the choir and raised his hands signaling to the choir to stand. Me'Shone excused herself from the choir and was making her way to Amen. After seeing Me'Shone make her way to him, he decided to meet her half way down in front of the congregation. Tears were streaming down Me'Shone's face as she and Amen embraced. She pulled back a slightly and grabbed Amen's face gently with both hands.

I love you baby and please forgive me. I'm sorry for doing those things to you. I'm going to need your help baby because of my past.

Don't worry about it Me'me. Let's go home.

As they were getting their wedding day kiss on, Keyshaun made his way up front and tried to wrap his arms around his mom and dad as the congregation watched on and the choir began to sing the song "Good days and Bad days" by the Merrills.

MY FIRST KNIGHT

He's my first knight
Sitting beside me at the round table
If I left this world today
I know he would be able

Able to handle anything before him
Because I gave him what he needed at birth
I whispered in his ear
And told him what he was worth

To me you're worth more than silver and gold
And when it's all over
Your story will be told
Amongst those in heaven

I get full of pride
Every time I look into the eyes of my son
I have so many great expectations
Of what I want him to become

I see him hungry to carry the torch
Because he's a big dog
And he won't waste time idle on a porch

I love him as only a father can
He has to know
That I'm his number one fan

He's my son
From my deepest aspiration,
Is where he came from
I know I have my expectations Lord
But it's your will that I pray be done

So hang on, young man
As life begins to take flight
I will always be there for you
Because you will always be My First Knight

KALEB'S 15 COMMANDMENTS

1. Always follow the Lord's Commandments!

2. Never treat anyone better than you treat yourself!

3. Never respect anyone that doesn't respect you!

4. Treat every event as if there is no second chance!

5. Never tell all of your business no matter how close a person is to you!

6. Work Hard!

7. Play Hard (Enjoy Life)!

8. Never use drugs!

9. Take care of your body (Always work out)!

10. Set standards in every relationship (Male or Female)

11. Be the best Man, Husband, Father that you can be!

12. Be honest with yourself. Assess yourself every 3 months! (4 times a year [written])!

13. Look everyone in the eye!

14. Always have a plan (include and expect change What If?)!

15. Never abuse a woman (verbally or physically). Chivalry goes a long way! Even if she does it to you, walk away!!!!

IF IT WASN'T 4 SOUTH CAROLINA

If it wasn't 4 South Carolina
My life would be filled with fortune and Fame
Or am I just kidding myself
And it would have ended up the same

If it wasn't for S.C.
I wouldn't have this drive and commitment to succeed
I really need to thank South Carolina
Because South Carolina didn't believe

It's time to face my past
Placing everything on the table
Because if I don't
I will never be able

Able to see past
Where I'm from
Because where I'm from
Doesn't set limits to
What I can become

New York can't do it for me
And neither can L.A.
Growing up problems are everywhere
You just have to find your way

A way out of no way
And it's never easy
Just ask the Lord to open your eyes
And enable you to see

See that I have to be a father
And a good husband
Because I don't want to repeat
The same cycle again

So many other states
Offer a plethora of opportunities
But just as many undetermined
Children fail in the city
As well as in the country

One day I'm going to make it big
And nothing will be fine-a
They may even put up a billboard of me
In Andrews, South Carolina

FINALLY

Finally she's here
And I'm going to cherish her all
I promise to be there for her
Whenever she calls

Though it's only been a week
Since we've revealed our true feelings
I wanted you long before that
But I had a hard time believing

Believing that you could ever be mine
So I wasted a lot of time
Trying to locate that perfect approach
Hell, I even thought about writing you a note

But it's okay
Because it's been well worth the wait
Every "MOMENT" from here on out
I will not let go to waste

Time with you is precious
Because of the situation in our lives
So every minute counts
From the time we say hello, till we say our goodbyes

I'm amazed about the feelings I get
When I look into your eyes
It's like we become one
And our individual lives die

I'm going to take my time
And I enjoy every moment we spend together
Because since the first day that I met you
Each moment gets better and better

So, baby, these are my feelings
I know it took me an eternity
But now I can sit back and sigh saying
I found her,
                    "FINALLY"

FIGHTING LIKE FOOLS

As time goes on
And the love disappears
You're contemplating why you're still here
And how you've lost so many years
You begin to ponder

Knowing from the beginning
That the relationship had no future
You stayed for the long haul
Afraid of departure

Afraid that you were being too picky
Figuring everyone has their issues
Later realizing there is a difference between
Issues and who a person really is

Every now and then
to confuse you even more
Love would stop by
And knock on the door

Eager for peace and hope
You blindly welcomed it
But always in the back of your mind
You could never forget

Forget the name-calling and flying objects
That were scattered over many years
What will happen next is one of your many fears
Lying in bed silently fighting back the tears

One day in the middle of life
You ask yourself an important question
What are we fighting for?
Is it to see who wins
And who has the highest score?

Are we fighting for the sake of remaining or regaining love?
Or to prove who's right or who's wrong
The constant battle to prove if
This is where I belong

Nothing hits harder
When in the middle of "Fighting like Fools"
That you stop and you think
I really don't love you

COMPLACENT

I don't know about everyone else
But I have to admit it
That at one time or another
I've become complacent

I used to think that
I was the perfect man.
I thought they should bottle me up
And put me into a can

Until I watched another man
Open the car door for his wife
It was a small gesture
Symbolizing her importance in his life

This led me to think of other gallantries
That over the years I stopped doing
Like rubbing her feet and kissing her softly
Things I did when I was pursuing

A woman doesn't want much
She just wants a sense of security
Knowing that her man is able to handle anything
And that he's full of possibility

She wants to be treated richly
Even with poor man's money
It's the effort and uniqueness that arouses her
Taking away her clouds and making every day seem sunny

Every day I should be thinking of something
To surprise her with
If it's nothing but a quick visit at her job
Or to come home with a sentimental gift.

Holding her while watching a movie
You'd never imagine how much that means
Things that we as men take for granted
Are parts of a woman's hopes and dreams

Sunshine Blues
My tribute to The Real King "BB"

I'm in love with sunshine baby
In her love I'm soaking wet
I said I'm in love with sunshine baby
How blue can I get?

Her love's as deep as the ocean
Sometimes I think I'm going to drown
But even when I'm drowning
She turns my frown upside down

Cause' I'm in love with sunshine baby
In her love I'm soaking wet
I'm in love with sunshine baby
How blue can I get?

Every man wants to flirt with her
It drives me insane
My jealousy won't let go of me
If she leaves I'll never be the same

Cause I'm in love with sunshine baby
In her love I'm soaking wet
I'm in love with sunshine baby
How blue can I get?

Anything she asks of me
I am more than willing to do
But when she asked me to make love to her
I didn't have a clue

Cause I'm in love with sunshine baby
In her love I'm soaking wet
I'm in love with sunshine baby
One day her love's going to save me yet

Robbing Me

I let you rob me
Robbing me of my innocence
It's funny that you committed the crime
And I'm living the life sentence.

Sentenced to make what's broken appear to be fixed
Taking licks intentionally, with my guard down
All the time I should be wearing a frown
Yet I still smile

Smiling with deep regret
Trying not to get upset
Because it was me who let you in

Playing the role of a school teacher
Teaching the crook how to deplete me
Wanting to let go
But I guess I don't really want to be free

It's funny 'cause I can't get mad
Not mad at you
You're just doing what I let you do

I began taking inventory of things stolen
And understanding wasn't one
If you had stolen some of that
You'd understand where I was coming from

Looking around for dignity I noticed that my
Self-respect shelves were also empty
I looked everywhere
But there was none left inside of me

What's sad is, if I leave now
And find someone else
They may pay the price
As I try to restock my shelves

It's ironic and really puzzling
Because they left all the good
Taking my get "mad and get even"
So I can't when I should

Now I have to ask the Lord
For some "Stand for something"
Because without it
I will "Stand for nothing"

The next time I'm going
To install an ADT
So I'll know when an intruder
Is trying to steal from me

I'll keep my head up and eyes open
Because finally I'm able to see
And look that person square in the eyes
The one that's trying to
                    Rob me!

Damsel in Distress

She wants me to save her
From silly games and lonely nights
Planning flights that lead
To her fantasy
She's my Damsel in Distress

I race across the moon
Because there is no time to waste
As I imagine the taste of her lips
While her fingertips caress my face
She's my Damsel in Distress

Rescue me, she cries
From this monotonous love
Wake me from this terrible dream
Because it's not what it seems
Looking in from the outside

She yearns for the kiss that
Would break the cold cold spell
Placed on her by bothers
Who took her through hell

She wants to let down her hair
Without the worry of judgment
She doesn't want to think about anything
She wants to be complacent

Complacency with her love
Is the greatest gift you can give her
With a side of honesty
And a whole lot of laughter

Knowing her knight can rescue her
From any situation she finds herself
No matter how far she sinks
He can save her from any depth

Freedom to be a queen
But in the same breath a mistress
There are bountiful wonders
Locked inside her treasure chest

Freeing her, frees me
I think that describes it best
I know because I've been freed
By my
        Damsel In Distress

I Blame

I'm all grown up now
With a whole lot of problems
I'm looking for someone to blame
Maybe that'll help me solve them.

I can blame it on my mother
She should have left his abusive behind
I try to escape the memory
But the images are locked in my mind

Would my mother leave though?
Because before she was my mother
He was her man
Choosing him over me
Yeah this I can understand

But I can't blame my mother
She showed me how to love
And her love and devotion
I place no one above

Anyway then she could blame her parents
Maybe they didn't do what they were supposed to do
They'll just blame their parents
Hey they have to blame somebody, too!

So I can't blame my mother
So I'll blame my dad
He didn't do the right thing
So I'll make him wish he had

They say that I'm lucky
Because I at least had a dad
I beg to differ
You can't miss what you never had

My dad looked at me and smiled
As he used the same excuse
Son we all have been traumatized
From a long history of abuse

I got angry because no one
Wanted to accept responsibility
Hey I've gotta blame someone
And it ain't going to be me!

I know who
I'll blame my sister or my brother
I've run out of immediate family members
Other than my father and mother

Though they were children just like me
They should've raised me like their own
Forget their childhood
And be the head of my parents' wonderful home

Better yet
I'll blame my aunts and uncles
Somebody should've taken the lead
Taken me by the hand
And showed me how to be

Wait a minute
I think I finally got it
They say it takes a village to raise a child
But what good are they though,
if they don't know how?

Standing in front of the mirror
I ran out of people to blame
Every excuse I had
They all told me the same

So I looked into the mirror
And said the buck stops here.
Right now, I know right from wrong
And it's finally clear.

Nobody's perfect
And I've knowingly done some wrong
When my children look for someone to blame,
Am I going to sing the same ol' song?

No I'm not
Because I want it to stop and start with me
Being accountable for my sins
So that my children will be free.

Free from shouldering the blame
For sins of generations
Making a new entry into our bible
And be the head of new nations

Being a man
Is standing alone with all guilt and shame
Saying there is a need for change
Taking responsibility for his family
And saying,
        I'll Take the Blame!

Is it Possible

I often dreamed of a perfect love
One that makes me quiver with thoughts of her
She would be the greatest promise
In her I would be safe and undoubtedly secure

Hopelessly I sought out this ideal love
Constantly being blinded by decorated trees
Dressing up to play the part
But only concerned with fulfilling their needs

Is it possible?
A love that's pure and has no bounds
I wonder if this love is looking for me
As crazy as that may sound

A love that kisses me
And the kiss is equal to that of making love
The entire time with my eyes closed
Inside smiling, this love I'm no longer deprived of

I would be her sand and she my ocean
Together we would make the perfect sunset
Our bodies providing the perfect silhouette
With no beginning and no end
We are the perfect duet

She is here
And I have found the impossible
I will shout to the world
That finding true love
            "Is definitely Possible"

I'm Ashamed

I hate calling on your name
When I know I've done some wrong
I feel like such a liar
Singing the same ol' song

Falling in the same pitfalls
Walking around with blinders on
Pretending like I've forgotten
where you've brought me from

No I can't call on your name, father
My tongue doesn't deserve your grace
Hide me, o'father
Because I'm ashamed to show my face

When will wisdom set in
And restrain this weak flesh
I can't seem to find the will
Or the obedience to do it myself

Run from me, O'Lord
Till I can lay everything at your feet
Confessing everything that's not holy
Leaving room for you inside of me

Chorus
I'm ashamed
So ashamed
I don't want to continue doing the same ol' thing
Lord, I'm so ashamed

Sing me a song, Lord
One with waters so deep
That they drown this dying man's soul
So that a living man may speak

See my soul, father
Tell me if I'm truly pure at heart
But I beg that you don't
Tell me, tell me to depart

I'll receive it, O'Lord
And I'll make amends
But protect me from those things unholy
So I won't do them again

I want to ask you for forgiveness
But at this moment just fix this broken vessel
I would say that I'm going to get better soon
Because I don't want to upset you

Thank you, O'Lord for listening
These are just some things that I wanted you to know
Oh there's one more thing, Lord
Your son loves you so

Chorus

One day soon
I'm not going to be ashamed
I'm going to shout
From the mountain top
The excellence of your name

Then I'll be able to hear
The words from you
In my son, I am not shamed

WHY GO TO HEAVEN?

Why go to heaven when
I can have life
And have it more abundantly
I can even serve God here on Earth
All while driving a Bentley

Go to heaven
Go to heaven for what
I'm doing all the right things now
I'm not living a life of greed and lust

I can gain the whole world
And keep my soul
Because I still have Jesus
And he makes me whole

All I have to do
Is give God his money
Yeah, Jesus as a pimp
Now that's funny

They say that it's easier
For a camel to go through the eye of a needle
Than for a rich man to make it into heaven
I guess the bible wasn't talking about people of today
Because they are sure they can make it in

But that was just one of Jesus' parables
You know something like a riddle
You just have to re-think it
And work it a little

A parable for me to know and quote
But to be smart enough to work around it
I just have to get on some camels and get low
I'm sure my money and me will fit

Pay your money to the church
They all scream and shout
I'd rather give my money to someone
That I know I can help out

I know I should give
Just let me know to who
Because right now I'm baffled
And Left without a clue

Don't get me wrong
I know that the church has bills to pay
But is that all they're doing with the money
For their sake I definitely pray

Why live so far above those
That come to hear the word
To believe that God wants us to have a Rolls Royce
Is definitely absurd

God wants us to be happy
And money is definitely not the key
But I see and hear more pastors talk
About achievement in prosperity

Sometimes I root for rappers
To make that cheese and get paid
Because everybody can't be a minister
And be laid in the shade

So why go to Heaven
When I can get everything right here
If you paid close attention to this letter
I think I made myself perfectly clear!

Why do I want to go to heaven? Simply put! No more Yesterdays. Mary Mary has a song entitled "Yesterday". The song mentions how they've had enough headaches and heartaches. How they've had so many ups and downs. Eventually the song says that they have cried their last tear. Now I said that Mary Mary said these things in their song but the song was meant for whomever that may be having a tough time. It's a very beautiful song that touched me. That's when I thought, "that's why I want to go to heaven." I'm tiered of yesterdays. It doesn't matter if the streets are gold or not. As long as I can have a piece of mind, I will be all right.

INDECENT PROPOSAL

I've been watching her for weeks now
I'm compelled to make my move
And if I don't do it soon
I don't know what I'm going to do

She's way out of my league
And her man has plenty of cash
But I can't take my mind off of her
She was someone I had to have

So I waited to see them together
I didn't want to approach her behind his back
Showing much respect to him
Before I spoke, I took off my hat

Excuse me sir
With all due respect
I'm going to ask you a question
That I hope I don't regret

I want to take your lady out
For a night on the town
His smile suddenly went away
And quickly became a frown

I waited for him to punch me
But his demeanor suddenly changed
A conceded smirk took over
As he accepted the challenge
To my silly game

She knew I had been watching her
So she decided to play along
We decided to set a date
And I happily went home

We met at an out of town restaurant
Confidently I began my conversation
You're beautiful I smiled and said
By any stretch of the imagination

Do you really believe?
That you can compete with my man
He's taken me all over the world
From the bridges of London,
To the beautiful gardens of Japan.

Well I can't take you to those beautiful places
But I already have reservations to ecstasy
And this trip won't be seasonal
As long as you're with me

How much will it cost me?
To kiss you with uncontrollable passion
Does your man kiss you like that?
Or do you have to ask him?

Does he massage your feet?
Or does he pay for massage therapy
If there's anyone touching your feet
It would have to be only me

Does he look into your eyes?
To search your soul
Has he touched every part of your body?
To see what treasures they hold.

Does he really see you,
Or are you just another beautiful face
Because if it's just your beauty he sees
You can easily be replaced

You know what I'm going to do for us
I'm going to put an end to this date
Because it's just a matter of time now
I just have to be patient and wait

I've planted my seed in fertile ground
In your heart it is sure to grow
Because you want the same things I want
And soon enough you will know

Know what true love is really about
You just need the freedom
And a reason to let it out.

Before I leave
There is one more thing I'd like to say
Right now I'll settle for only being your friend
and that'll be good enough
Until I see you again.

"Amen"

It's me, Father
Calling on your holy name
I know I committed some negative acts today
But if you give me a second
I'll try to explain

First I would like to give you thanks
For guiding and protecting me
From the things that were right in my face
To the things I could not see

It's amazing when I look over my life
How you designed my each and every step
The only time that things went wrong
Was when I tried to do things myself

Tonight I forgive those, Lord
Who have done me wrong
It's hard sometimes, Jesus
But I hope you understand
Where I'm coming from

I pray that they forgive me
For things that I said or did
Forgetting is one thing
But sometimes it's hard to forgive

From the moment you woke me, Lord
To the setting of the sun
I pray that it was your will, Father
And not my will that was done

I meant every word in my prayer to you
From the beginning to the end
In Jesus' Name I pray
       Amen

Printed in the United States
by Baker & Taylor Publisher Services